Praise for the novels

"Evocative . . . fascinating history and an
involving tale."—*Booklist*

"A gripping, convincingly imagined
historical . . . told with page-turning verve, as
Conley uses his extensive historical knowledge
of Cherokee life and culture to spin a lively,
informed piece of speculative history."
—*Publishers Weekly*

"Conley has shaped a touching, powerful
vision of Indian life past and present, of abiding
love, and of a national disgrace."
—*Kirkus Reviews*

"An unforgettable adventure of love, death, and
nature that entices you with each page."
—Max Evans, author of *The Rounders*

MEDICINE WAR

Robert J. Conley

A SIGNET BOOK

SIGNET
Published by New American Library, a division of
Penguin Putnam Inc., 375 Hudson Street,
New York, New York 10014, U.S.A.
Penguin Books Ltd, 27 Wrights Lane,
London W8 5TZ, England
Penguin Books Australia Ltd, Ringwood,
Victoria, Australia
Penguin Books Canada Ltd, 10 Alcorn Avenue,
Toronto, Ontario, Canada M4V 3B2
Penguin Books (N.Z.) Ltd, 182–190 Wairau Road,
Auckland 10, New Zealand

Penguin Books Ltd, Registered Offices:
Harmondsworth, Middlesex, England

First published by Signet, an imprint of New American Library,
a division of Penguin Putnam Inc.

First Printing, October 2001
10 9 8 7 6 5 4 3 2 1

To Cherry

Prologue

In the years leading up to Oklahoma statehood in 1907, the Cherokee Nation was a unique place in the history of the world. A small, independent republic, the Cherokee Nation had been re-established in its new location in what is now northeast Oklahoma following the forced removal of the Nation from their ancient homeland over what became known as the Trail of Tears in 1839. Once relocated, the Cherokees wasted no time in rebuilding. A national capital was quickly established at Tahlequah.

The Cherokee Nation suffered an internal civil war following the removal, between the two major factions of the Nation known as the Ross Party and the Treaty Party. Members of the Ross Party, so named because they were followers of the then Principal Chief, John Ross, had assassinated the leading members of those Cherokees who had signed the Removal Treaty. Treaty Party members retaliated.

The conflict was finally resolved and relative calm prevailed until the Civil War of the United States intruded. Cherokees divided once again into two factions, largely the same two as before, but this time the Treaty Party appeared under the guise of

Confederate Cherokees. The Civil War devastated the Cherokee Nation, and the treaty that followed was even worse. In a first step toward Oklahoma statehood, the treaty created Indian Territory, made up of the lands of the so-called Five Civilized Tribes. It established a federal court at Fort Smith, Arkansas, which was given jurisdiction over Indian Territory, severely limiting the sovereignty of the Cherokee Nation.

In spite of this adversity, the Cherokee Nation, by the time of Oklahoma statehood, had produced more college graduates than did its neighboring states of Arkansas and Texas combined. It had created perhaps the world's first free, compulsory, public school system. It had built the first institutions of higher learning west of the Mississippi River, the Cherokee National Male and Female Seminaries. The Nation continued to publish its own bilingual newspaper, which it had been doing since 1828. A Cherokee, Elias Boudinot, wrote the first novel ever penned by an American Indian. A Cherokee, E. D. Hicks, installed the first telephone line west of the Mississippi River.

While all of this "progress" was going on, pockets of Cherokee conservatism remained strong in full-blood, or nearly full-blood communities. The result was that the population of the Cherokee Nation became incredibly diverse, ranging from the traditional full-bloods to the nearly white mixed-bloods and even white Cherokee citizens by marriage. Some Cherokees had been slave owners before the Civil War, and freed slaves had also become citizens of the Cherokee Nation.

Entertainment in those days reflected the diversity of the population. In conservative communities there was the traditional game of Cherokee marbles and corn stalk shoots. In the capital at Tahlequah there was a literary society, and traveling Shakespearians performed there while on tour. There were barn dances, fiddling contests and foot races. There was something for everyone. But the one thing that brought people together from all walks of life was a horse race.

Chapter 1

Charlie Horse woke up with a pounding head and a chirping cricket sitting on his left cheek. He squinted one eye, trying to focus his vision on the annoying black bug. His cheek twitched from the tickle of the bug's legs as it rubbed them together. Slowly, Charlie raised his left hand to gently brush the invader away from his face. It hopped away into the dew-covered grass. Charlie tried to sit up, but he moaned with pain and lay back down, putting his left hand to his throbbing head. He waited a long moment before trying it again. He told himself that he had not had too much to drink the night before. That was not the problem. The problem was that the stuff he'd had to drink was from a bad batch. It was tainted. Had to be. It was a chance one took if one wanted a drink. It was against the law to buy or sell liquor in the Cherokee Nation—in fact, in all of the Indian territory—so enterprising white men in Kansas and in Arkansas found ways of smuggling the stuff in and selling it on the sly. Of course, there were also illegal stills scattered throughout the thickly wooded hills of the Cherokee Nation. One purchased whatever was available on faith, hoping that it would be safe to get drunk on. Charlie's head hurt too much, he thought. He told himself he was lucky to be alive. He had heard of men dying from drinking bad booze.

He got up slowly on unsteady legs and stood reeling for a moment, getting used to the change in altitude. At last he started to walk, each step placed carefully, almost gingerly. He was somewhere in the woods. He tried to remember just where it was he had been the night before and who he had been there with. In a few short steps he came to the edge of the woods and found himself looking out onto a prairie. Everything was fuzzy in his brain and to his eyes, but at last he recognized the place. It all came back to him as if a lamp had been lit in his dim brain. He was there in the thick woods at the edge of the field where they had recently built a new racetrack. It was the place where the big horse race was scheduled to begin that very afternoon, the first race held on the new track. Charlie and his friends had talked about the upcoming race the night before when they had started drinking that bad stuff. They had talked about the horses they knew would be running, and they had speculated on how many other horses might run, as well as how many people would show up to watch the race and make bets. Some white people would be there, they said, and Blacks, and even some of those wild plains Indians from out west.

They had talked about where they would put their money, if they had any. Charlie felt in his pockets to see if he had any cash left. He found a little. If he put it on the right horse, he might have more before the day was done. Then he might be able to find someone else with some whiskey to sell, but not the same white man who had sold them the bad stuff last night. He would find good liquor this time. He could drink lots of good whiskey and not get sick. Maybe he could find that Hinton out by Lost City who made such good stuff. He thought about the conversation with his friends last night when it had still been early enough in their long evening of drinking to remember what had been said.

They had all agreed, Charlie remembered, that the winning horse would be the big white stallion owned by George Panther, the horse that George called Anagalisgi—Lightning. And they all agreed that the big white horse did in fact run like a flash of lightning and was therefore well named. There was no horse around, they said, that could outrun Lightning. And besides that, they said, George Panther was a powerful Indian doctor, or medicine man. He was bound to have come up with something to help his horse win the race, they said. There was where to put your money. Bet on Lightning, and you were sure to win. Charlie made up his mind right then that what little cash he had left to him would be placed on Lightning to win. He would surely have more money later on in the day after the race had been run, after Lightning had won. It was beginning to look like it would be a good day after all, in spite of his throbbing head. Charlie thought that he had better go see George Panther about his head and tell him about the bad batch of whiskey. George would be able to take care of that, too.

Charlie stepped to the edge of the thick brush there where it met the prairie, and looked out over the racetrack. He started to step out into the clearing, but he stopped again, startled. He stood still, frozen with cold fear at what he saw. There was a figure all in black and all alone, sprinkling something on the racetrack as he walked around. Charlie thought that he was safe there in the brush. He thought that he would be hidden from the view of the dark apparition if he just stood still. But then the figure turned and looked in his direction, and Charlie felt something cold run through his veins. The figure's eyes were red, and Charlie was sure that those red eyes were looking right at him there in the brush. He could feel them burning into him, and that burning caused an obnoxious odor to fill his nostrils and his lungs, a foul odor that also felt sickly. He was afraid to breathe, to draw into his lungs the uncleanness of the air around him, the air that had just been fouled by that stench. He had to do something. He had to get away. Charlie forced himself to pull his feet away from the ground where they seemed almost to be stuck. He turned and ran blindly through the thick woods and tangled bramble, running as hard and as fast as he could. Vines and brush tore at his hands and his face and his clothing as he ran. He fell, but he scrambled to his feet quickly and looked behind himself once before tearing off again.

Gwed' was packing the wagon with food and water and blankets, things they would need for the long afternoon at the racetrack. The whole family would be going, and they would spend the rest of the day, possibly even the night, before beginning the trip back home after the race was over. It promised to be a full and exciting day. She was confident that her husband's horse Lightning would win. She was excited about the race, but even more, she looked forward to the gathering. She would see relatives and friends whom she seldom saw because of the distance between their homes. People would come to the big race from all the far-flung districts of the Cherokee Nation. And there would be strangers too; new people to meet, new friends to make. They would camp around the racetrack and cook their meals right there. It would be a good time.

She had just put a basket of food into the wagon bed when she looked up to see Charlie Horse running in her direction. She could tell that he had been running long and hard, and as he drew closer, she could see the fear in his eyes. The old gray mare, standing patiently, already hitched to the wagon, could also sense his terror. She wobbled her head and blew air out from between her lips. Charlie ran on up and stopped beside the wagon, gasping for breath. He put a hand on the side of the wagonbed to steady himself and keep from falling.

"Tsali," she said, speaking to him in Cherokee, "what is it?"

"I have to see George," he said. "I'm sick, and I've been hurt. Is George here?"

"Come on," she said, and led Charlie around the corner of the log house to an arbor, where a bench and a couple of wooden chairs sat. A small fire burned just beside the arbor. "Sit down," she said. "I'll get George for you."

Gwed' went into the log house, and Charlie sat waiting there under the arbor, sucking in great

breaths of air, trying desperately to replace the foul
air he had drawn into his lungs beside the racetrack
with good clean air. There was, of course, a little
smoke in the air under the arbor, smoke drifting in
from the small fire, but it was good, purifying
smoke because it was coming from George
Panther's fire. Charlie had been afraid that he
would not make it to the home of George Panther,
afraid that the piercing red eyes had already pene-
trated him too deeply, that the putrid air had already ruined his lungs, and that the bad booze he'd
had the night before had made him too sick to run
that far. He had been terrified as he ran that he
might drop dead before reaching his goal. He was
relieved to have made it all right, but he was also
still filled with horror at the evil he had seen that
morning with his own eyes, smelled with his own
nostrils, and now felt seeping its way into his body
through the pores in his skin.

"*Siyo*, Tsali."

Charlie jumped at the greeting and looked up to
see George Panther walking over to him, a friendly
smile on his face. Panther was a large man, about
fifty years old. He was probably carrying on him an
extra one hundred pounds, but it didn't seem to
slow him down any. He was always cheerful, always friendly, and his manner put Charlie at ease. It
gave one confidence just to be in the medicine
man's presence. Charlie felt as if he had just escaped
the company of evil to find himself in the company
of solid, warm protection. He just hoped that he had
made the change fast enough.

"Hello, George," he said. "I wanted to come and
see you because I drank some bad stuff last night. It

hurt my head. I was going to come and see you because of that, but I woke up there in the woods by the racetrack, the new racetrack, you know, and when I was coming out of the woods, I saw him there."

"Who did you see, Charlie?" George asked.

"I don't know," Charlie said. "Someone bad. He was dressed all in black. He wore high-topped black boots, and he had a black suit coat. He had a wide-brimmed black hat, too. He was walking on the racetrack, sprinkling something around. I couldn't tell what it was. But then he looked right at me, and his eyes were red. I could see them from that far away, and he could see me even back there in the woods. When those red eyes hit me, I felt them. They burned me, but I turned cold inside. And there was a nasty smell in the air. It was heavy. It filled the air, and it felt like the air I was breathing was full of some kind of sickness. I thought it was going to kill me, but I ran here as fast as I could. I was afraid that I wouldn't get here to you in time."

"You did right to come here, Charlie," George said. "It'll be all right now. You relax. Wait right here, and I'll be back. I'll get something for you."

As George walked toward his log house, Gwed' appeared there beside the house. He stopped and spoke to her briefly, then went on inside. Gwed' stepped around to the back of the house and returned shortly with some sprigs of cedar. She went under the arbor with Charlie, held the cedar sprigs in the fire until they began to smolder, then walked around him a few times, filling the space under the arbor with the purifying smoke of burning cedar.

Charlie thought that he could feel the cedar doing its work right away.

"George will be inside for a little while yet, Charlie," she said. "Can I get you some coffee?"

"Yes," Charlie said. "Thank you."

Charlie was almost finished with the coffee by the time George came back out to the arbor, carrying a bowl in one hand and a small bag in the other. He sat down in a chair facing Charlie.

"I couldn't tell who it was you saw," he said. "I saw him, like you said, all in black with little red eyes, but he was just a shadow. That's all. He was like a shadow. I couldn't see him clear. I couldn't make out his features. But that's all right for now. We'll take care of it. Here. Drink this."

He handed the bowl to Charlie, and Charlie drank it like a man who had been in the desert and just received his first drink of water in days. He drank it down greedily, desperately. Some of it ran down his chin. He didn't stop drinking until the bowl was empty. He did not know what he was drinking. It tasted mostly like good, clean water, but there was something else in it. He knew that. He could tell. He didn't care though. George had given it to him, and he knew that it was what he needed. It would save him from the evil that had touched him that morning. Charlie lowered the bowl and took a deep breath. Then he put the bowl on the ground beside the chair.

"That will help you with the stuff you drank last night," George said. "It'll make your head feel better. Now, do you have your pipe with you?"

Charlie patted his pockets and after a brief mo-

ment of panic came out with his short-stemmed
pipe. He held it up for George to see. George
handed him the small bag.

"Go on and smoke some right now," he said.
"Smoke it again three more times today, the last
time just before you go to bed tonight. Smoke it first
thing in the morning, too. Keep it up until the tobacco is almost gone. Then come back, and I'll check
into it again and see if you need any more. You'll be
all right."

"But what was he doing?" Charlie asked as he
filled the bowl of his small pipe from the bag
George had given him.

"He was doctoring the racetrack," said George.
He stood up and walked to the fire and took up a
burning twig, holding it out for Charlie to use to
light his pipe. Then he tossed the twig back in the
fire and resumed his seat. "He was trying to fix the
race so that his horse, or the horse he's planning to
bet on, would win. He might hurt the other horses
if they're faster than his, or he might hurt a jockey.
That's what he was doing. But what I gave you just
now will protect you from his medicine, and I have
something for my horse, too. We'll be all right. Just
relax. Okay?"

"Okay," said Charlie, puffing on his pipe. "Thank
you. George, I only have a little bit of money. I don't
have anything else to give you. I was going to bet
this money on Lightning today, but I'll give it to you
instead."

He reached into his pocket for the money, and
then he held out his open palm toward George.
George looked at the money for a long while. He finally reached over and took one penny.

"Go ahead and bet on Lightning," he said. "You'll win."

"*Wado*," said Charlie, "if you say so, but you know, I'm just a little bit afraid to go back over there."

"Ride along with us," said George. "We'll be leaving here in just a little while. My boys are in the house finishing up their breakfast. There's plenty in there. Go on in now and eat something."

Charlie finished smoking his pipe. Then he got up to go inside and eat. He was feeling much better.

George stayed under the arbor staring into the fire. Who was it Charlie saw? he asked himself. He had looked into his crystal, but all he could see in there was a vague and dim shadow, a mysterious and sinister form, all black but with glowing, red eyes, just as Charlie had said. There was no doubt that poor Charlie had found himself in the presence of palpable evil that morning, and he was indeed lucky that he had escaped it.

But this was only the beginning. George knew that. Whoever this evil personage might turn out to be, it was someone who had been caught by surprise doing his mischief. Now, if his mischief was going to be thwarted, which it would be now that George knew about it, he would be angry. He would work harder. He would throw some really bad medicine at Charlie for having interfered, and if he could tell that it was George who was working against him, he would put all the power of his evil to work against George. That was the way it always happened with these bad doctors, these practitioners of evil. George had been forced to deal with them before on numerous occasions. He knew the type. He knew their methods.

George also knew that he had his work cut out for him now. He would be busy night and day fending off the evil spells woven by this malevolent personage. Thinking about the mystery, George came up with several possibilities. He knew the medicine people, good and bad, throughout the Cherokee Nation. He knew some in the Creek Nation and some even among the Choctaws. He knew a few farther west, out among the plains people there, but there he did not know so many. But there was no telling where a man—or a woman—might go for that kind of dark help. Often they would go far from home. And so far, George could not see the enemy. The door to the house flew open, then a moment later slammed shut. George knew that it was Tom coming out.

"What's wrong with Charlie?" Tom asked.

"He had a bad experience this morning," said George, looking at his grown son, his oldest. "I helped him though. He's all right."

"Is he riding over to the races with us?"

"Yeah, he is."

"Good," Tom said.

George knew what Tom was thinking. Charlie always seemed to know where to go for whiskey, and Tom would be looking for the same thing. His boy was twenty years old, but he was still a boy, and he was still a problem. George helped everyone else around for miles with their problems, but he couldn't seem to control his own son. And Gwed' did not have much more luck than he. Sometimes when they were alone, which was not often, they

would talk about their two boys. They would share
with each other their worries over Tom. He had a
wild streak, and he seemed always to be just on the
verge of getting into serious trouble. George had
talked to him. So had Gwed'.

And Tom listened. And he agreed with everything they said to him. He was respectful. And then
he would go out and find some rowdy companions,
get hold of some whiskey and get drunk, and finally
start a fight. He would come home bloody and
bruised and all hungover. Sometimes George
thought that they were too easy on the boy.
Sometimes he thought that they should throw him
out of the house and let him find out if he could
make it on his own. But they never did. He was
their son. Instead, they would talk to him again, and
he would listen politely and agree and promise to
do better in the future.

"Does your mama need any more help packing
up the wagon?" George asked Tom.

"There's not much more to do," Tom said.
"Andy's helping her."

George nodded slowly. Andy was two years
younger than Tom, but Andy was by far the more
mature and responsible. Andy was just about the
opposite from his older brother in every way. A stu-
dent at the Cherokee National Male Seminary, Andy
had aspirations of becoming a lawyer. George had
never gone to school. Neither had Gwed'. They
were both proud of Andy for his educational ac-
complishments and goals. They helped and encour-
aged him in every way they could. George had even
made medicine for him to help him learn better and

faster, and to hold harder in his mind those things that he had learned.

George had never gone to school, but he knew about learning. He had learned his life's work from his grandfather. He had studied all of the plants and all of their uses. He had learned the correct words to say or the right songs to sing over the right plants for any problem that might come up, for an illness or for a wound or for bad medicine inflicted from an evil source. When anyone came to him with a problem, George knew what to do to help. And when the source was unknown, he knew how to look into it to find the answer. Sometimes it was easy. Sometimes it was most difficult.

The door opened again, and Gwed' came out with her arms full. She was followed by Andy and by Charlie, each also loaded up. George looked at them, and then he gave a disapproving look at Tom.

"Why aren't you helping them?" he asked.

"They got it all," Tom said. "Hey, Mom, anything else to do?"

"We're ready now," she said. "Just close the house up and get in the wagon."

Charlie piled his load in the back of the wagon and walked over closer to George.

"Where's Lightning?" he asked.

"Adam will be bringing him along," George said.

"Adam Diwali?"

"That's right. He's going to ride him in the race, so I let him take the horse home with him for a few days."

"Adam's a good rider," Charlie said.

George laughed. "He's little and skinny, too," he said. "He'll win this race riding Lightning."

George meant what he said. He had confidence in his horse, and he had confidence in Adam. Adam was one of the best riders in the Cherokee Nation. He was not only George's choice to ride Lightning in the race, he had also trained Lightning. Adam Diwali knew Lightning better than anyone else, with the possible exception of George. More important, Lightning knew Adam. George was almost certain that Lightning and Adam would win the race for him that day.

Chapter 2

The crowd was already huge by the time George Panther and his family drove their wagon up to the racetrack, and people were still arriving from all directions. They came on foot, on horseback, on mules and donkeys, in buggies and in wagons. People were gathered all around the circular track, and farther back wagons were parked and tents had been pitched. Cooking fires were burning in front of the tents, and women were busy cooking. Children ran and played, mostly ignored by the adults. Young men and girls walked or stood around talking. Neighborhood dogs had wandered in, looking for someone to pet them, or children to run with or waiting for someone to toss out a scrap of food. Some nipped at horses' legs, and a few men had to drive them away from the horses and from the track with long willow switches. Bets were being placed. George drove his wagon around the large circle of the gathered crowd to the far side.

"There's my sister, Polly!" Gwed' cried out, and George drove in that direction. His sister-in-law already had a tent up and a fire going, and appetizing smells wafted out from her fire. Polly saw the wagon coming and ran to meet it.

"Come on over and join us," she said. She showed George where to park the wagon, and then she and her children, who were not quite as old as those of Gwed' and George, helped to unload the wagon. "Food will be ready in just a little while," Polly said.

"I'm ready for that," said George. "Where's Big Joe?"

"Ah, he's over there somewhere, looking at the horses," said Polly. "I guess he's planning on betting some money."

"It'd better be Lightning," George said, "unless he wants to lose it all."

"I told him that already," Polly said.

Gwed' did not get around often to visit her sister, and George was glad that she had this opportunity. The two women always had a good time when they got together, and he liked seeing his wife happy. He enjoyed the visits, too, and the company of Polly and of her husband, Joe, the one they called Big Joe. By the time the wagon was unloaded and the gray mare unhitched, Tom had already disappeared. Charlie, too, made his excuse and wandered away somewhere into the crowd. Andy stayed to visit with his aunt, uncle and cousins. George looked around until he spotted Adam Diwali and Lightning.

"I have to go talk to Adam," he said, and walked away from the little family camp. As he did, he took note of the people in the crowd. Many of them were his friends, and they smiled and greeted him as he walked by. He had to stop a couple of times to visit with someone. He also noted that there were white people and mixed-blood Cherokees in the crowd.

Often, one could not tell if a person was Cherokee or white simply by looks, and it was getting to be more that way all the time. There were Blacks there too—Freedmen, they were called now. They had been made citizens of the Cherokee Nation when they'd been given their freedom, and many of them could speak Cherokee, and for some it was the only language they spoke. He also saw some Indians wearing blankets and with their hair in long braids. Finally, George made his way to where Adam was preparing Lightning for the big race.

"*Siyo*, Adam," he said.

"*Siyo*, George."

"How is Lightning?"

"He's never been in better shape, George," Adam said. "He'll run real well today."

"Have you looked at the other horses?"

"I haven't had time," Adam said.

George rubbed Lightning's neck and face and whispered in his ear.

"I think I'll walk around and have a look at them," he said.

He turned to begin his stroll around the park, and he thought that he saw a white man watching him. The man was a stranger to him. He shrugged it off and walked on. He stopped by a Creek man he knew and said hello, speaking to the man in his own Muskogee, or Creek, language. The man had a paint horse standing by.

"You have a new horse?" George asked him.

"Yes," the Creek man said. "He's going to give your Lightning a run for it, too."

George laughed and wished the man luck. He moved on, passing by a Comanche with a little buf-

falo runner. George remembered them both from
the last race. The quick little pony had come in second just behind Lightning. The Comanche scowled
at George, and George smiled in return. Then he
saw Go-Ahead Rider, the high sheriff of the
Cherokee Nation, walking toward him. They
greeted each other and shook hands.

"Are you planning to win yet another race?"
Rider asked him.

"Adam and Lightning will do their best," George
said. "We always plan to win. You wouldn't expect
me to plan to lose, would you?"

"It looks like you've got some stiff competition
this year," Rider said.

"I know most of these horses," said George, "and
most of the riders, too."

"There's a few new ones," said Rider. "If Adam
was riding my horse, I'd tell him to watch out for
that big black over there."

Rider nodded over his own right shoulder, and
George looked in that direction. A small crowd was
gathering around a big black stallion. The horse was
stamping and fidgeting, raring to go. George did
not recognize the horse.

"I'll take a look at him," George said, then he
walked over there. He did not know the people who
were gathered around the black horse, and he had
not seen the horse before either. New blood. As he
was studying the horse, a man stepped up behind
him and slightly to his right.

"*Siyo*," the man said. "You're George Panther."

George looked at the man, another stranger to
him.

"Yes," he said. "And you?"

"I'm called Big Forehead," the man said. He was an average-size man, shorter and much slighter than George. His skin was dark, and he wore a thin mustache. He was dressed in a black suit with the trouser legs poked down into the high tops of a pair of black boots, and he had on a wide, flat-brimmed black hat. His cheek bones were high, and his eyes, mere slits in appearance, were slightly slanted.

"I haven't seen you here before," said George.

"I come from up north," Big Forehead said. "They tell me the big white stallion belongs to you. You call him Lightning. They say he's never lost a race."

"He hasn't so far," George admitted.

"I'm betting on this black one," said Big Forehead.

"Well, good luck to you. Is he your horse?"

"No, but I'm betting on him to win."

George made an excuse and bade good-by to Big Forehead. He walked the rest of the way around the track, but he was no longer studying the horses. He was thinking about Big Forehead. He recalled Charlie Horse's description of the man at the track early that morning, and he thought about the image he had seen in his crystal. He couldn't quite say that Big Forehead was the one, just because he was dressed in black. But there was something about the man. He spoke Cherokee well enough, but he had a touch of a strange accent. It was something unidentifiable. It was not like a white man speaking Cherokee, nor a Creek, nor a Shawnee. George had heard examples of all of those. It was something else, and he couldn't put a finger on it.

And Big Forehead had been vague about where

he came from. "Up north" he had said. Most Cherokees would have said "Delaware District" or "Saline District" or "Cooweescoowee District." They would likely even have mentioned their home community. But Big Forehead had just said "up north." And he had known George. Of course, that could be explained. If he had been talking horses, there were many in the crowd who might easily have pointed George out to him and talked with him about Lightning. George Panther and his Lightning were always a big topic of conversation around the racetracks.

All George had to go on concerning Big Forehead was a vague yet matching description, and a feeling, but it was enough to make him suspicious of the man. He headed back toward where Adam Diwali waited with Lightning. It would be time for the race to begin soon, and George wanted to be there with them. On his way back, he could see Big Forehead looking at him from across the way, smoking a pipe. George took note of the smoke. It was drifting in his direction.

Back with Adam and Lightning, he took some papers and some tobacco out of his pocket and rolled himself a cigarette. He brought a wooden match out of a tin in his pocket, struck the match and lit the smoke.

George was not making medicine to help his horse win the race. He would not have considered that a fair way to win, and besides that, he was sure that Lightning needed no such extra help. But someone might be making medicine to stop Lightning from winning. It could be aimed at hurting Lightning or Adam. George was smoking to protect them—that was all. It was getting closer to time for the race, and the betting in the crowd was almost furious, with people trying at the last minute to get their money down on their favorites to win or place. Many were betting on the horse they thought would come in second, having already made up their minds that Lightning would be first. But there was some betting, besides Big Forehead, in favor of the black stallion.

Soon, the horses and jockeys were called to the starting line. George gave Lightning a final nuzzle and a last whisper in his ear. Then he slapped Adam on the thigh.

"It's all up to you and Lightning now," he said. "Show them how to run a race."

"We'll give it everything we've got," Adam said.

Adam rode the horse to the line. All the jockeys were having trouble holding the skittish horses back. The starter raised his pistol and fired a shot, and they were off. The little buffalo pony ran out in front, but very quickly the Creek's paint caught up with it, and they were running neck and neck. Both Lightning and the big black stallion were hanging back, mixed in with the crowd of horses behind. Then about halfway around the track, the black shot out. With long strides, it quickly caught up to the two smaller horses. It pulled ahead, running with seeming ease. Lightning then seemed to shoot out of the pack. The people around the track were yelling and screaming encouragement to their favorites.

Lightning came up beside the big black, and they ran side by side for several long strides. Lightning pulled ahead, then he stumbled, as if over something invisible, and Adam flew forward out of the saddle. A huge gasp came from the throats of all in the crowd of spectators. Adam grabbed desperately for Lightning's neck, and he somehow managed to hold on, hanging down under the big horse's head. Lightning caught his balance and kept running. The spectators breathed a uniform sigh of relief. It had been a thrilling moment, one which could have easily ended in disaster. As Lightning moved to pass the black stallion, Adam struggled to pull himself back around Lightning's neck and get himself into the saddle again. The crowd cheered as Lightning, with Adam now securely in the saddle, crossed the finish line well ahead of the black. The Comanche pony came in third, with the Creek's paint just a nose behind. George smiled. Charlie Horse came walking up.

"You won, George," he said. "I did, too. I bet on Lightning against the black horse, and I won." He held out a handful of cash.

George took hold of Charlie by the shoulder and turned him to look across the track and into the crowd over there. "See that man?" he said. "In black. You see him?"

Charlie squinted around for a moment before answering. "Yes," he said, "I see him."

"Is that the man you saw this morning?"

"It looks like him," Charlie said, "but so would someone else dressed like that. His eyes aren't red."

"They wouldn't be red out here in public like this," said George. "So you can't be sure?"

Charlie shook his head slowly. "It could be," he said, "but I can't say for sure. I wasn't seeing too clearly then, George. But I did see his black clothes and his red eyes. I saw that much."

"Okay, Charlie," George said. "That's all right. We'll find out."

George started to turn around and look in another direction, but before he moved his gaze, he saw his son Tom walk up to the strange man in black. He wondered if Tom knew the man, and if so, what they were talking about. He was a little ashamed of himself for his next thought. Big Forehead was likely dealing in whiskey. Why else would Tom be talking to this stranger from "up north"? Then George saw the white man again, the one who had been watching him earlier. The man walked slowly past Big Forehead, and he thought that Big Forehead said something to the man, but he couldn't be sure. The distance was too great, and even if Big Forehead had said something to the man, it might have been something perfectly innocent—a greeting maybe. George tried not to let his suspicion get the best of him. But he also meant to stay alert. Adam came riding up on Lightning then, and he had a big smile on his face.

"Lightning did it again."

"You did a fine job, Adam," George said. "You and Lightning both."

"I thought I'd lost it there for a minute," said Adam. "It really had me scared. But Lightning kept his feet. He was great. He outdid himself today."

"And you got back in the saddle," said George. "That was a pretty good trick, too."

"Well, anyhow, we made us some money today," Adam said.

"Come over to my sister-in-law's camp," George said. "We'll eat something."

Adam dropped down to the ground from Lightning's back, and leading the white steed, he walked along with George. All along the way, they were slapped on the back by many in the crowd. At Polly's camp, everyone congratulated them some more, and they all happily counted the money they had won betting on Lightning. It had been a good day for all. The women dished out great heaping plates of food, and soon everyone was eating.

"Where's Tom?" Andy asked.

"He left right after we got here," said Gwed'. "He hasn't come back."

"Well, he'll just go hungry then," said George. "I just saw him across the way there. He was talking to that stranger. He'll manage by himself. If he gets hungry enough, he'll be back around."

George tried to put the troublesome boy out of his mind. It did no good to worry about him and what he might be doing, what kind of trouble he might be getting himself into. The food was good and so was the company. Lightning had won the race. George tried to concentrate on the positive things about the day, and there were plenty of them. But there had been something else. Someone had been at the track that morning, someone sinister. There was this suspicious man in black, this Big Forehead, this man with the troublesome dialect. And there had been something invisible in Lightning's path during the race. George was convinced that bad medicine had caused that near mishap, and that the only thing that had saved Lightning and Adam was his own protective medicine. Someone had deliberately caused the horse to stumble, unconcerned about possible injury to either horse or man.

A horse race was a small thing, a day of entertainment, a time for visiting, one happy day out of the year for a few of the people who walked this earth, whose lives came and went, making way for the next generations. It was an insignificant thing in the universe. It was a small thing except in the mind of one who had great amounts of money invested and wagered, for whom money was all-important, and there were too many who fit this category.

George suddenly wondered who the owner of the black horse might be. Big Forehead had said that it was not him. But could Big Forehead or someone else be working for the horse's owner? That was a possibility. He decided to make some discreet inquiries. He knew though that there were other possibilities. Someone could have it in for George or for Adam. There was no way yet of telling just why these things were happening and who was behind them. It might be anyone. Even if he could determine the identity of the bad doctor, he still might not know who was paying the doctor to cause harm out of vengeance, jealousy, greed or any number of other petty kinds of motivation. He saw Sheriff Rider going by, and he called out to him.

"Come and eat with us, Go-Ahead."

Rider came over and sat down beside George, and soon Gwed' had a plate full of food on the makeshift table in front of him. He thanked her.

"Congratulations," Rider said. "It was a pretty spectacular win."

"Yes," said George. "It was, wasn't it? I have a good horse and a good jockey."

"I'd say the best, on both counts."

"Have you seen my boy, Tom?" George asked.

"Not since early," Rider said. "You worried about him?"

"Naw, he'll be all right."

Rider knew of Tom's problems, and knew that George was worried about him. He'd had to throw the boy in jail on more than one occasion. Neither man said anything more about it though. This did not seem to be the time or place for it.

"That black horse gave us quite a run," George said.

Rider nodded. "It was close there for a while. I told you that was the one to watch."

"Yes, you did. Whose horse is that anyway?" George asked.

"The man who was riding him," said Rider. "He's a Shawnee from somewhere north of here. I met him a little while ago. He seems like a nice enough man. He's a pretty good rider, too."

A Shawnee from up north, George thought. Big Forehead had said that he was from "up north," and he talked Cherokee with some strange kind of dialect. He also had bet his money on the black horse. It might not mean anything, but it was interesting to think about. Perhaps there was a connection of some kind between the owner of the black horse and the mysterious man in black. Rider finished his meal and got up to leave. He thanked the women and said good-by to George, then went on his way. The women began preparing the camp for the night.

George decided that he had better do the same thing, in his own way, just in case.

Later, George was just finishing his last walk around the camp site, smoking as he walked, when he saw the white man. He finished up what he was doing casually, as if he had just been taking an evening stroll and smoking for pleasure. The white man came walking straight toward him.

"*Siyo,*" he said.

"*Siyo,*" said George. "*Tohiju?*"

He was a little surprised that the white man had greeted him in Cherokee, but the white man's next comment took away that surprise.

"How you doing there?" the white man said, speaking English, and obviously unaware of what George had said to him following the common greeting. George figured then that the greeting was the only Cherokee word the man had picked up. Maybe he was a mixed-blood citizen, or a white citizen by marriage, a man married to a Cherokee woman.

"Doing all right," George said, switching to English himself.

"Your horse ran a hell of a race today," the man said.

"He did all right," George said.

The man stuffed a hand into his jeans pocket and pulled out a wad of bills, which he then fanned out to impress George. George wasn't impressed.

"You interested in selling that horse?" the man asked.

"He ain't for sale," George replied.

The man fanned the money out some more.

"He ain't for sale for no amount of money," George said.

The man shrugged, stuffed his money back into his pocket, then turned and walked away.

That night George slept on a blanket out under the stars. The rest of his family and in-laws did the same. All except Tom. He had not come back. The night sky was clear and bright, full of shining stars and a full moon. George thought that he was probably the last one awake in the camp. He was lying on his back, looking up into the sky, when he saw the first purple light flash. It was like a shooting star, but it came from the ground and shot up into the air, making a large arc before heading directly for the camp. Coming close, it exploded as if against something solid. George smiled to himself. Then another flashed, and another. They seemed to come from all directions, and it looked as if there was an army somewhere firing cannons at the camp, as though a small war were in progress.

George relaxed and watched the purple flashes crash against the invisible barrier, the barrier he himself had created earlier, "just in case." He smiled, knowing that his camp and his family were all well protected, knowing that his own medicine was more powerful than that of his unknown enemy, knowing that the rest of the camp slept soundly, comfortably, completely unaware of any outside danger. George was relaxed, but he knew that it was only a momentary relaxation, for he knew that the fight had just begun.

* * *

Tom Panther was only a few miles away in a small community just a short distance outside of Tahlequah. He was in the middle of a circle of young men and boys about his age, and he was fighting another man. Blood ran from his nose, and his lower lip was swollen. His opponent swung at him with a right cross, but Tom backed up just in time and the blow missed. He shot out a left jab that caught the other man on the side of the head. The man staggered back, and Tom moved in fast. He connected with two more left jabs. The other man was off balance. He was hurt. Tom swung a hard right and knocked him down.

"That's the way, Tom!" someone in the circle shouted. "Finish him off."

Tom moved in, kicking the man while he was down. The man on the ground covered his head with both arms and rolled over, facedown. Tom kicked him in the ribs. Finally, two of the young men in the crowd stepped in and grabbed Tom by his arms, pulling him away. Tom struggled with them.

"That's enough, Tom," one said. "That's enough. You'll kill him."

"Son of a bitch," Tom spat.

"Hey," said another one, "let's go get some whiskey and celebrate. You whipped his ass real good."

Tom stopped struggling. He shrugged the boys off his arms. He wiped at his bloody nose with a shirtsleeve.

"Yeah," he said. "It's a good thing for him you pulled me off. I mighta killed him. Okay. Let's go get that whiskey."

Chapter 3

George and the others spent the night in the camp by the racetrack, and in the morning the women prepared breakfast. Everyone ate and then visited. They were not the only ones. Several other families were still there. It was early afternoon before the camps began to break up and everyone headed home again, leaving the racetrack and the surrounding camp sites abandoned.

George and his family made it back to their house in the late afternoon. George decided that it was too late for a nap. If he went to sleep, he knew he would sleep on into the night, and there was a great deal of work to be done. The kind of work George had to do was best done at night. Gwed' made some coffee, and George relaxed under his arbor, drinking coffee and smoking, thinking about the work ahead of him.

He waited until dark before going to work, and then he began selecting herbs from his collection around the house and boiling water over the fire outside. He timed his work so that he was ready for the most important part around midnight. Then he sang special songs to the medicine; to the tobacco and the herbs. There were a good many songs to sing. He was not finished until that time of morning just between darkness and dawn, that ambiguous time when it is neither night nor day. Then he walked around his home in a wide circle, sprinkling a liquid he had brewed. As he made his way around the house his circles became ever smaller and smaller until at last he went inside the house to use up what was left of the medicine. He sprinkled the floor, the corners of the rooms and the doorway. Gwed' and Andy were still asleep. Tom had not yet reappeared.

Finished with his administrations, George went back outside and returned to his arbor. He filled a pipe bowl with tobacco that had been infused with the songs, lighting it with a burning branch from his fire. He smoked to the four directions, and he covered his own body with the smoke. Then he went inside and blew the smoke over the sleeping bodies of his wife and his youngest son. With the tobacco used up, George went to bed.

It was after noon when George woke up. Gwed' had cooked much food, and there were already people waiting to see him. She was feeding them on a plank table outside in front of the house. George greeted the visitors and sat down at the table. Gwed' filled a plate and put it in front of him. He ate voraciously, and when he was done, he drank two more cups of the steaming black coffee. Ready to go to work, George stood up.

"In just a few minutes," he said to Gwed', "I'll be ready for Canoe over there under the arbor."

Gwed' nodded in response, and George went into the house into a back room. He found a stash of tobacco he had worked on the night before and took it with him out to the arbor. Canoe had been over to see him before, and George knew what it was that had been tormenting Canoe. The medicine was ready. Under the arbor, George sat in his favorite chair. In another few minutes, Canoe came around from the front of the house and walked into the arbor.

"Sit down," George said.

Canoe took a chair and sat facing George.

"What's been happening since you were here last?" George asked.

"My little girl is sick now," Canoe said. "We don't know what's wrong with her. I woke up this morning and my leg was stiff and sore. It still is. I was going to drive the wagon over here, so I hitched up my mule and started out, and then a wheel came off. I couldn't fix it, so I just crawled up on the back of my old mule and rode him over here."

"I looked into all that last night," George said, "and I think I know who's doing it to you. I don't know who he's gone to, though. But it's your neighbor just south of your house. About a mile or so, I'd say."

"That's Billy Fire," Canoe said, astonished. "We've always been friendly enough. He even ate at my house once."

"When was that?"

"A couple of weeks ago, I guess."

"Did he leave anything behind when he went home?"

"No, I don't think so," Canoe said, musing. "Wait a minute—he did. He left a little bear he'd been carving. It looks pretty nice."

George handed the tobacco to Canoe.

"Take this home and smoke it like I told you before," he said. "And try to bring me that little bear, but try to bring it over here without touching it. Pick it up with a stick or wrap something around it. Don't touch it, and tell your wife and your little girl not to touch it. If anyone's already handled it, bring that person over here to see me, too. We'll clear this all up."

Canoe sensed the finality in George's voice, and he knew that others were waiting. He stood up and extended his right hand for George to take. George gripped his hand lightly.

"I have brought some good ears of corn," Canoe said.

"Thank you," said George. "Take it over there and give it to Gwed', and tell her to send Henry out here in about ten minutes or so."

Canoe nodded and went back to his mule. He took a sack off the back of the mule and headed for the table in front of the house.

George had a few minutes before the next person would be with him. He rolled a cigarette and lit it. He pondered the amount of bad medicine being used in the neighborhood lately. Something bad was going on. Of course, that sort of thing had always existed among the Cherokees. George was well aware of it and knew well how to deal with it, but this intensity was something new. There was too much going on. He wondered why. He also wondered about the source. He recalled the image of the mysterious figure in black with the red eyes, and he thought about the man Big Forehead.

As he sat there thinking, he saw Canoe move out

from in front of the house and go back to his mule
to leave. Down the road, a wagon was approaching.
It was full of people. As it drew closer, George could
see that it was a whole family. He knew the people
were coming to see him. This promised to be a busy
day. As he finished his cigarette, Gwed' came out
from around the corner of the house, bringing him a
cup of coffee. He took it and thanked her.

"Are you ready for the next one?" she asked.

"Yeah. Send Henry on over," he said.

George knew Henry well. Henry was a regular.
Hard-luck Henry, George sometimes called him.
Henry's only problem was that he was lazy, and he
never managed to finish anything he started. He
never accomplished anything. And because Henry
could not admit to anyone, including himself, that
he brought all his troubles on himself, he always
blamed his problems on someone using bad medicine against him. They were doing that, he said, because they were jealous of his abilities. There was
not much that George could do for Henry. He always gave Henry tobacco to smoke for protection.
The tobacco eased Henry's mind. When it was all
smoked up, he'd be back for more. What he brought
in exchange was more tobacco, for the only thing
that Henry seemed to be able to do well was grow
and cure tobacco.

Henry came around the corner of the house and
took the chair facing George. "I'm just about out of
my protection tobacco," he said.

"I have some for you right here, Henry," George
said. He held the bag out for Henry to take.

"Thank you," Henry said. "I brought you some
here."

He handed George another bag, much like the one he had just taken. The difference, of course, was that the tobacco George had given Henry had been doctored.

"Henry," George said, "why don't you sell your tobacco? It's good. You could have a fine business going. Take it into Tahlequah and sell it to those storekeepers there. They'd mark the price up some and sell it out of their stores. You ought to do well at that. It would make you some good money."

Henry shook his head slowly.

"I would, George," he said. "It's a good idea, but I just can't make it to town at the right times. Last time I tried to make it into town, my leg was hurting me so bad, I couldn't even walk at all."

"I'll tell you what, Henry," said George. "You get a good batch ready to go, and I'll bring my wagon over to your place. We'll haul it into town and get it sold for you. What do you say?"

Henry thought for a minute, trying to find a reason that George's offer wouldn't work. At last, unable to find an excuse, he said, "Well, I could do that, I guess. It will take me a few days to get enough ready. I don't know, though. Something might go wrong. I'll see."

"What if I come over to your place in just about a week?"

Henry thought and scratched his head. "I don't know," he said. "Make it two weeks?"

"Two weeks then," said George.

"Well, all right."

"Henry," said George, "there's no reason for this not to work. You have all the protection you need right there in that tobacco. Whoever it is bothering you can't get to you. What I gave you is strong medicine. Remember that."

As Henry left, George wondered if that really would work. He wondered if Henry would find some other excuse to cause the plan to fail. George decided to give it a try. His life's work was helping people, and this was the only kind of help Henry needed. It might work.

He kept seeing people, hearing their troubles and offering up solutions. Some had physical ailments, cuts, sore throats, arthritis, back pains—and George provided cures for all. Some of the cures he had on hand. For some of the people, he had to prepare medicine, and so they had to wait. Some medicines would take longer and had to be prepared overnight. Those people were told to come back. Individuals came. Couples came. Whole families came. All had their problems. And George was obligated to do everything he could to help them all. No one was turned away.

He could not remember a time when he had not been in training for this role. His grandfather used to take him for long walks in the woods when he was just a small child, and he showed him the different plants and told him their names and their uses. At night Grandfather sat with him by the fire and sang the songs to him until he learned them all. It was a lifelong process. There was always more to learn.

Once, when George was still a young man, he had come home drunk. He had been out with some friends, and they had found a whiskey peddler. When George came staggering into the yard, Grandfather had been there waiting for him. George could still remember the fear in his heart when he realized he'd been caught. He had fully expected a beating, but instead, Grandfather had taken him to the chairs under the arbor and told him to sit down. Grandfather sat facing him.

"George," Grandfather had said, "your life is already laid out for you. You will become a healer. Your life will not be your own. It will belong to the people, just as mine now belongs to the people. I guess you had to do what you did tonight. You're young. Maybe you think you have to do it some more. So go on. Do it. Do it now while you're young, and get it out of your system. One of these days, you'll have to cut it out. You won't be able to do it ever again, because your life will belong to the people."

And George had done just that. He had run with a wild bunch. They drank and they got into fights and they chased women. Now and then they found themselves in jail in Tahlequah, sometimes for more than just one night. Then there came a time when Grandfather had told him to stop. It was time. And George had given up his wild ways. He had gone into a period of serious study with his grandfather and became his assistant. He made medicine. He washed people off when they had been around the dead. He built the fire and heated the rocks for the sweat lodge, and he carried the rocks into the lodge.

"One day when I am gone," Grandfather had said, "you will take over. This will become your life."

The day had eventually come when Grandfather was old and weak. He still saw people, still helped them, but George was fifty years old by that time, and Grandfather had told him that it was his time. And George had begun working with some of the people on his own. Grandfather left the earth not long after that, but he left George with his medicine books, small notebooks filled with Cherokee writing, and George had been fascinated with the information in the books. Some of it was so powerful that it frightened him. He was amazed at how much more he had yet to learn from the books.

George still thought about the days of his wild youth, especially when he worried about Tom. And he thought that maybe Tom would come out of it one of these days, just as he had. He had tried to teach Tom, as Grandfather had taught him, but Tom wasn't interested, and finally George had been forced to admit to himself that Tom just wasn't cut out for that kind of life. And neither was Andy. Andy was responsible, but Andy's ambitions led him in another direction. So George worried about what would become of the medicine when it came his time to go. He wanted someone to teach, someone to leave the medicine with. It was too important to be lost when he was gone.

He was visiting with the family that had come together in a wagon, when Tom came walking down the road. Tom glanced at George there in the arbor, then disappeared around the corner to the front of the house. Tom would sit down out there, George knew, and ask Gwed' to feed him, and she would. He would not say anything about where he had been and what he had been doing, and Gwed' would not press him for that information. George did not blame Gwed' for that. He himself had stopped trying to make Tom tell him those things. If he were to insist, Tom would just lie. George tried to keep his mind on his business. He couldn't afford to let worries about his son interfere with his work.

He had almost finished with the family. He had given them their medicine and was telling them how to use it, when Tom came back around the corner of the house.

"Hey, Dad," Tom said, speaking English. "Can I see you a minute?"

"Excuse me," George said to the family. He got up out of his chair and walked over to Tom. He was burning with anger, a state he did not like. He stopped close to Tom and looked him hard in the face.

"You know better than to bother me when I'm talking to the people like that," he said. "What do you want?"

"I need some money, Dad," Tom said. "Skinny Johnson's in jail in Tahlequah. I need to bail him out."

"Why should I give you money to bail Skinny Johnson out of jail? Let him stew in there for a while. I'm not Skinny Johnson's keeper."

George wanted to add, *and I may not be your keeper much longer,* but he chose to swallow those words.

"Well, it's kind of my fault he's in there," Tom said. "And besides that, I owe him some money. I promised him I'd come back with it."

"What happened to your face, boy?" George asked.

"Ah, I had a little argument with a guy. That's all. Hell, you oughta see him."

Reluctantly, George dug deep into his pocket and pulled out some bills. He handed one to Tom, but

Tom kept his hand out. George gave him another and then another.

"Thanks," Tom said. "Say, can I take Lightning to town?"

"Take that old gray mare," George said. "You leave Lightning alone."

"Aw, Dad."

"You heard me, boy," said George. "You keep away from Lightning. If you think you were in a fight last night, you just touch my horse. I'll show you a beating."

Tom walked toward the corral, which was behind the house out of sight. George returned to the arbor to rejoin the family that was waiting there. He finished talking to them, and they left, loading up in their wagon and driving off. George rolled himself a cigarette and lit it. He needed to relax. As he smoked, Tom came riding out right between the arbor and the house. He looked disgruntled. He was on the mare, but he had saddled her with George's best saddle. George heaved a sigh, trying to figure out whether he was relieved to see Tom leaving again, or relieved that Tom had not tried to take Lightning in spite of what had been said. That boy was nothing but trouble. George thought again about his own rowdy youth, and he decided that he was probably being punished for what he had done to his grandfather. There's a payback for everything, he told himself.

Gwed' came around to the arbor with another cup of coffee, and George was glad to have it. She asked about Tom, and George told her what had happened. They both were quiet for a moment, each one knowing what the other was thinking.

"How many's left around there?" he asked her.

"There's just that young Creek man and his wife," she said. "You know, the ones with the little boy? Then there's a white man. I never saw him before."

"Wait a few minutes," he said. "Then send out the Creeks."

The young Creeks were not in trouble. They just wanted assurance that their son would stay healthy and grow into a fine young man. George could understand the feeling. He talked to them in Creek, and he told them to come back to see him in a few days and he'd have some medicine ready for them. They thanked him, promising to return as they left. They were nice young people, and they had a beautiful little boy. George liked them. In another few minutes, the white man came around. George did not recognize him.

"How can I help you?" he asked, speaking English.

"I just moved home from California," the man said. "I went out there back in '50, you know, for the gold rush. I didn't strike it rich out there, so I came home to go into business. I'm just not making the kind of money I ought to be making. I've done everything the right way. I've made all the right contacts, but I'm just not getting the customers. I don't know what's wrong. Maybe someone's got it in for me. I don't know."

"What line of business are you in?" George asked.

"I just opened up a mercantile in Tahlequah," the man replied. "I know there's others already there, but I studied the situation, and there's plenty of business to go around. I have some family connections. I'm a Cherokee citizen. My mother's half Cherokee."

"What clan?" George asked.

"We don't know," the man said.

"What's your name?"

"Tom Grimes."

"Well, I'll look into it," George said.

He made Grimes wait a few more minutes, then gave him some tobacco to smoke for good fortune and told him how to use it. Grimes thanked him and paid him with cash. As he watched Grimes climbing onto the back of his saddle horse, George thought that though the man might have a half-blood mother, he's still a white man. He only thinks about money. But then, he guessed that the man was raised that way. He couldn't help what he was.

The last of them were gone, and George was relieved. It had been a long and busy day, and it promised to be an even busier night. He could already see that he would be up and at it all night long again, preparing the medicine for all the different people he had seen. He stood up slowly and walked around to the front of the house. Gwed' filled a plate for him and put it on the table.

"You going to be working all night again?" she asked.

"It looks that way."

By the time he finished his meal, it was dark. He thanked Gwed' for the meal, then got up and went back around to the arbor. Gwed' went along with him.

"Is there anything you want me to do?" she asked.

"You might build up the fire and put a pot of water on to boil," he replied.

Just then they saw a streak of purple shoot up from the horizon and arc through the sky toward them. It stopped abruptly and fragmented, smashing itself against the invisible shield that protected the house. Other flashes followed, ending the same way. They watched for a moment. Then George looked at his wife.

"He's found me," he said.

"And you don't know yet who he is?"

"No," he said. "So far, I can't find him."

"The difference," she said, "is that you're not hiding. He is. He's got reason to hide because you're looking for him. And you'll find him, George. I know you will. Sooner or later, you'll find him."

In the meantime, they were both glad that George had made the time earlier to perform the extra protection ritual on the house, for the danger was present. It was immediate, and it was out there all around them.

Chapter 4

In a back room in his house, George concentrated hard, staring into the crystal. He would be able to bring much of the bad stuff to a quicker end if he could find out for sure just where it was coming from. There was a darkness in the center of the crystal, but it had no definite shape. It was like a tiny gray cloud floating in there. He looked harder, squinting his eyes, trying to bring some form out of the dark shadow. His eyes were hurting from the intense gazing. Then the shadow slowly began to move, almost imperceptibly at first. It changed its shape, twisting and turning. It settled into a long oval. Then it developed two legs and a torso and arms, but there was no head on the dark figure, and no more details revealed themselves. Suddenly it vanished.

George blinked his eyes and shook his head. He wrapped the crystal up and put it away. He went outside to the arbor. For a moment he stood staring up into the sky. The sky was clear, lit by moon and stars, and the purple flashes were no longer falling down at him. He smiled. The enemy had worn himself out with his barrage. Those kinds of attacks used a great deal of energy. It was not the kind of thing that George engaged in. He would do no deliberate harm to anyone. But he knew about it, all right. He also knew that the other doctor, the evil one, would rest up, gather new strength and energy and try it again. George could not afford to let down his guard, not for a minute. If he did, that was when the evil would surely attack him.

George took his seat in the arbor and gathered up some herbs. The water in the pot was already boiling. When he had what he wanted, he got up and moved to the fire to drop the mixture in. Then he gathered tobacco into three piles on a smooth tree stump in the center of his arbor. The tobacco was for three different people with three different needs. He would have to sing different songs to each pile of tobacco. The song cycles would take most of the night. He had been tired earlier, but when he sat down to his work, he found new energy and wakefulness. It always happened that way. He was just about to start the first song when he heard a noise from behind the house.

He sat still and listened, and he could hear a horse stamping. Lightning and the other horses in the corral were usually quiet at night unless something was bothering them. George thought at first that it must have been Tom returning home late on the gray mare, but if it were Tom, why hadn't George seen him ride up? Why would Tom have ridden around the long way and through the woods to get to the corral rather than coming back in the way he had gone out, right between the arbor and the house? George stood up and moved slowly, careful not to make any noise. He walked to the edge of the house, and then he crept silently along the wall until he had reached the back corner. He eased himself forward to take a peek. Lightning was stamping and snorting in the corral, startling the other horses. It was then that George saw the man.

In the light of the moon, he could see him clearly. It was the same white man who had tried to buy Lightning at the racetrack. He held a coil of rope in his hands, and he was stalking slowly toward the corral. He couldn't buy the horse, and so he was going to try to get him another way. George backed away slowly. He made it around to the front door of his log house and opened it very cautiously. Stepping softly inside in the darkness, he found his Winchester rifle, cranked a shell into the chamber, then turned and went back out the door as easily as he had come in, careful to make no warning sounds. He slipped back along the wall and peeked around the corner again.

The white man was at the corral gate, and he was swinging a wide loop at the end of his rope. He was planning to go into the corral and throw that loop over Lightning's head and get away with the big horse. Lightning seemed to sense the man's intentions. His stamping and snorting protests were getting louder. George had seen enough. He stepped boldly out in the open and raised the rifle to his shoulder.

"Hold it right there," he called out in English.

Caught in the act, the white man pivoted and slung the coiled rope through the air at George. The rope coil stung when it hit. Some loops went around George's head, others around his arms. At the same time as he threw the rope, the white man pulled out a revolver, and just as George was recovering from the initial assault, the man fired. George flung himself back against the house just in time. The bullet whizzed harmlessly past him. In spite of the tangle of rope, George managed to raise the rifle up to his shoulder. He took quick aim and fired.

The white man yowled and jerked as the hot lead crashed through his sternum and tore its way through his body, smashing a vertebrae on its way out his back. He stood on wobbly legs. His revolver fell to the ground and the man staggered forward. His eyes opened wide, and his mouth opened as if he were about to say something. His right arm rose and his right hand reached toward George as if he were pleading for something. Then his knees buckled and he fell forward, landing hard on his face. He did not move. He was dead.

"George?"

Gwed' had come running out of the house. She came to George's side and took hold of his arm with both her hands, looking ahead at the body on the ground. Andy came running out of the house right after her and stood at his mother's side. He too saw the body. They all stood silent for a long moment.

"What happened, George?" Gwed' asked.

"It's that white man from the racetrack, the one who tried to buy Lightning. I guess he wanted that horse real bad. He was getting ready to throw a loop around Lightning's neck. When I came up on him, he threw the rope at me and took a shot at me. I shot him back."

"What do we do now?" Gwed' asked.

"You go on back in the house," George said. "Pack me up some things I can take along with me. I'm driving the body on into Tahlequah right now."

"In the dark?" she asked.

"I don't want to leave it laying there overnight," he said. "Andy, hitch up the wagon for me. The work will just have to wait. I couldn't make medicine with that dead man right over there anyway. I should get into Tahlequah by daylight. I'll tell Rider what happened out here and let him take it from there."

Andy headed for the corral, walking in a wide circle around the dead man.

"I'll go with you, George," his wife said.

"No," he said. "You don't need to do that. Just help me get ready to go."

"You want to take Andy?"

"No. I'll do just fine by myself."

Gwed' went into the house. George kept staring at the body lying there. He found a way to get to me after all, he thought. Whoever it was trying to break George's protective barrier had sent the white man. George knew it. The white man had been a pawn. He had come out to the house to steal the horse, not knowing that his motions were being guided by a powerful evil force. George almost felt sorry for the foolish white man, but of course, if the man had not already had larcenous thoughts in his head, the evil wouldn't have been able to use him in that way. A man like that is always vulnerable, always ready to be made use of for someone else's nefarious purposes.

Andy brought the wagon, and George, though he hated to do it, loaded the body into the wagon. He would have to purify himself later. This thing had to be done now. Gwed' came out with his travel bag. George took it and put it into the wagon. He put his rifle on the seat, thinking that Go-Ahead Rider might ask for it. Then he picked up the tangle of rope the man had thrown at him and tossed that in, too. He looked at his son and then at his wife.

"I'll be all right," he said. "As soon as I get back, I'll have to wash off. You know what I need. Go ahead and get it ready for me, will you? We'll all have to wash off. I expect I'll be back around noon."

George climbed onto the seat, took the reins and started the wagon rolling. He was glad of the bright moon high in the night sky. It would light his way along the winding road into Tahlequah.

Some miles away, in a small log cabin, Big Forehead sat at a table where a candle burned. Big Forehead dangled a milky crystal between the candle flame and his own eyes, and he stared into the crystal. He saw the body of the white man lying bloody on the ground, and he saw George Panther standing nearby, a smoking Winchester rifle in his hands. Big Forehead gave a sinister smile. George Panther had trouble coming his way. More trouble than he could know about, and it would be coming from a direction he would not even be watching, from a source he had never imagined would bother him. Big Forehead felt as if he had won the war. The final battle plan had been laid. Now all he had to do was sit back and watch and wait.

Tahlequah was bustling with people. Wagons moved in both directions on the street. Men on horseback rode this way and that, and pedestrians were bustling everywhere. George managed to turn his wagon with its grim load off of the main street and rode over one block onto the street that ran alongside both Wolf Creek and the back of the capitol square. That would take him directly to the National Prison and Sheriff Rider's office anyway, but even that street was busy. The going was slow. George noticed that there were camp sites all along the creek just across from the square. He didn't like it that so much traffic was on the streets so early in the day, and that people passing him by were looking nosily into his wagon bed at the body there.

At last he made it to the National Prison. He saw Beehunter, Rider's sometime deputy, standing at the front door, and he stopped the wagon just in front of the prison and set the brake. "Beehunter," he called out in Cherokee. "Is Rider inside?"

"He's in there," Beehunter answered. "Do you want him?"

"Yes. I need him to come out here."

Beehunter went inside, and a moment later he reappeared with Sheriff Go-Ahead Rider. The two Cherokee lawmen walked out to George's wagon. George climbed down from the bench. He did not offer to shake hands. Rider and Beehunter looked in the wagon bed and knew why.

"Who is it, George?" Rider asked.

George shrugged. "I don't know him, Go-Ahead. He was at the racetrack though, and he tried to buy Lightning off me. Of course, I wouldn't sell. He had a pretty good wad of money in his pocket. He showed it to me. Maybe it's still there. I didn't touch him any more than I had to—just enough to get him loaded into the wagon. Anyhow, he came out to the house last night and tried to steal Lightning. I heard some noise and when I went to look, I saw this man at my corral. He had his rope ready. This rope here. I went back for my rifle, and then I came up on him and told him to stop. He turned and threw his rope at me and took a shot at me. I shot back. I killed him. That's all I know."

Rider looked at the Winchester on the wagon seat. "Is that the gun you got him with?"

"Yeah. You want it?"

"I don't think there's any need for that," Rider said. "Just keep it. You might need it for something else. I'll let you know if we need it for evidence."

"All right."

"Beehunter," Rider said, "get some help and take care of this body. George, let's you and me go inside. I'll have to fill out a report."

Beehunter looked hesitantly at the body.

"Ride back home with me when we're done here," George said, "and I'll do the washing off for you."

Rider led the way inside the prison to his downstairs office and offered George a chair. He went behind his desk to sit down. He also offered a cup of coffee, but George declined. Rider rummaged through some desk drawers until he found the right papers. Then he asked George to repeat the story, and this time, Rider wrote it down in Cherokee, using the syllabary that had been developed by Sequoyah. Finished, he handed the paper to George to read. George read it over and nodded.

"That's just how it happened," he said.

Rider handed George the pen, and George signed the paper, using the Cherokee syllabary to write his name.

"We'll try to find out who the man was," Rider

said. "There will have to be a trial. We have so many mixed-blood and white intermarried citizens now that they're impossible to keep up with. I meet new ones every day. Anyhow, when they get the date set, I'll either ride out or send someone out to let you know. You can go on back home now if you want to."

"Rider," George said, "why are there so many people in town?"

"Oh," Rider said, "there's a council meeting today. They'll be talking about a big lease with some Texas cattlemen for some of our land out west. Some other things, too, I guess."

"Oh," said George. "Well, it's too many people for me. I'll be glad when I get back out of town."

"I wish I could go with you," said Rider.

"You know, Go-Ahead," George said, "talking about all the white people who have come in here, and the council meeting going on now, it all reminds me of what I've been told. One of these days, and it's not all that far away, the white people are going to take over this Cherokee Nation. They'll take it all away from us, and they'll make it into a state or a part of a state just like Texas or Arkansas or Kansas or North Carolina. They'll take away our government, too, and they'll put us all under their own laws. They'll take the land. They'll mark it all off in little squares and put fences around it and across it. They'll cut down the trees and dump all kinds of stuff into the rivers until the water won't be fit to drink. They'll even burn things that will fill the air with poison smoke. They'll take everything away from the Cherokee People."

"I hope you were told wrong, George."

"It'll happen, Go-Ahead. And it will stay like that for a while. Maybe our children or our grandchildren will have to suffer through that time. Things will be like that for seventy years, maybe more, and then we'll start to get it back. It'll be slow, but it'll happen. You and me won't be here to see it, but we will get it all back. That's just some of what our council's going to have to deal with on down the road."

As George left the yellow sandstone building, he saw Beehunter coming back. He waited at the wagon for the deputy.

"You going back with me?" he asked.

"Let met tell Rider," said Beehunter. "You go on. I'll catch up to you on horseback."

George managed to get the wagon turned around. Then he had to wait for some time before he could get it back into the heavy traffic on the road out of town. Seeing a break at last, he snapped the reins and the horses pulled the wagon out in front of a water wagon that was coming along at a pretty fair clip. George had to ease up to keep from running his team into the rig ahead. He drove by the capitol building on the square again, past the many camp sites along Wolf Creek. At last he came to the far end of the street and turned onto the country road. There was even traffic there, but it was all going into Tahlequah. George moved freely ahead.

Back at the prison, Beehunter told Rider that he was going to catch up with George Panther. Rider knew why Beehunter was going and so made no objections.

"Beehunter," he said, "have you heard that prophecy that George tells?"

"About the white man taking over the Cherokee Nation?"

"Yes," Rider said. "That one. Do you believe it?"

"George says it will happen," Beehunter said. "I believe George. It seems bad, but we'll get over it."

Beehunter left the office, and Rider leaned back in his chair. Yeah, he said to himself, in seventy years or so. He thought about his own words to George Panther, about how it was impossible to keep up with the number of white citizens in the Cherokee Nation anymore. He thought of changes he had already seen in his own lifetime, and it seemed as if George was right. The way things looked, it was all going in that direction. Seventy years, he thought. My children will go through the worst years. Maybe their children will see the better ones again. If not, then their grandchildren.

Out on the road, George heard a horse coming up behind him, and he looked over his shoulder to see Beehunter coming up close to him. Beehunter tied his horse onto the back of the wagon and climbed in to sit beside George on the bench.

"You said you saw that white man at the races?" he asked.

"That's right," George said. "He tried to buy Lightning."

"Ever see him before that?"

George shook his head. "I don't recall that I'd ever seen him before," he said.

"Rider doesn't know him," Beehunter said. "I

don't either. He sure had lots of money in his pockets."

When they reached the house, Gwed' and Andy were sitting under the arbor. George pulled the wagon up close by and he and Beehunter climbed down. Beehunter greeted Gwed' and Andy. A bucket was there with the long handle of a dipping gourd sticking out. George didn't offer any explanations. Everyone knew what was going to happen. He sat on his chair and pulled off his shoes. He then rolled his trouser legs up to his knees and pushed his shirtsleeves up over his elbows. Andy and Beehunter did the same. Gwed' took off her shoes.

"Gwed'," George said, "you do me."

She stepped over to the bucket and dipped out a gourd full of the brew that it held. George cupped his hands and held them out. Gwed' poured the liquid into them, and George washed his forehead and the top of his head with one swift motion, then held out his hands for another dipper full. He washed his head four times. Then Gwed' poured the liquid on his right arm, and he washed it downward with his left. That was done four times. Then four times for the left arm, and four times for each leg.

George took the dipper from Gwed' and washed her off. Then Andy, and finally Beehunter. George then took the bucket and moved to the wagon, which he sprinkled liberally, as well as his rifle, and then the horses. He sprinkled the place where the body had fallen, and finally, going into the corral, he sprinkled Lightning and the remaining horses. Walking back to where the others waited, he put the bucket and the gourd dipper on the ground beside Beehunter.

"When you go back to Tahlequah," he said, "take this for Go-Ahead to use."

"I will," Beehunter said.

"But have coffee with us first," said Gwed'.

Beehunter agreed. They sat in chairs under the arbor, and in just a few minutes, Gwed' came out with coffee and cups. Then she went back in the house.

"I think that white man was a fool to try to steal from you," Beehunter said.

"Well, my Lightning is safe," George said.

"One thing I'll say for that white man," Andy said. "He had good taste in horses."

They laughed, but not uproariously. A death was not a thing to take lightly. And George knew that the foolish white man was only partly to blame. He didn't bother telling that to the others, though. If he were to tell them that much, he would have to reveal more, and he wasn't ready. He didn't know it all himself. There were still too many unanswered questions. Why was so much evil in the air? What was the source of it all? Was it really Big Forehead, and if so, why was he after George?

George realized that last question was the most easily answered. If Big Forehead, or someone else, was busily engaged in making harmful medicine, then George was the man to whom his victims would go for help. If George's medicine were stronger than that of the evil doctor, then the evil one's medicine would not be effective and his reputation would suffer. If his reputation suffered, then the people who came to him for help would stop coming. They would say, "I tried to do something to so and so, and I went to this man for medicine, but so and so is just fine. Nothing ever happened to him."

George also knew the evil doctor did what he did out of pure greed. People paid him to do harm to their perceived enemies. He took their money and, in an absolutely cold-blooded fashion, he worked the medicine and the spells to bring harm, even death, to the ones they had named. He had nothing against his victims. They might be old and helpless or young and innocent. But bringing harm to them gave some kind of pleasure or satisfaction to those who had paid him, and that was all that mattered. If they were pleased and satisfied, they would be back. It was in their nature. In the mind of George Panther, such a man—or woman—was pure evil.

"I'd better get back to Tahlequah," said Beehunter. "It's real busy in there today because of the council meeting. All kinds of people are in town. Rider has put on extra deputies. He won't like it if I'm just taking it easy out here."

"You take that medicine to him to wash off with," George said.

"I will."

Beehunter headed for his horse, but he stopped. He was looking down the road at a rider who was approaching.

"Who is it?" George asked, walking over to stand beside the deputy.

"It looks like Swim," said Beehunter. "Maybe Rider sent him to hurry me back."

Swim was another of Rider's part-time deputies,

usually hired during events like the council meet-
ings when hundreds of people flocked into
Tahlequah. With that many people packed into the
small town, almost anything could happen. Mostly,
though, the deputies would be hauling drunks into
jail and breaking up fights. That was usually about
all. Beehunter and George met Swim as he rode
into the yard. Andy walked over to say hello as
well.

"Did Rider send you out here to get me?"
Beehunter asked. "I was just about to go back when
I saw you coming."

"No," Swim said. "Rider sent me out here with a
message for George."

"What is it?" George asked.

"Just after you left," said Swim, "the sheriff from
Illinois District came into Rider's office. He had
some kind of business with Rider, and he wanted to
attend the council meeting, too, for some reason.
But that's not the message. You have a sister in
Illinois District?"

"My sister, Sally, moved there with her husband," said George. "Is it about her? Is she all
right?"

"Her husband is dead," Swim said, "and she's
alone with her little girl. She's having a hard time.
The sheriff told Rider that he stopped by to see
them, and they hadn't had much to eat for a few
days. Rider said you had to know about that."

"What happened to her husband, Cob?" George
asked.

"I don't know, George. All I heard is what I told
you."

"All right. Thanks for coming out here to tell me. I'll have to do something about that right away."

"Well, we'd better go back to town," Swim said, looking at Beehunter.

"Yes," said Beehunter. "I'm sorry to hear about your sister, George. Let me know if I can help you."

As Beehunter and Swim mounted their horses and rode off, Gwed' came out of the house and walked over to stand beside George and Andy. "You want something to eat?"

"Yes," George said. "Thank you. Gwed', Cob is dead. Swim just rode out to bring me the message."

"Sally's Cob?"

He nodded.

"That's what Swim came to tell me. Sally and her little girl are alone and not doing well. They're going hungry. I'll have to go get them and bring them home with me so that we can take care of them here."

"Yes," she said. "We can do that. When will we go after them?"

"Right away."

"Well, I'll get us all something to eat first. Then I'll start packing the wagon."

She went into the house and left George standing in the yard with their son. In another moment, Andy excused himself and went inside to help his mother. George sat alone considering recent events. He thought about the night's work he had lost. Some of that work had to be done at night, and so it would have to wait. But there were some things he could do during the daytime. He had figured that he would eat his noon meal, then relax with coffee and a cigarette. As soon as that was done, he'd get to work and try to make up for the time lost the night before. But now he had something else to do, something even more immediate, something that could not wait. If Sally and the little girl were going hungry, his trip south could not be postponed. He would just have to put everything else off and get them. He wondered what had happened to poor Cob.

Chapter 5

It was a long, slow ride in the wagon down to Illinois District in the southern part of the Cherokee Nation. They'd had to stop and camp out along the way at night. Gwed' had packed plenty of food for them to eat along the way, and some extra for Sally and her little daughter, Annie. George was anxious to get there for he had no idea how his sister and his niece were doing. According to what the district sheriff down there had told Rider, the situation seemed dire. It had been a long time since George had seen them, but he knew where their house was, and he found it again with no trouble.

As the wagon rumbled and rattled up to the house, the door opened a crack, and a forlorn face peeked out. George recognized little Annie, even though he had not seen her for several years. He thought that she must be six years old by now. He felt a lump in his throat as he set the wagon brake, seeing how sad she looked, how frightened.

"Annie?" he said. "Is that you?"

The little face disappeared, and a moment later Sally showed herself, looking out with curiosity.

"George?"

George had lumbered down off the wagon bench,

and he hurried to his sister with open arms. Sally embraced him, tears in her eyes.

"Oh, George," she said. "What are you doing here?"

"We came to get you," he said. "What else?"

"But how did you know?"

"We heard about you from the sheriff. We didn't know until then. We came to take you home with us."

Sally stepped back and wiped her eyes.

"I'm sorry," she said.

"For what?"

"For crying like that."

"Don't be," said George. "Everything's going to be all right now."

"Annie," said Sally. "Come on out. It's your Uncle George."

Annie came out of the house and stood behind her mother, peering out suspiciously at the strangers.

"You remember Uncle George?" Sally asked.

Annie nodded silently.

"She's being shy," said Sally.

Gwed' had come over by then. "She'll get over it all right." She hugged her sister-in-law. "We were awfully sorry to hear about Cob," she said.

Andy stepped up then, and Sally hugged him. "My, you're big," she said. "Annie, this is your cousin Andy."

"I know you're both hungry," said Gwed'. "We brought some food. Let's all eat."

They ate until all of them were satisfied, and then they began packing up the things that Sally and Annie wanted to take along with them. Annie did not have much to say, and when she did, it was only to her mother and in a very quiet voice. George watched her without her realizing she was being watched. It hurt him to see her so sad at such a young age. She had been such a happy little girl the last time he had seen her. But he could expect nothing else. She had lost her father, and then she and her mother had been struggling just to survive. George realized he could not bring back her father, but he could help in almost all other ways. He swore that they would always have a home. He swore that they would never again go hungry.

They were only halfway back home when Annie started talking. Her eyes were bright again. Sally was in much better spirits, too. George was grateful that the sheriff had brought word to Rider, and that Rider had sent Swim out to his house with the message. He hated to think about his sister and little Annie out there in that house alone, going hungry, and all on top of their great loss. Cob had been a decent man. He had taken good care of his wife and daughter, and they both had loved him dearly. But that was all behind them, and now they would be a part of his family.

"Sally, I wish I had known sooner," he said as they rolled and bumped along the road. "I came as soon as I heard."

"I know you did," said Sally. "I just didn't know how to get word to you. I just hate to crowd in on you like this."

"We have plenty of room," said Gwed'.

"And if we get to thinking that we need more," said George, "we'll just put up another house. We've got room for that, too."

"That's so much trouble for you."

"It's no trouble at all. We have friends who will be glad to help."

And it wasn't much trouble. Tom was still nowhere to be seen, and Andy was usually in Tahlequah at school. He did come home most weekends, and on school holidays he would be home for several days. Then it was a little crowded, but they made do. Sally helped Gwed' with the work around the house and outside in the garden, and Annie helped, too. She played outside as well. Everyone was pleased with the little girl's recovery. She was healthy and happy, and her cheerful disposition reflected that fact. Sometimes in the evenings she would sit close to her mother and cry a little because she missed her father. It was sad, but it was as it should be, as it had to be.

But they decided that a new house should be built, and George prepared the ground not far from his own house. They would be close neighbors. When Canoe and some of the other friends around the countryside found out about it, they pitched in to help. Sally and Annie would have their own house real soon.

It was a day of big celebration. It was Andy's birthday. People had been invited from all around, and most of them had come. Gwed' and Sally had cooked enough food to feed an army: venison, beef, pork, fish, corn bread, bean bread, biscuits, beans, corn, squash, soups. Out in front of the house, long planks had been laid out across tree stumps, sawhorses and whatever was available to make temporary tables and benches. Some of the men who had already eaten their fill were playing *diga-dayosdi*, the game of Cherokee marbles. The field had been laid out not far from the front of the house, over one hundred feet long with five holes spaced out in an L shape every thirty-five feet or so. The men were playing with smooth round stones, slightly smaller than billiard balls, trying to toss their own marble into a hole or knock an opponent's marble out of line. Small bets were made on the outcome of the game. People stood around cheering and jeering, making jokes and generally enjoying the game.

Back at the long tables, there were still plenty of others eating or sitting with full bellies, drinking more coffee. George Panther finished his meal, having waited until all of his guests had been served. He finished a last cup of coffee, then got up from the table. Going into the house, he found his fiddle and bow and went back outside. He sat down in a straight wooden chair, drew the bow across the strings tentatively a few times, made some adjustments, tuning the fiddle, then launched into a rousing version of "Soldier's Joy." When that was done, he changed the mood sharply with a wailing rendition of "Amazing Grace." His guests called for more, but just then George saw Beehunter come riding up. He looked around and found Andy, who was also an accomplished fiddler, got up out of his chair, handed the fiddle and bow to Andy, then walked over to meet Beehunter.

"Welcome," he said. "I'm glad you came."

Just then Andy began to make the fiddle sing.

"He's a good boy," Beehunter said. "And he makes good music."

"Go sit down at the table," George said. "We'll get you some food. Do you want some coffee?"

"Yes," Beehunter said, "that would be good."

He walked to the nearest long table and sat down on the bench there. Gwed' soon brought him a plate full of food and a cup of steaming coffee. Beehunter began wolfing it down as if he had not eaten for two days. George got himself another cup of coffee and sat down next to Beehunter. Canoe came walking over and sat next to George on his other side.

"It's a good party," Canoe said. "Lots of children. Where's your niece?"

George pointed at Annie where she was running with a group of children. "She's right over there. Yes, a lot of people showed up today. It's good."

"The little girl's doing all right then?"

"Yes. Fine. She's happy here."

"Andy's almost as good as you with that fiddle."

"Before long," said George, "he'll be better. He's learned a lot of songs—almost as many now as I know. How are things with your family?"

"My little girl is well," Canoe said. "Have you seen her? She's just over there playing with the other children. Over there where your niece is. They'll be good friends, I'll bet."

George smiled. "I saw her," he said. "How's your leg?"

"Oh, it's just fine."

"No pain?"

"No. None."

"I had to leave for a few days, you know, to go get Sally and Annie, but before we left, we took care of that stuff that was bothering you," George said. "They'll keep trying, but you just keep doing what I told you to do. You'll be all right."

"On my way here," Canoe said, "I passed by Billy Fire's house. He was sitting outside just staring straight ahead. He looked kind of lost. Really strange. I don't think he even saw me when I walked by him."

George smiled again and nodded. "That's how it happens," he said.

"George," said Canoe, "I don't want to hurt Billy."

"You didn't do anything to him," George said. "What he did to you is coming back to him. That's all. You didn't do it. I didn't do it. He did it to himself. If he'll let it go now, he might get back to normal."

Canoe nodded in understanding, and George slapped him on the back. "Don't worry about it. Have a good time," he said.

"*Howa*," Canoe said. "I'm okay."

When Canoe got up to go visit with someone else, Beehunter took a last long drink of coffee, then put the cup down. "George," he said, "I came out here to tell you about the trial."

"Has the time been set?"

"Yes. In one week in Tahlequah. That's what I came to tell you."

"Do you know who the judge will be?"

"Judge Sixkiller, it looks like."

George nodded. "He's a good man. I'll be there," he said.

"I'm sure there won't be any problems," Beehunter said. "Rider told me that. He told me to

tell you it will start at one o'clock in the courtroom
in the capitol. Rider said he doesn't think it will last
very long. Everyone knows what happened out
here."

"*Wado*," said George.

"Well, I have to go back now," said Beehunter.
"Rider will be looking for me. This has been a good
party."

The people began gathering up in the square
around the capitol in Tahlequah several hours before the trial was scheduled to begin. Some were
just curious. A trial was good entertainment, especially when it involved a murder. Others were
George's friends and so were sincerely interested in
the outcome of the proceedings. They talked together in small groups. Some said that there was no
way in which George Panther could be convicted.
His medicine was too strong. Some said simply that
he was clearly innocent of any wrongdoing, and because of that things would go well for him. Others
said that if for any reason they found George guilty,
they would fight to free him and help him escape.

"Would you fight Rider?" someone asked.

"If he tried to put George in jail, I would."

Sheriff Go-Ahead Rider, high sheriff of the
Cherokee Nation, and several of his deputies were
present to make sure that order was maintained.
They did not expect trouble. They just believed in
being prepared. Rider and Beehunter were standing
together beside the back door of the capitol building, watching over the crowd. The trial would take
place in one of the courtrooms inside. They had
heard the talk. Rider was thinking that if the un-

thinkable happened and the jury found George guilty, he did not know what he would do. He did not think that he would fight Cherokee people who wanted to free George. He did not think that he would be able to put George in jail. If the unthinkable should happen, he told himself, he would just have to turn in his badge. Of course, it was not going to happen, he knew. Those were just idle thoughts.

George Panther, dressed in his best suit of clothes, said good-by to Sally, Annie, his wife and son Andy. Tom had still not come home. George told them not to worry. Everything would be all right, and he would be back home soon. They all asked if they could ride in and be there with him through the trial.

"There's no need. I'll be back before dark," he said. "This is just a thing that we have to go through. They have to have all the papers fixed up just right when a thing like this happens. I'll tell my story, they'll fill out the papers, and they'll tell me to go on back home. That's all."

He went out to the corral and saddled Lightning, then mounted up and headed for Tahlequah. He wondered briefly where Tom might be, and if Tom would even care one way or the other about this trial, but he put the thought and its accompanying worries out of his mind. He instead reflected on his most immediate problem, the trial itself. He had made medicine to affect its outcome in his favor, of course, but only as a precaution. He had faith in the Cherokee court system and in Judge Sixkiller. He knew that he had not done wrong, and Rider and

Beehunter knew what had happened and were confident that everything would turn out well.

Even so, riding in to stand trial for murder, one could hardly help but worry at least a little. After all, murder was a hanging offense. The gallows stood just behind the prison, a constant reminder to all who passed by. It was an ominous sight. George imagined hanging to be a horrible death. He pushed the thought out of his mind and concentrated on a happy outcome for the day.

"Look, Go-Ahead," said Beehunter, speaking in Cherokee. He nodded ahead, and Rider looked up to see two white men walking determinedly toward him. He could see that they wore revolvers on their hips, which was against the law in Tahlequah. They arrived at the porch and made their way up the stairs. Rider could see then that they were both heavily armed, with extra revolvers tucked into their belts, and as they approached him, they pulled aside their jackets to reveal deputy United States marshals' badges pinned on their vests. The law against carrying sidearms in Tahlequah did not apply to these men. Both men wore high-topped boots with their trouser legs tucked into the boot tops.

"Hello, boys," Rider said in English. "What can I do for you?"

"I'm Glendon Jones," said the tallest of the two men. His face was red, and he sported a bristly mustache. He was maybe forty years old. "You Sheriff Rider?"

"That's right," Rider said.

"My partner here is Amos Adams. We're deputy

United States marshals out of Fort Smith. We've come about George Panther. Understand he's supposed to be in court here today. We have a warrant for his arrest for murder."

"Like you said, we have George scheduled for trial right here," Rider said. "I don't understand what the United States has to do with it."

"A complaint was filed in Fort Smith," Jones said. "That Heflinger that Panther killed? He was a white man."

"He was not a Cherokee citizen?" Rider asked.

"No," said Jones, "he was not. So the case goes to the federal court in Fort Smith. You want to hand him over to me now?"

"Well, he ain't arrived yet," Rider said. "You can wait here for him if you want to. He'll be along directly."

"You mean to say you're about to try a man for murder," said Adams, "and you don't have him in jail? You're trusting him to come in here on his own?"

The man was short and stout and probably not yet thirty. He needed a shave, but only to wipe the fuzzy stubble from his round face. Straggly blond hair hung down from under his flat hat brim.

"Sure," Rider said. "I know George personally. He's a good man, and he's honest. What's more, he ain't guilty. This trial's just a formality. He'll be here. It ain't time for the trial yet. Crowds gather up around here early."

Rider pulled out his pocket watch and looked at it for a moment, then put it back in his vest pocket.

"I just bet he'll be here," Adams said sarcastically.

"He will," said Rider.

"Come on. Would you just ride in and turn your-self in on a murder charge?"

"That's not exactly the case here. Ever'one knows what happened out there wasn't his fault," said Rider. "I know it, and the judge knows it. So does everyone on the jury. Hell, George was only de-fending his property, and he was shot at first. This is more like a formal hearing. That's all."

"That's his story," Adams said. "That's what a trial's for. To figure out the real truth of a thing."

"George brought the body in and told me what happened," said Rider. "If he was a murderer he'd have been more likely to have hid it somewhere. He sure wouldn't have told me it was him that did the killing. Hell, if it wasn't for George, this trial wouldn't even be going on."

"Well, it's not our business anyhow," Jones said. "All we do is arrest them and take them in. The rest is up to the judge."

"And the jury?" Rider asked.

"What do you mean by that?" said Adams.

"Oh, nothing much," Rider said. "I just heard someone say once that over there in Fort Smith, what the judge wants is what the judge gets. Said the jury's in his back pocket. Something like that."

"Now, you listen here—" Adams started.

"What're all these people doing here?" Jones in-terrupted, changing the subject. Older, more mature and of a calmer nature than his younger partner, Jones did not want to get into an argument with the Cherokee authorities. He might also have wanted to remind the hotheaded young deputy that they were tremendously outnumbered in Tahlequah and that it might not do to upset the crowd. He realized George Panther must be a very well-known and popular man among the Cherokees.

"They're just waiting for the trial," said Rider.

"Well, you might just as well send them on home, Sheriff," Adams said. "There won't be any trial here today. The United States claims jurisdiction in this case. We'll be taking Panther along with us back to Fort Smith. If the son of a bitch even shows up."

Rider turned to Beehunter and spoke in Cherokee. "Beehunter, these white lawmen just now told me that the man George killed was not a Cherokee citizen. He was a white man. They want to take George back to Fort Smith to be tried in the white man's court. I don't think that's a very good idea. Ride out and meet George and tell him. He should be on his way here by now. Tell him to go on back home. Tell him to stay away from here today."

"Howa," said Beehunter. He walked down the stairs of the back porch and headed off through the crowd.

"What did you say to that man?" Adams asked.

"What man?" said Rider. "You mean my deputy?"

"Yeah. If that's what he is. What did you say to him?"

"I told him what you said to me," Rider answered. "That there won't be any trial here today. He'll tell the rest of the people here, and we'll get this crowd dispersed."

"Why didn't you tell him in English?" said Jones.

"Beehunter can't understand English," said Rider. "Many of these people here speak only Cherokee."

"You got a deputy that can't talk English?"

"You are in the Cherokee Nation, you know."

Adams, clearly the less patient of the two deputies, pulled a watch out of his pocket and studied its face. "When do you expect Panther to show up?"

"The trial's not scheduled to start for another hour yet," Rider said. "He ought to be here by then." He was watching the road carefully in case George should ride in early. He checked his watch again. Beehunter should be well out on the road, he thought. He had seen no sign of George, so it was pretty clear that Beehunter would successfully intercept him along the way. He put the watch back, leaned back against the building and relaxed.

Riding along casually toward Tahlequah, knowing that he had plenty of time to get there, George Panther saw Beehunter come riding toward him in a great hurry. The two riders met and stopped their horses side by side.

"Beehunter, what brings you out this way?"

"Rider sent me to meet you."

"To escort me into town? Doesn't he trust me to show up on my own?"

"That's not it," said Beehunter. "Rider said to tell you to turn around and go back home. That man you killed was a white man. Two white catchers are waiting to take you to Fort Smith with them."

"You mean that man was not a Cherokee citizen?"

Beehunter shook his head. "No, he was a white man. There won't be any trial in Tahlequah today."

"And they want to take me to Fort Smith?"

"That's right. They have the papers."

George understood the jurisdictional situation with the United States, and he knew about the court in Fort Smith. From everything he had heard, it was not a good place for an Indian. It seemed that the judge had already made up his mind any time an Indian was brought into his courtroom.

"They'd throw me in jail there," George said. "They'd keep me there until the time for the trial, and there's no telling how long that would be. Then they'd probably convict me just because that man was white. They'd say I killed him, and they wouldn't worry about the why of it."

"Rider said don't come to town today," said Beehunter.

"Thanks, Beehunter," George said. "I won't. I'll turn around right now and go back home. Thank Rider for me, too."

Both men turned their horses and headed back in the directions from where they had come. As George made his way toward home, he thought about the mysterious, shadowy, amorphous figure he had seen in his crystal. Was that shade—whoever or whatever it might be—responsible for this troublesome new development in his life? Had he or it somehow caused this white stranger to go to George's home to cause this trouble, to try to steal Lightning and to shoot a gun? George realized he was now about to become a fugitive from white man's justice. It would considerably complicate his life. It would interfere with him in his duty to help the people. He also had a larger family to care for now.

George was not afraid, but this new complication

was very troublesome and most unwelcome. There were things he could do to keep the U.S. deputies away from him. He also felt confident that he would eventually get to the bottom of all this trouble. His grandfather had trained him well. But these complications were making it more difficult. It would take more time to get things settled.

Back at the capitol square in Tahlequah, the two deputy marshals were becoming increasingly impatient. Adams, especially, was getting irritable. He pulled out his pocket watch again and looked at it for what seemed to be the hundredth time. He snapped the cover shut and shoved the watch back down into his pocket, then turned to Rider. "Your man is late," he said.

"My man?" Rider said.

"That damned Panther," Adams said. "He's late. He should have been here over fifteen minutes ago."

"Maybe your watch is fast," Rider said.

"My watch is right on time," Adams said. "I don't believe he's coming. I think you're a damn fool to expect him to come in on his own like that."

"Amos," Jones said, "take it easy."

"Well, shit, Glen," Adams said, "do you think he's coming in? Do you believe that?"

"I don't know, but there's no call to go insulting Sheriff Rider there. There's no call to start making accusations. We'll just wait awhile longer here. Fifteen minutes ain't all that late."

"Ever'one here is looking right at us," Adams said.

"Yeah," Jones said, "I reckon they are. So try not

to give them nothing to talk about. Try not to act like a damn fool. You know, the Cherokees got a newspaper, too. I bet there's at least one reporter out there."

By this time, Rider knew that George would not be coming in. His goal at this point was to delay the deputies as long as he could. Every minute he could keep them right there in Tahlequah was another minute George would have to prepare himself for them. Before much longer, the two would come to the end of their patience, and then they would go looking for George. Rider meant to give George as much time as he could.

"It's been an hour now, Rider," Adams said. "He's a whole hour late. What do you say now?"

Rider shrugged. "It takes time for people to get into town," he said. "Sometimes things don't get started for two, maybe three hours, after they've been scheduled. We wait for people to show up, and then we get started. That's just the way things are done around here."

"That's bullshit," said Adams. He turned to Jones. "What do you say, Glen? You still want to just hang around here getting stared at by a bunch of Cherokees for another hour or so just waiting to see if that honest Injun's going to come riding right on in here bigger'n shit and give hisself up to us?"

Jones heaved a sigh. "No," he said, "I reckon we'll just mount up and ride on out to ole Panther's house. We can arrest him out there."

"You know where he lives?" Adams asked.

"I know," said Jones. "Come on. Let's get going. It'll be dark before we can get out there and back."

"It wouldn't have been if we'd left earlier," Adams mumbled, following his senior partner down the stairs.

Rider watched them go. He had done all that he could. He hoped that George would be ready for them when they arrived at his house. Beehunter came back just after that and walked up to join Rider. The crowd around the square was beginning to break up. Word had gotten around that the trial was called off.

"Did you meet George?" Rider asked.

"Yes, I did," Beehunter said. "He went home."

In the back room of his house, George took out his crystal. This new problem was not just a streak of bad luck, and he did not believe in coincidence. There was a reason for it. Someone was trying to make trouble for him, bad trouble. It could only be the one who was responsible for all the recent bad medicine. When George helped the evil one's victims, that meant that his bad medicine was unsuccessful. That would mean fewer people coming to him to have their mischief done as the word got around. George stared hard into the crystal. For a long moment, he saw nothing there. Then once again, the dark cloud formed, and it twisted and turned. George watched it intently.

Slowly, an arm came out of the right side of the cloud, and then another out of the left side. The cloud continued to pulsate. A leg grew down from its left side, and then another shot down out of the right. George kept staring, studying, but nothing more would come.

"Show me his face," he said to the crystal.

The form began to dissipate, and it became a gray cloud again. Finally, George blinked his eyes several times, then rubbed them. He put the crystal away. He would have to try it another time. Whoever it was, he had strength. He had to give the evil one that. It was as strong as anyone George ever had to fight before. He would have to catch him in a weak moment. And he would have to cause that weak moment himself, by doing something to sap the other man's strength. Then he would look again.

He walked into the other room, where the family was sitting around the table. He pulled out his chair and sat down heavily.

"Are you all right, Uncle?" Annie asked.

"I'm just fine, baby," he said. "I'd like a cup of coffee."

"I'll get it."

The little girl jumped out of her chair and ran for a cup. She picked up the pot and poured the cup full, then walked very carefully with it to the table, placing it in front of George.

"Thank you," he said.

"George," said Gwed', "I'm worried. They said it was a white man. Will those white lawmen be after you now?"

"I guess they will," he said. "I'll just have to be ready for them. That's all."

Glen Jones and Amos Adams stopped their horses. Jones pulled out his Smith & Wesson six-gun and checked its load and the spin of its cylinder. Adams watched him curiously.

"You think he's going to give us trouble?" he asked. "Put up a fight?"

"Just being cautious," Jones said. He put the revolver back into its holster. "I don't expect any trouble. George Panther is a highly respected medicine man. A good citizen, they say. I imagine he'll come along without giving us any problems."

Adams took out his own revolver to check it over. "I always heard they were the real troublemakers," he said. "The damn medicine men. How much farther is it to his house?"

"It's just up there around the bend," said Jones. "You ready?"

"I been ready ever since we got to Tahlequah," the young man answered.

Chapter 6

Gwed' heard the horses ride up in front of the house. She went to the front door, wiping her hands on her apron, and then she opened the door. She was surprised to see the two white men out there. They wore many guns, and they were dismounting as she called out to them from the front door. She knew who they were, of course, but she hadn't expected them so quickly.

"Hello," she said in English. "What do you want here?"

"You Mrs. Panther?" Jones asked.

"Yes. Who are you?"

"Is your husband home?"

Gwed' hesitated, not knowing exactly what to expect from these men. She knew that she did not like their looks. She also knew that she had no intention of cooperating with them. Their expressions were stern, and there were all those guns. She would try to convince them that George was not at home.

"Don't you understand English?" asked Adams. "He asked is your husband home? Is George Panther here?"

Now it was more than their looks and more than their mission. They were rude. She knew that she did not like these white men. She did not trust them, and she certainly would not tell them anything about George—or about anyone or anything else.

"What do you want here?" she demanded.

"Our business is with George Panther," Jones said. "We don't want to bother anyone else if we don't have to."

George stepped out the door just then and put a hand on Gwed's shoulder. He moved around her, gently pushing her back out of the way. Sally and Annie had stepped up behind Gwed' protective.

"George," said his wife, speaking in Cherokee, "what did you come out here for?"

"It's all right," he said. "I'll take care of it." Then he looked at the white men and spoke in English. "I'm George Panther, and I am at home. Just who are you, and what do you want here?"

Jones pulled his jacket aside to reveal his badge. Adams did the same, and then he lowered his right hand to rest meaningfully on the butt of his revolver. He squinted his eyes and scowled at George.

"I'm Glendon Jones, Deputy United States Marshal," said the older man. "This is my partner, Deputy U.S. Marshal Amos Adams." He paused and pulled a folded paper out of his inside jacket pocket, unfolding it and holding it out for George to look at. "We have here a warrant for your arrest, Mr. Panther, for the murder of one Omar Helfinger, a white man. We're here to take you back to Fort Smith to stand trial."

"When will the trial be held?" George asked.

"We don't know that, Mr. Panther," said Jones. "All we do is bring you in."

"So I just sit in your jail and wait till it comes up?" George asked.

Jones shrugged, and Adams said, "That's the way it goes. We don't just call for a trial and then set and wait to see if you'll show up on your own. You didn't show up in Tahlequah today, like they told us you would."

"Someone told me that the trial was called off," said George. "So why should I show up?"

"We called it off. We're taking you to Fort Smith," Adams said.

"I didn't murder that man," George said. "He was right here on my property after dark, and he was trying to steal my horse. When I called out to him, he shot at me. He shot first. I reported the whole thing to Sheriff Rider. I can show you right where it happened. My wife and my son were here. They can tell you how it happened."

"You and them can tell all that to the judge," Adams said. "You know, the one they call the Hanging Judge? Just come on along now and don't give us no trouble."

"I won't give you no trouble," George said. "Let's go then."

"George?" said Gwed'.

He turned to face her, and he put his arms around her and held her close for a moment. "Don't worry," he said, speaking Cherokee in her ear. "I'll be back tonight."

He released Gwed' and turned back to the deputies. "You want me to take my own horse?"

"Unless you want to walk all the way to Fort Smith," said Adams. Jones frowned at Adams as the three men walked outside.

"He's just back there," said George, pointing toward the corral behind the house. "I'll go saddle him up."

"We'll just walk along with you," Jones said.

"Yeah," said Adams, "just to make sure you don't decide to ride off in the wrong direction."

Gwed' followed them out, a worried look on her face. Andy stepped out of the house to stand beside his mother, and as George, followed by the two lawmen, disappeared around the corner, he put an arm around his mother's shoulders. "Should I get father's rifle?"

"No."

"What should I do?"

"Nothing," she said.

"Will we just let those men take him away?"

"Your father said he'll be back home tonight. He said don't worry. Everything will be all right. We have to believe him."

Little Annie came out to stand with them, and she looked off in the direction of the lawmen and her uncle back at the corral.

"Uncle George will be back," she said. "He'll be all right. And those men will be in trouble."

George saddled Lightning and led him back to where the deputies' horses stood waiting. All three men mounted up. They turned their horses and rode back toward Tahlequah. Gwed', Sally, Annie and Andy watched them ride away. Unseen by anyone, Tom Panther also watched from the dark shadows in the nearby woods. He wondered what was happening to his father, and, failing to recognize his aunt and cousin, he wondered who the strangers were at his house. Standing there in the dark, he suddenly wondered why he had even come back. He turned and disappeared back into the woods.

They were perhaps halfway between George's house and Tahlequah, and the sun was low in the western sky. Deputy Marshal Jones spotted a likely camp site beside the road. He knew that a stream ran nearby, and he pulled back on his reins. "Hold up," he said. "We'll make our camp here."

"You don't think we can make it on into Tahlequah?" Adams asked.

"We're only about halfway," said Jones. "I'd rather not ride in there in the middle of the night. Come on. Let's get the horses unsaddled."

George took the saddle and blanket off of Lightning while the deputies unburdened their own horses. All three horses were set out for the night near the edge of the clear running stream where there was plenty of grass around. The deputies built up a small fire and laid out blanket rolls. They prepared a meal of sausages and beans and served it up with hard rolls. They also made a pot of coffee. If not well fed, George thought, at least he had been fed. The coffee was good enough, though, and he had two cups. Ready to bed down for the night, the deputies bound George hand and foot. The ropes were tight, and the knots were hard. They leaned him up against a tree and wrapped another rope around him and the tree, pulling it tight, leaving him to sleep through the night in that uncomfortable position, sitting up.

"That oughta hold you," Adams said. "Medicine man. Shit."

"Take it easy, Amos," Jones said. "Come on. Let's turn in. We'll get us an early start in the morning. Sorry we can't make you more comfortable, Mr. Panther, but we can't take chances. You understand?"

"I understand," George said.

As the two deputies crawled into their bedrolls for the night, George Panther sang softly. The lawmen could not hear his songs. They had caught him by surprise this time. He had not been prepared. He had not thought they would be out at his house so fast. He was not worried though. He had said that he would be back home that night, and he had meant it. He was confident in the songs and in the medicine. He kept singing quietly, to himself, to the spirits. He heard the deputies begin to snore. They would be in a deep sleep well before the songs were done. He continued singing into the night. Somewhere in the distance a whippoorwill whistled its tune, and in a nearby tree a night owl hooted softly.

The sun was up but still low in the eastern sky when Deputy Jones woke up the next morning. It was a hard waking. He knew that the sun was up, and he wanted to get up himself and get back on the road. He stretched and rubbed his eyes. He rolled over, wrapping himself in his blanket and almost drifted back to sleep. His eyes were still closed, almost glued together by the crust that gathers on them in the night. He rubbed them again. Finally, he opened them, squinting against the light. Adams was still sleeping. Jones could hear the younger man's snores. He sat up slowly, his body stiff. Why was it so hard for him to wake up? he wondered. He reached for his boots and pulled them on, glancing over at the snoring Adams.

"Amos," he called out, "wake up."

He looked at what was left of the small fire, thinking about morning coffee. They would have to gather sticks and build the fire up again. He wondered if coffee would be enough to get started on. They didn't have much for breakfast, just cold biscuits. Maybe they could wait until they reached Tahlequah, and then buy themselves a real breakfast. He wasn't sure what to do about Panther, though. Of course, they would be reimbursed for the meals of a prisoner, but they did not like to spend the full amount they were allowed for prisoners' meals. It was a way of putting a little extra cash into their own pockets.

Jones was hungry, though, and he thought that he would have to have a breakfast. But maybe coffee would do for now, to help him wake up. He could not remember having such a hard night's sleep. It would take a whole pot of coffee to get him going. Breakfast would wait until Tahlequah, but coffee could not. He coughed up a wad of phlegm and spat it out.

Jones stood up stiffly, stretched again, and looked over at the tree where George had been tied the night before. The ropes that had bound George's hands and feet were lying in a pile on the ground. The second rope was still wrapped around the tree. The knots were still tied. There was no sign of George Panther. Jones blinked. He shook his head. Then he rushed over to the side of the still sleeping Adams and kicked him rudely.

"Get up, Amos!" he called out. "Get up. He's gone."

Adams sat up quickly, rubbing his eyes. "What?"

"The son of a bitch is gone!" Jones shouted.

Not waiting for Adams, Jones ran over to the tree, dropped to his knees, and picked up some rope in his hands. He stared at it, unbelieving. He ran the rope through his hands, examining the knots. They were still fast. All of them. And the rope had not been cut. It did not make sense. It did not seem possible. Yet it was so.

"Come over here, Amos," he said.

Adams walked gingerly on bare feet over to the side of Jones. He too knelt and examined the ropes. "How the hell did he get loose?" He looked around in all directions as if he might see some sign of the escaped prisoner or perhaps some evidence of what mysterious thing had taken place during the hours of darkness.

"Well, hell, you see the same thing I see," Jones said. "Goddamn it. How should I know? We just didn't tie him good enough, I guess."

"The damn knots are still tight," Adams said. "And I checked them over last night. I checked them real good. He was secure, Glen. Someone must have slipped in here last night and turned him loose."

"If someone did that," Jones said, "why the hell would they have tied the knots back the way we had them?"

"How the hell should I know?"

"Check his horse," Jones said.

"You check it," Adams said. "I ain't got my boots on yet."

"Well, get them on. We've got to get going. We've got to run the son of a bitch down right now."

While Adams hobbled back to his bedroll and sat on the ground to pull on his boots, Jones ran over to the streambed where they had left the three horses the night before. The deputies' horses were still there, grazing contentedly. But Lightning was not there. His saddle and blanket were also gone. And there were no telltale signs.

"Goddamn it," Jones said, hurrying back to the camp. Back by his bedroll, he picked up his shirt and started pulling it on. "Get it together, Amos," he said. "We got to get moving. No time for coffee this morning."

An owl hooted from somewhere very near, and Adams jumped and grabbed his revolver. He looked around up in the trees.

"Don't be so damn jumpy," said Jones. "It's just an old hoot owl. Hurry up and get ready now. We don't have all day here."

They rode slowly, looking carefully for any signs they might find along the way. They were unable to find anything to indicate with any certainty in what direction their escaped prisoner had gone or if he had any company. Neither man wanted to give voice to his thoughts. It was as if man and horse had simply vanished.

"What do we do now, Glen?" Adams asked.

"Hell, let's ride on back over to his house," said Jones. "These Indians are funny that way. Even if they know you're after them, half the time they just go right on back home. Anyway, it's worth a try. We got no other leads."

"Well, I don't care what you said about that damn medicine man before, Glen," said Adams. "This time we'd best be ready for a fight."

George and his son were standing outside the house at the corral.

"Andy," George said, "I want you to take your mother and your Aunt Sally and your cousin and get them over to your Aunt Polly's house. I've already told your mother and Sally, and they're packing up what all you'll need to stay there for a few days. Those lawmen will be coming here for me again, but don't worry. They won't see me, and I don't want anyone else to be around. You understand me? I don't want any trouble here, and I want all of you to be where it's safe."

"Are you sure you don't want me to stay here and help?" Andy asked. "I'm not afraid, and I don't like leaving you alone when there might be trouble. You know I can shoot a gun almost as well as you."

"Just do like I say," George told him. "There won't be any shooting here. Hitch up the team and take the wagon. You'll need it. I want you and all the rest of this family to stay with your Aunt Polly till this is all over. Then I'll send word for you to come back home."

"*Howa*," Andy said. He did not like it, but he would do as his father said.

As Andy moved to catch up the team, George wished silently that he knew where Tom was hanging out. He didn't want Tom to come wandering home and blunder into the deputy marshals. Of course, Tom was not wanted for anything, so far as George knew, but he did not trust the federal lawmen. There was no telling what they might do if they came across any member of his family. He did not trust Tom either, although he hated to admit it, even to himself. His thoughts were interrupted when Gwed' came out of the house carrying two bundles. She walked around to the corral and stepped up close to George.

"You be careful," she said.

"I'll be all right," he said. "They won't catch me by surprise again. I just want you and the rest of this family away from here. As soon as this is all over, I'll come for you or send word to you. One way or the other."

"All right," she said. "Just be careful."

George stood and watched Andy drive off in the wagon with Gwed', Sally and Annie. He would miss them, but knew it was best this way. When they were finally out of sight, he went to work. This kind of work was best done at night, but there was no time to waste. George knew that the two lawmen would be back before nightfall. The work had to be done. He boiled herbs in water, and while he waited for the mixture to cook long enough, he mixed tobacco. He sang songs into the medicine he made, and he sprinkled the liquid medicine and smoked the tobacco. When he was done, he went into the house. He rolled himself a cigarette, lit it and moved a straight-backed wooden chair to a position at the back wall of the house directly in line with the front door. Leaving the front door open he sat in the chair staring straight out to the yard in front of the house.

Jones and Adams pulled up short of the house. They sat in their saddles for a long moment, looking at the house. They saw no sign of human life other than a curl of smoke rising from what was left of a small fire beside the arbor at the side of the house. Birds sang in the trees and fluttered about the yard. Squirrels chattered. A lazy hound lounged beside the house, seemingly unconcerned about the approach of the two strangers. Slowly, keeping his eyes on the house, Jones swung out of the saddle. He drew his revolver out of the holster and held it ready as he took a couple of steps toward the house. Adams got down to follow him. About halfway across the yard, Jones made a motion with his left arm, and Adams started a wide circle around the house to approach the back. Closer in, Jones stopped. He could see that the front door of the house was standing wide open.

"George Panther," he called out. "Are you in there?"

He waited, but receiving no answer, moved on to the door. He stood there for a long time, staring in through the open door.

"Anyone home in there?" he called out.

Still he received no answer. He stepped inside cautiously and shut the door behind himself stepping back so that his back was against the door. Waiting a moment for his eyes to adjust to the dimmer light inside, he peered around the room. He saw no one. There was a doorway leading into another room, a blanket tacked over it to serve as a door, so Jones stepped toward it. He moved slowly, constantly looking around and back over his shoulder. Reaching the doorway, he shoved the blanket aside and ducked under it, stepping quickly into the next room. Seeing no one, he walked back into the main room and over to the back door. Adams was waiting outside, a cocked revolver in his hand.

"There's no one in there," Jones said.

"There's no one out here," said Adams, "but that big white horse is right over yonder in the corral. He come back here all right. But where the hell did he go without his horse?"

"I don't know," Jones said.

"So what do we do now?"

"There's nothing we can do," Jones said, "but just go on back to Fort Smith and report the truth of what happened here. Damn. I hate it. George Panther is the first prisoner I ever lost, and it sure ain't going to be easy telling the marshal how it happened."

"Maybe we ought to make up some lie," said the younger deputy.

"You come up with a good one," said Jones, "and maybe I'll consider using it."

The two deputies mounted up and turned their horses back toward Tahlequah. As they moved away from the Panther home, George stood up from his straight-backed wooden chair. He walked to the front door, where he stood briefly looking after the lawmen. As they rode out of view, he stepped out into the yard. He could see them for a few more seconds before they rounded a bend. Then they were gone. He was well satisfied for the moment. He had won that round, but he knew there would be more to come. They had come after him that first time with an arrest warrant. The next time, it would be a fugitive warrant. He was now not only a wanted man—he was also an escaped prisoner. He knew that it made the deputies from Fort Smith look bad.

They would surely come back, and they would come after him with their best, with all they had. He would have to stay ready for them from now on. There would be no rest for George Panther.

In his small, dark cabin, Big Forehead stared into his murky crystal. He knew that George had been arrested, and he had watched his escape. He had even seen the deputies approach the Panther home and leave disappointed. He knew what George had done, knew that he had simply made himself invisible to the eyes of the white lawmen. He had heard that George had that power, and now he knew it to be true. He knew that his chosen enemy was formidable indeed.

He would have been happier, of course, if the lawmen had taken George away and successfully delivered him to the jail in Fort Smith. But he knew, as did George, that the lawmen would be back. They would not give up so easily. Most important, Big Forehead knew that George Panther's life would now be taken up with his own problems, and his energies would all be directed at keeping himself safely out of reach of the deputies from Fort Smith. For the time being, that was victory enough for Big Forehead. He was content. He smiled as he stared at the lone image of George Panther that floated inside his crystal.

Chapter 7

At the track just behind his house where he trained horses, Adam Diwali led a spirited gray stallion through the gate. The horse was saddled and ready to go. In fact, it was more than ready. It was anxious. Adam could tell. He knew the horse well, having trained it for racing for its owner. He knew that the horse loved to run, and it was a good one. It would take on any challengers, and it had a good chance at winning any race—unless George Panther's Lightning was entered. And even if the gray horse was running against Lightning, it often came in a close second or third. Adam was fond of the horse and was ready to put it through its paces. As he mounted up, the gray horse nickered and stamped its front feet, then pranced around in a circle.

"Steady now," said Adam

There was something wrong with the horse. Adam fought to control it.

"Steady," he said.

Overhead a ragged-looking raven circled in the sky. Its circles grew ever smaller as it soared closer to the earth, and in the center of its circle down below was Adam on the gray horse. The horse reared and came down hard. Adam, taken by surprise, was thrown off balance, his head coming dangerously close to the horse's neck. He straightened up and fought to steady the animal as the raven swept closer.

"Ka! Ka!" it screamed.

The gray horse kicked up its hind legs. It spun in a circle going to its left. Then it began bucking in earnest.

"Ka! Ka!" the raven crowed.

Adam hung on tight. He couldn't figure out what had gone wrong with the horse. It had never given him any problems before this. Was it frightened or just bad-tempered? He couldn't tell, and he didn't have time to worry about it. He was holding on for his life, being jerked first this way and then that way, flung upward, then coming down hard with a jolt that shook all his bones.

The gray horse jumped high in the air and came down hard, jolting Adam loose from the saddle. Before he had time to settle himself again, the horse leaped forward. When it hit dirt, it jumped again, this time rearing backward. It started to spin, then suddenly it flung its rear end sharply to the right, and Adam went flying through the air. He landed hard, and as he hit the ground, he heard his leg bone snap. He screamed in pain. He tried to sit up, but found that the pain was too much. He moaned out loud, and he looked over at the gray horse, standing calmly, as if everything was all right, as if it had done nothing wrong or even out of the ordinary. Then Adam heard the raven.

"Ka! Ka!"

It was an unusually loud cry, and Adam looked around to see where it was coming from. The ugly black bird had settled on a low tree branch just outside the track. Adam felt a chill run over his entire body. He stared at the bird, and it seemed to be looking back at him with red flaring eyes. It ruffled its ragged feathers and lifted its wings slightly. A loose feather fell to the ground. Then the nasty-looking bird spread its wings, gave a slight push with its skinny legs and took flight. As it flew over Adam's head, it screamed out once again.

"Ka! Ka!"

George Crump sat at his desk in his office in the United States Courthouse at Fort Smith, Arkansas. In front of him was a stack of papers through which he was fumbling. There were just too damn many open cases, he thought, too many fugitives, too many unsolved crimes and too few deputies to patrol the vast Indian Territory. The notorious Crawford Goldsby, known as Cherokee Bill, was still on the loose. Henry Starr was running around the country robbing banks. Jim French, Mose Miller, Bill Cook, and other lesser-known outlaws were also out there somewhere, still terrorizing the citizens of Indian Territory. And there were the white outlaws who invaded the Territory, knowing that the Indian lawmen could not touch them, and the deputy marshals from Fort Smith were just spread too thin. Crump had been appointed United States marshal for the Western District of Arkansas by President Cleveland in 1893. His boss was Judge Isaac C. Parker, infamously known as the Hanging Judge. Crump looked up from his papers when he heard a sharp rap on his office door.

"Come in," he shouted.

The door opened and three deputies stepped into the room. They took off their hats and moved to the edge of the desk.

"Grab some chairs," Crump ordered, and they did, pulling them up close to the desk. "I called you in here to give you a new assignment," said Crump. "You might have heard that Glen Jones and Amos Adams went over to Tahlequah to arrest an Indian named George Panther. They said they found him at home, and he went along with them peacefully. It was late, and they made camp by the side of the road. They said they tied him up real good for the night, but when they woke up in the morning, he was gone. But the ropes were still tied around the tree.

"They said this Panther is well known and highly thought of as a medicine man. The Cherokees believe that he got loose by some kind of Indian magic or conjuring. Now I don't believe that, and neither do you, but I just want you to know. Anyhow, Panther killed a white man. He claims the man was trying to steal his horse and that he shot in self-defense. Maybe so. But that's not our concern. Our job is to find him and bring him in for trial. That's all. The rest is up to the court.

"Now the Cherokee sheriff over there at Tahlequah is a full-blooded Indian named Go-Ahead Rider, but he won't be any help to us at all. He'll make like he doesn't know anything, doesn't have any information to help us. He's lying, of course. He's protecting one of his own. Check in with him anyway. It's protocol. So I want you men to look up Glen and Amos. Have them tell you everything they know about Panther. Get directions to his house. And then I want you to bring him in. That's all."

The sun was out of sight, but the sky was not yet dark. George Panther sat underneath the arbor beside his house. The fire was going, and a pot of water was boiling over the flames. George was singing low to some tobacco in front of him, putting a song into the healing plant. He sang the song seven times, then he put the tobacco into a pouch. He stood up, picked up some twigs of various kinds from beside his chair and walked over to the fire. He put the twigs into the pot of boiling water and said some words over them. Then he went back to his chair and sat down. The sky was a little darker, and suddenly there was a flash of purple. As before, it rose in an arc and then seemed to smash itself against something before it could reach the air over George's house. Other flashes shot through the night air and exploded against the same invisible barrier.

George smiled to himself. The evil one was still trying. He was still aiming his bad medicine at George, but the protection that George had provided for himself and his family was still firmly in place. He would keep that protection strong, and make it stronger. The other one would not get through. But as long as the barrier was holding, there were other things to deal with first.

The business with the white lawmen was an inconvenience and an annoyance. It took time and effort to prepare and use the medicine needed to protect himself from them, and that meant time and energy taken away from the people who needed his help, the ones who depended on him. And it meant time taken away from his family. Still, it had to be done, for if George failed to protect himself, he could be taken away and locked up, and that would deprive everyone else of his administrations. He would do what he had to do to protect himself, and then he would work on what he had to do for the people. He knew that he would be up all night long, maybe even longer.

George thought about Big Forehead, and he wondered still if that man was the source of the evil. He was almost convinced that was the case, but he had been unable so far to see clearly, and he could not aim his own medicine at Big Forehead without having that final proof. No matter how strongly he felt about it, no matter how much his reasoning power told him that Big Forehead must be the guilty one, there was always a possibility that he could be wrong. He had to see the man in action. He had to know for sure, beyond any doubt, before he could do what had to be done.

Tom Panther was just in the woods outside of Tahlequah. He was with four other young Cherokee men, drinking whiskey they had purchased from a Cherokee woman who lived on the outskirts of town. They figured that she got the stuff from some white man who brought it in illegally from Arkansas, but they really didn't care. None of that mattered to them, so long as they could buy it when they wanted it. They had gone into the woods a little ways just to avoid being seen. It was against the Cherokee law to buy, sell or consume liquor, and they did not want to get thrown in jail by Sheriff

Rider. They had all been in Rider's jail before, most of them more than once. The boys knew that the deputy marshals who rode into their country out of Fort Smith, Arkansas, carried with them blank warrants, which they called "whiskey warrants." That way any time they ran across any illegal use of whiskey, they had their warrants handy. Even worse than being caught by Rider or his deputies would be getting caught by the U.S. deputy marshals. Tom took a long drink and passed the jug to another boy, a young mixed-blood who looked like a white boy.

"Hey, Skinny," he said, speaking English, "let's go over to that little gal's house, and let's all get some of that stuff. You know."

"Who're you talking about?" Skinny asked. "What little gal?"

"You know who I mean," said Tom. "That Velma you know. If she puts out for you, she ought to put out for all of us. We'll have us a good time, and she'll like it, too."

"She ain't like that," Skinny said. "She's my girl."

"We're all friends here," Tom said. "Come on. Let's go over there. We'll show her a good time, all right."

"You stay away from Velma," said Skinny. "Besides, if we was to go over there at night like this and half-drunk the way we are, her daddy'd shoot us. He'd kill us all."

"We could handle him all right," said Tom. "I ain't scared of him. Are you?"

"Tom," said another of the boys, a young full-blood, "leave Skinny alone. Have another drink."

"Don't go telling me what to do," said Tom hotly.

"You think you can make me? Just come on and try. I can take you and Skinny both. Hell, I can take all three of you. I ain't scared of all of you or of Velma's old man neither. Come on. Try to make me shut up. Just try it."

"No, I don't want to try to make you do anything. I'm just talking. That's all."

"Well, don't try to tell me what to do."

Skinny held the jug out toward Tom. "Have another drink?"

Tom took the jug and tipped it up for a long while. When he lowered it, he almost fell forward on his face. He staggered and caught his balance. He laughed to try to cover his embarrassment. One of the other boys reached for the jug, but Tom jerked it back. He took a deep breath and tipped it up again. He wanted to show them that he could handle it, that he could outdrink them all.

"Hey, Tom," said one of the boys, "let me have a drink of that stuff."

Tom hugged the jug close to his chest. "Try to get it," he said.

"Never mind," the boy said. "Hell, I'm going home."

"Me, too," said Skinny. "I've had enough of this."

The two boys turned to walk away, and the third one joined them without having said anything. Tom was left standing alone, watching them walk away. "Hey," he called.

The boys kept walking. They did not look back.

"Hey!" Tom shouted. "Where the hell are you going? Come back here."

Skinny stopped and looked back over his shoulder. "You're too drunk, Tom," he said. "You're no fun to be around. We're going home."

"Fuck you!" Tom shouted, and he threw the jug at Skinny. Skinny jumped to one side and the jug fell harmlessly to the ground. The other boys stopped walking and turned to face Tom. They looked at one another.

"Let's teach him a lesson," one of them said.

Sober, Tom might have taken on all three of the boys and had at least a chance, but Tom was far from sober. He was staggering drunk. The three boys walked up close, and one of them moved around behind Tom. Skinny kept his distance. He did not want any part of this. The first boy hit Tom with a hard right to the jaw that spun him around, and then the second boy did the same. Tom bounced back and forth between them several times before he fell. Then they took turns kicking his ribs.

"Hey," said Skinny, "cut it out. You might kill him. I think he's out cold already anyway."

The two boys stopped.

"Ah, to hell with him," one said. "Let's all get out of here."

George had just dozed off in his chair when the sound of an approaching wagon startled him awake. He sat up straight, stood up and walked to the window to look out. There was Andy driving the wagon loaded up with the rest of the family. They were coming home. George jerked the door open and went outside.

"What are you doing back here?" he said, his glare directed at Andy.

"We just thought—"

"Don't try to take the blame, Andy," said Gwed'. She looked at George. "I'm the one. It was my decision. I said our place is here, with you. This is our home. All Andy did was be a good son. He did what his mother told him to do. That's all."

"Aren't you glad to see us, Uncle?" asked Annie.

George reached out with both hands to take the little girl and lift her out of the wagon. He held her and hugged her to him, and her arms went around his neck.

"I'm always glad to see you," he said. "All of you. You're my family, and I love you. I just don't want you to be around here if there's any trouble. I don't want you to get hurt. That's all."

"George," said Sally, "we all feel the same way about you. That's why we came back."

George heaved a long and heavy sigh. "Well, then," he said, "let's get this wagon unloaded. Then we'll fix some food. I'll bet you're hungry after that long ride. Aren't you?"

"I'm starving," Annie sid. "Let's get busy."

It was early morning when Canoe arrived at George Panther's house. Gwed' had just stepped out the front door to toss out a pail of sudsy water. She looked up to see Canoe coming, and she stood waiting to greet him.

"*Siyo*, Gwed', is George at home?"

"Let me go see if he's awake," she said. "You can wait over there." She gestured toward the arbor and went back into the house. Canoe went into the arbor and sat in the chair meant for guests. He knew which chair was George's chair.

He waited for perhaps half an hour before

George came out of the house, rubbing his tired eyes. George walked into the arbor and shook hands with Canoe. Then he sat down. "That's the first time I fell asleep in four days," he said.

"Oh, I'm sorry to wake you. I didn't know."

"That's all right," said George. "I have work to do. I can't be sleeping the day away like that. I'm glad you came. Is there something the matter?"

"Yesterday morning," Canoe said, "I stepped out my front door and a copperhead was right there in front of me. It looked at me and hissed. I backed up real careful inside the house, and I got a long stick. I used the stick to move the snake away from my house.I threw it out into the woods. I went back in my house and had my breakfast.The next time I walked outside, it was back. Right where it had been before. I got my stick and moved it again. This time I took it way off and left it.

"I was feeding my animals a little later, and when I went inside my barn, I saw a feather on the floor. It was a black feather, and it had been tied."

"Did you touch it?" George asked.

"No," said Canoe.

"Did you bring it with you?"

"No. I didn't touch it."

"They're fighting back," George said. "We'll have to use stronger medicine. How's your leg?"

"It's all right."

"And your little girl?"

"She's well."

"That's good. That medicine I gave you is still working, and that's why they're fighting back harder now. Do you still have some of that medicine left?"

"Yes."

"Go on back home then," said George, "and keep using it just the way I told you before. While you're gone, I'll make up something stronger for you. I want you to bring me that feather. Don't touch it. Find something to use to pick it up and carry it. Bring it back here, and when you come, I'll have the other stuff ready for you. Did you see Billy Fire yesterday or this morning?"

"He was the same way as when I saw him last time," said Canoe. "Just sitting and staring."

George smiled. "You're going to be all right," he said. "Just do what I told you. And if you see the snake again, or snakes—there are probably two of them—kill them and burn them."

As Canoe was leaving, a wagon came rolling up into the front yard. It stopped just in front of the house. George recognized the driver, and then he saw that Adam Diwali was sitting in the wagon bed. He knew immediately that something was wrong. He stood up and walked over to the wagon.

"Adam," he said, "what is wrong with you?"

"My leg is broken," Adam said. "Jonas found me and we straightened it up the best we could."

"Let me look at it," George said, and he crawled up into the wagon. He felt Adam's leg, and Adam winced with the pain. "You did a pretty good job of straightening it and everything," George said. "I'll finish it up for you."

Gwed' came out. She had heard the wagon roll up.

"Adam's got a broken leg," George said. "I need to wrap it up."

"I'll bring what you need," she said, and went back inside.

"How'd this happen?" George asked.

Adam told George the story about how the gray horse had suddenly gone crazy and thrown him.

"I know that horse real well," he said. "I trained him from the time he was a colt. He's a good horse. He never did anything like that before."

George knew it was the same evil at work. It had to be. Something had to have spooked that horse to make it behave in that way. George knew how good Adam was with horses, and if Adam said the horse was a good one, one that he knew and had trained, then something had made the horse act like that. But why had the evil one come after Adam? He thought some more. He was after George because George was blocking its evil. But it was unable to do much damage to George. It could only inconvenience him. Adam was George's friend. He was also his trainer as well as his jockey for Lightning. So the evil one had chosen to go after anyone close to George. That was the only explanation.

Gwed' came out of the house with a bucket and some long strips of white cloth, and she lifted them up for George to take into the wagon.

"All right," George said. "We'll get this fixed up in a few minutes."

"Oh, George?" Adam said.

"Yes?"

"I forgot to mention—there was an ugly black raven flying around in circles."

Tom Panther woke up that morning with a thick head. At first he did not know where he was. He sat up slowly, and then he remembered. He was in the woods just outside of Tahlequah. He had been drinking there the night before with Skinny and some others. He looked around and found that he was alone. He guessed that he had passed out and the others had just left him there. He noticed the empty jug lying on the ground a few feet away.

"Assholes," he said, speaking out loud and in English.

The movement had hurt his lips. He reached up and found them swollen and crusted. To touch them hurt. He winced. Then he felt the rest of his face, and he found a swollen eye. He felt more crustiness on his face. What was it? Dried blood? He started to get up, and he felt a pain shoot through his side. It was from his ribs. He could tell he had bruised or broken them. He let himself fall back on the ground and moaned. He took a few deep breaths and tried to sort things out in his mind. But it was a tough job. His head was throbbing and swimming.

He could not recall the events of the night before. He vaguely remembered arguing with Skinny, but he could not even remember what the argument had been about. But maybe it had gotten worse. Yes—now he remembered. He had wanted to go to Velma's house and get into her pants, and Skinny had objected. What kind of a friend was that? More of the events of the night came back to him. The others had taken Skinny's side in the argument. Tom thought hard, but he couldn't sort out any further details.

But he reasoned it out. The argument must have continued. They'd had a fight. Skinny, and the others, all taking his side, had beat Tom up, left him lying alone and unconscious in the woods. He could not remember it, but there was no other explanation. Well, by God, he thought, they wouldn't get away with that. He'd show them that Tom Panther was not a man to be fooled with. He vowed swift and terrible revenge on them all, but especially on Skinny. He would figure out something dreadful to do to Skinny, something real special. It would have to be so bad that it would scare the shit out of the others, and they would be worrying about when Tom would come after them. That was the way he would work it.

Big Forehead sat alone in his small cabin, and he gazed into his crystal. Suddenly, he burst out into satisfied and raucous laughter at what he saw there. He stood up and walked around inside his small, dark room laughing. He laughed so hard that his sides began to hurt, and he held onto them. Tears ran down his cheeks, and his jaws began to ache. At last he sat down again in his chair and sucked in deep breaths, trying to calm himself and recover from the fit of hilarity. Settled down finally, he stood up and walked to a cabinet. He opened it and took out a glass and a bottle. He went back to his chair and put the glass on the table. Then he poured it full of dark whiskey, set the bottle on the table, leaned back and took himself a long and satisfying drink.

Chapter 8

The three deputy United States marshals rode up in front of the Cherokee National Prison in Tahlequah. They sat in their saddles a moment, exchanging glances with one another. Then they dismounted and wound the reins of their horses around the hitch rail. They walked up the steps to the front door and went inside. Sheriff Go-Ahead Rider looked up from behind his desk as they stepped into his office. He saw their badges, and he knew who they were.

"Howdy," he said. "What can I do for you fellows?"

The tallest of the three men stepped forward and extended a hand. Rider took it, prepared for the hard grip of a white man's hand shake. "I'm Silas McGee," the man said. "These here are Hiram Billings and Kit Harper. We're deputy U.S. marshals."

"I can see that," Rider said. "I knew it when you came through the door."

"How'd you know?" McGee asked.

"Why, you all look alike," said Rider. "Besides, your badges are showing."

"Oh."

McGee pulled a paper out of his inside coat pocket and handed it to Rider. Rider took his time studying the paper.

"We're carrying that warrant there for the arrest of George Panther," McGee said. "We stopped by to see you out of courtesy. Lawmen coming into another lawman's territory, you know. That's really about all. Just wanted you to know that we're going to be out there looking."

Rider handed the warrant back to McGee. "You might have a time finding ole George," he said. "Especially if he don't want to be found. From what I hear, everyone who's gone out there looking has found an empty house is all."

"They got him one time," said Billings. "He can be got again."

"They didn't hold him very long though, did they?" said Rider.

"He pretty sneaky is he?" McGee asked.

Rider gave a shrug. "You could put it that way," he said.

"They say he's knowed as a medicine man of some kind," said Harper. "That so?"

"I've heard that said."

"Is that how he came to be so sneaky like that?" Harper said. "He make some kind of Injun medicine and throw us off the track or something?"

"I've heard of such things happening," Rider said. "I couldn't comment as to the truth of it one way or the other."

"I don't think we have to worry about anything like that," said McGee. "If we don't find him at home, he'll likely be hiding out in the woods somewhere. We'll just have to track him down. That's all."

"We were sort of hoping that you might be able to help us out a little," Billings said.

"In what way?" Rider asked. "I can't help you serve a federal warrant."

"We know that," said Billings. "Just thought that you might have some advice or some information or something. Anything that might help us do our job, you know. If we don't find him at home, where might we ought to look for him? You know him personal, don't you?"

"Yeah. I know him. George is usually home," Rider said. "If he's not there, he could be anywhere. He could be off visiting someone. No telling who. I know a lot of people, but I don't know where they're at all the time. It's none of my business."

"If it was you looking for him," Billings said, "where would you look?"

Rider gave another shrug. "I reckon I'd ride out to his house," he said.

"Well," McGee said, realizing that the conversation was leading nowhere, "we just wanted to let you know we're here. That's all. We'll get Panther all right, one way or another. Don't worry about that. Be seeing you."

"Good luck to you," said Rider. "You'll need it. And be careful."

As the three deputies walked out the door, Beehunter came into the office from the hallway. He looked at Rider, and he spoke in Cherokee. "They're after George Panther?"

Rider nodded.

"They won't find him," Beehunter said.

"No," Rider agreed. "But they're sure causing him a lot of inconvenience."

Outside, the deputies climbed back into their saddles. As McGee was turning his horse to ride north, Harper spoke up. "I knew we wouldn't get no cooperation here. He might be a lawman, but he's siding with his own kind against us."

"I guess you can't blame him for that," Billings said.

"Well, it was a waste of time trying to get any help out of him," said Harper.

"I didn't really expect it," said Billings. "Just thought I'd try."

"Like I told the sheriff," said McGee, "it was a courtesy call. That's all. Forget it."

They were on the road about three miles from George Panther's house when they heard a loud shout echo through the tree-covered hills that lined the winding and shaded country road.

"Go back!" it called out.

They hauled in their reins and sat in the road, looking around. The hills suddenly seemed taller and steeper, and the woods appeared to be so thick and lush and dark as to be virtually impenetrable. The shout could have come from anywhere.

"Who are you?" McGee yelled.

"Go back!"

McGee waited for the echo to subside.

"You're interfering with deputy U.S. marshals in the line of duty," he called out. He could hear his own voice resounding on the hills. "Come on out and show yourself."

A shot sounded just then, and dirt was kicked up

a few feet in front of the deputies. Their horses jumped and nickered with fright.

"Take cover," said McGee, dismounting quickly. Harper and Billings were not far behind him as he ran toward the thicket on the side of the road. All three lawmen jerked out and cocked their revolvers.

"Where the hell is he?" said Harper.

"I'm not sure," McGee said. "Somewhere up ahead. That's all I can tell."

"I think he's up on that hillside," said Billings. "Up there where the road curves."

"You think it's Panther?" asked Harper.

"I don't think so," McGee said. "It's not his style. At least, not from everything we been told so far."

"Maybe it's a friend of his," Harper said.

"Yeah," said McGee, "maybe."

"Well, what the hell are we going to do here?" Harper asked.

"We need a rifle," said McGee. "It's too far for six-guns to be of any use. Either one of you think you could get to a rifle?"

Billings looked out into the road where his horse was still prancing nervously about, his Winchester in a scabbard at its side.

"I think I can," he said.

"All right," McGee said. "Go get it. We'll cover you."

Crouching low, Billings ran to the side of his horse, jerked the rifle loose, and turned to run back just as a shot rang out and a bullet sprayed dirt a few feet in front of him. He hesitated. McGee and Harper fired their revolvers in the direction of the spot on the hillside where Harper thought the man was hidden. Billings ran back into the edge of the woods with his two companions.

"That was close," he said.

"It wasn't all that close," McGee said. "Whoever he is, the man's either a bad shot or he's not aiming to kill anyone. He just wants to slow us down or scare us off. That's how come he shouted that warning."

"Well, warning or no, if I could spot him," Harper said, "I'd damn sure shoot back to kill the son of a bitch."

"Well, I'll just kind of pepper that hillside," said Billings. "Maybe I'll get lucky."

He cranked a shell into the chamber and raised the rifle to his shoulder. He took casual aim and fired. Then he fired again. And again.

Canoe ducked behind a tree trunk and pressed himself hard against it as bullets started pinging into the hillside. One thunked into the very tree he was hugging. He waited until the shots stopped, and then, clutching his own rifle, he ran. Crashing through the woods, he reached the top of the hill, ran across it and started down the other side. He knew that cutting through the woods that way, he could get to George's house before the deputies, even though they would be on horseback. He hadn't stopped them, just slowed them down a little, so he had to warn George. He would not allow the white lawmen to capture or kill George Panther. Not if he could help it. He ran as hard as he could.

George was sitting under his arbor, smoking a cigarette, when Canoe came running up, gasping for breath, his skin scratched and his clothes torn from running through the thick woods. George expected someone to be coming along. He had heard the gunshots. But he was a little surprised to see Canoe. George stood up and walked to meet him. Nearly exhausted, Canoe almost fell down when he came to a stop, but George grabbed him by the shoulders and held him up. Canoe tried to talk.

"Hold on and catch your breath," George said.

Still panting, Canoe said, "The white lawmen are coming to get you. There are three of them. They're close, too. Just down the road around that bend. I tried to scare them away, but they kept coming."

"Was that the shots I heard?" George asked.

"Yes. I shot twice. Then they started shooting."

"I appreciate your trying to help me, Canoe," said George, "but I can handle this thing for myself. I'm ready for them. I'll be all right. Now you go home. Stay out of this. I don't want you getting yourself hurt or getting into trouble over this. Don't do anything like that again. Go on home now."

He stood and watched as Canoe walked into the woods. Then he turned toward the house and called out in a loud voice. "Andy, get out here!"

Andy came out of the house fast and ran to George's side. "Yes?" he said. "What is it?"

"Get everyone out of the house," George said. "Take my rifle with you, and take everyone way out in the woods. Hurry it up now. There's no time to waste."

Andy ran back into the house to obey his father. In a moment, Gwed' came out questioning.

"There's no time for that," interrupted George. "Just do what I say. Go on with Andy now."

He watched as his family disappeared into the thick woods behind the house, and then he turned to face the road. That was the way the lawmen would be riding in. After another moment, he turned and walked into his house.

The three deputies stopped their horses when they came around the bend, in full view of George's house. They sat and looked at it off in the distance. Harper, his patience running thin, finally spoke up. "Well, what the hell are we going to do now? Just sit here and stare at his house?"

"The chances are, Panther's been warned we're coming," said McGee. "If nothing else, he likely heard those shots awhile ago. My guess is that we won't find him at home."

"So what do we do?" asked Harper.

"The first thing we do is act like he might be home," McGee answered. "Just in case. Let's ride up a little closer, then dismount. Two of us will spread out wide in front of the house. The other will go around back. Then we'll call out for him. Give him a chance to come out peaceful."

"And if he don't?" questioned Harper.

"Then we go in and search the house," McGee said. "Hiram, why don't you go around to the back? Me and Kit will approach the front. Don't do anything unless someone tries to get out the back door."

"Sure thing," Billings said.

Without another word, McGee urged his horse forward at an easy walk. The other two lawmen moved along with him. They rode about half the remaining distance to the Panther house, then stopped and dismounted. Sweeping their eyes back and forth to keep watch on the house, they tied their mounts to some brush beside the road. Then they pulled out their revolvers and started walking toward the house.

Once they were in the front yard, they stopped. McGee looked at Billings and gave a nod. Billings started a wide circle around the house. McGee made a gesture toward Harper, and he and Harper began moving away from each other. When McGee thought they were spread out enough, and Billings had had plenty of time to be in place behind the house, he stopped, motioning for Harper to do the same. He took a deep breath, steeling himself for whatever might be about to happen.

"Hello in the house!" he shouted.

He received no answer.

"George Panther," he called out. "You in there?"

Again his only answer was silence. A squirrel chattered from somewhere in the trees and then began vaulting from branch to branch, rattling the leaves overhead. A blue jay called out in its loud and raucous voice. The woods around them suddenly seemed alive to the three lawmen. McGee moved toward the house, and as he did, Harper moved in from his position. When McGee reached the front door, he motioned for Harper to stop.

McGee called out once more. "Panther. You in there? I'm giving you a chance to come out without any more shooting. We don't want anyone to get hurt here if we can help it."

There was still no answer—only the rattling and

chattering from the surrounding dark woods, growing seemingly louder and louder.

"Anyone home?"

There was no human response. McGee clenched a fist and pounded hard on the door. No one came to open it. He pushed the door into the house. It opened easily, swinging all the way back to bang into the wall on the inside. McGee squinted through the open door. He could see no sign of life. He looked back over his shoulder and motioned for Harper to follow him. Then he stepped inside, taking just a couple of steps. He stood still, looking all around the room. No one was there. Harper stepped in to stand beside and a little behind him. McGee gestured toward the blanket-covered doorway across the room, and the two deputies walked over to it. McGee shoved the blanket aside and held it for a moment. Nothing happened. He walked through into the next room and found it as empty as the other one. The silence inside the house was in sharp and eerie contrast to the noise of the woods outside. Harper stepped up beside him. "You was right," he said. "He ain't here. Let's get out of here. I don't like it."

"Let's go out the back way," McGee said, "and join up with Hiram."

They walked back through the house to the back door and went outside. Billings was standing ready, revolver in hand. He relaxed a bit when he saw who it was coming out.

"Put it away, Hiram," McGee said. "No one's home."

Looking over Billings's shoulder, McGee noticed the corral with six horses enclosed. One was a big, beautiful white stallion. The white stallion looked at McGee and blew air out between fluttering lips, making a loud and almost obscene sound.

"Son of a bitch is making fun of us," McGee said.

"What?" Billings said.

"Never mind," said McGee. "Reckon how many horses ole Panther has anyway?"

"Got six right in there," said Harper.

"Wagon's sitting right over there," McGee said. "I'm guessing that Panther's somewhere close right around here on foot. He might even be watching us right now."

The other two men looked around nervously at that thought, and from somewhere near, an owl hooted. Harper shivered.

"How come that owl to be hooting in the daytime?" he said. "Owls don't hoot in the middle of the day, do they?"

"I don't know," McGee said. "It happens sometimes, I guess."

"It's spooky out here," Harper said. "I heard one time that them Indian medicine men can turn theirselves into hooty owls and such. You ever hear that?"

"I wouldn't place too much stock in those kinds of tales," McGee said.

"Well, it's spooky," said Harper.

"Look around," McGee said. "See if you can find any tracks leading out of here. Horses or human. If Panther's not here, he had to have gone somewhere. There might be some tracks we can follow."

The three deputies ambled around in different directions, studying the ground for any telltale tracks. Harper looked up in the trees as much as on the ground. The owl hooted again, and Harper jumped, jerking out his revolver. He turned in a circle, looking up into the trees all around.

"Relax, Kit," McGee said. "It's just an owl."

"If I can spot the son of a bitch," Harper said, "I'll kill him."

"Either one of you find any tracks?" McGee asked.

"No," said Billings.

"I didn't find nothing," said Harper.

McGee heaved a heavy sigh.

"Well," he said, "we might as well head on back. We'll just have to tell Marshal Crump we couldn't find hide nor hair of George Panther, that's all."

"He's not going to like it," Billings said.

"You got any other ideas?" Harper shot back. "Come on. Let's get the hell out of this spooky sonofabitching place."

They walked back to their horses, Harper almost running. He was the first to mount up, and without waiting for the other two, he started riding back toward Tahlequah.

"Hey, Kit," McGee called out as he was mounting his own horse, "slow it down, will you?"

McGee and Billings turned their horses and started after Harper just as a big screech owl came off a low branch at the side of the road. Its wings made no sound. It swooped low, coming within inches of Harper's face as it swept in front of him and went on across the road to disappear into the woods on that side. Harper screamed, and his horse went into a frightened dance.

"Goddamn!" said Billings. "Silas, did you see that?"

"Goddamn sonofabitching hooty owl," said Harper. "That was him, Silas. That was Panther right there in my face."

"It was just an old hoot owl flying across the road," McGee said.

"I tell you, it was him."

Chapter 9

Tom Panther washed himself in cold creek water as best he could. His face and his ribs were sore. He could tell that he had really taken a pounding, although he still could not remember it. Skinny and those other two guys must have beat him up and left him that way. Anyone could have come along and taken advantage of his helpless situation. Some bum might have come along and robbed him. Of course, he had nothing to steal. The bum might have killed him, though. A hog could have come along and eaten him. A cold snap might have come and he might have frozen to death, or at least caught pneumonia.

It was all Skinny's fault. There was no doubt of that either. It was Skinny who had started it all. Tom wanted to get Skinny back for what he had done. His sense of outrage focused squarely on Skinny. The other boys were all but forgotten.

Tom was hungry, and he wanted a gun. He could go home and eat and get his father's gun, he knew, but it was a long walk back to his parents' house, and he could not remember where he had left his father's horse and saddle. He would have to find someplace closer, someplace where he could easily walk and get some food—and a gun. His stomach was growling and causing him pain. He walked aimlessly through the woods, holding his head and moaning from the aches. There had to be someone he knew nearby, someone who would help him out. Then he thought of Bood Trainor over in Dog Town just north of Tahlequah.

Tom had not seen Bood for a while. Bood was a breed Cherokee, about Tom's age. He looked more white than Indian. There had been a time when they ran around together, drinking, chasing women and getting into fights. They'd had a lot of fun together, too, in those days. But then Bood had gotten married to another breed, and he had settled down. The last few times Tom had gone by to see him, Bood had refused to go out running with him. Tom resented Bood's reformation and wrote him off as a man who simply was no longer any fun to be around. It made Tom sick just to think about it. But just now Bood would be useful. It wasn't too long a walk to Dog Town, and Bood would not refuse Tom a meal. Tom was sure of that. He changed directions. He knew a shortcut through the woods to Dog Town.

Tom had not gone far before he began to feel as if the walk was longer than he had anticipated. He discovered along the way that it was not just his face and his ribs that were sore. He was bruised all over not just from the beating, but from sleeping on the hard, rocky ground all night. He was sore and tired, hungry and broke, and now on foot, and it was all the fault of that damned Skinny Johnson. Hell, Skinny probably even knew where he had left the horse. The more he walked, the more the soreness grew in his bones and muscles, and the more Tom's anger at Skinny grew into hatred. He was determined to make Skinny pay for his treachery. He could not allow anyone to do him the way Skinny Johnson had done. But first things first. He was hungry, terribly hungry.

At last he arrived in Dog Town, limping slightly from a sore foot caused by so much walking. He was breathing hard, too. He walked down the street, and dogs barked as he passed by. Children playing in the yards in front of the houses stared at him. One old man sitting on his front porch waved. Tom did not bother waving back. As he approached the house of Bood Trainor, a wretched-looking red hound seemed to rise up out of the ground and let out a deep-throated, menacing bay.

"Shut up, you shit," said Tom.

The door opened and Bood Trainor stepped out to see who it was that had aroused the hound. When he saw Tom, a look of surprise came over his face. "Tom," he said, "what are you doing over this way?"

"I was out late last night," Tom said. "I'm on foot, and I'm hungry. It's a long walk back to my dad's place."

"Well, come on in," Trainor said. "We can fix you up with something to eat. It's been a long time, pal."

The Trainor house was small, built of native sandstone. Inside, it had a living room, a kitchen and one bedroom. Tom followed Trainor into the house. There did not seem to be anyone else at home. Tom looked around. The place was neat and clean. "Where's your wife?" he asked.

"Oh, she went over to visit her mother," Trainor said. "We've got a kid now, you know."

"Oh, yeah?"

"Yeah. A little girl—she's one year old. She's something special. It's really different being a husband and a father. You ought to find yourself a nice girl and get married, Tom. Settle down. It's great. Well, sit down there and I'll get you something to eat."

Tom ravenously ate everything that Bood Trainor put on the table before him. Trainor also boiled up some coffee, and he poured out two cups. He sat down across the table from Tom.

"You had enough to eat?" he asked.

"Yeah," Tom said. "Thanks. That's a whole lot better."

"Say," said Trainor, "you still running around the way we used to do?"

Tom laughed. "I guess so," he said. "I tied on a pretty good one last night."

"You look like someone tied into you," said Trainor. "Who did that, and what does *he* look like this morning?"

Tom laughed again, more nervously than before.

"It was late," he said. "It was dark. I couldn't hardly tell."

"Well, I bet he looks worse than you do. I know the way you can fight. I remember that time you took out two guys all by yourself down by the river. You remember that time?"

"Yeah. I remember it all right. They weren't too tough."

"But you took them both on at once," Trainor

said, "and you whipped their ass good. I never seen anything like it."

"Hey, you got a change of clothes I can borrow?" Tom asked, changing the subject. "I'm kind of messed up here."

"Sure," said Trainor. "I'll fetch them for you."

Trainor got up and went into the bedroom, and Tom looked quickly around the room. He knew that Trainor had an old Navy Colt. At least, he used to have one. It was nowhere to be seen, which meant that if he still had it, it was put away somewhere. Tom felt a powerful urge to get up and rummage through some drawers, but he did not know how quickly Trainor would return from the bedroom. And the gun might even be somewhere in the bedroom.

"Hey, it's sure good to see you, Tom," Trainor called from the bedroom.

"Yeah," said Tom, glancing toward the bedroom door. "Same here."

He spotted a solid rolling pin in the kitchen on a cabinet, and he moved quickly to pick it up. Holding it behind his back, he stepped over to one side of the door that led into the bedroom. He pressed his back against the wall beside the door and waited, trying to keep from breathing too loudly, listening to his own heart pounding. He felt beads of sweat trickling down his forehead.

"These ought to fit you," said Trainor, coming through the doorway.

Tom took a hard swing with the rolling pin, banging it against the back of Trainor's head.

Trainor dropped the clothes he'd been carrying and staggered forward. He caught himself with his hands on the table, then sagged into the chair where he had been sitting. He took his head in his hands and moaned. Tom stepped up behind him and swung again. The thud was sickening, and Trainor fell forward to lie still. Blood ran from his head and pooled on the tabletop. Tom hit him again and again, making sure that he was dead. He stepped back and stared at his gory handiwork with wide eyes. Then he threw down the rolling pin and hurried to the nearest bureau, jerking open drawer after drawer in search of the Navy Colt.

With every drawer in the living room tossed to the floor, Tom went into the kitchen. Soon he had all the drawers pulled out and thrown down. Frantic, he ran into the bedroom. He jerked the bedclothes off the bed and turned over the mattress. Then he moved over to another bureau. He pulled out the top drawer, and there he saw the elusive revolver. He pulled it out and looked at it, holding it in both hands, feeling its weight. It looked just the way he remembered it. It was beautiful, a fine example of the workman's craft.

He checked and saw that it was fully loaded with powder and ball, with a cap on each nipple of the cylinder. He cocked it, listening to the clicks and watching the cylinder rotate. Then, carefully holding the hammer back with his thumb, he pulled the trigger and eased the hammer back down. The gun was in good working order. It was old though, thirty or forty years. He wished for a newer model that would take bullets. Hell, he thought, maybe he would use this one to trade for a newer one. He tucked it into the waistband of his trousers and rummaged some more through the contents of the drawer. He found a bag of shot, and the caps and powder. Grabbing them up, he ran through the house and out the back door.

In the yard, he stopped. He hesitated a moment, thinking. Then he turned and ran back into the house. He picked up the clean clothes that Trainor had brought out for him, rolled them into a bundle and ran out again, straight for the woods. A dog barked. In the house next door to Trainor's house, a window curtain was pushed slightly aside from the inside, and a woman's face peered cautiously out, watching Tom run into the woods.

Beehunter came walking around the corner of the National Prison. He saw Go-Ahead Rider standing there in the street, talking to another man. The man had two saddled horses. Beehunter recognized one of the horses, but he did not know the man, so he sensed that something was wrong. He walked over to join them, and he stood aside listening politely. The problem was that they were talking in English, and Beehunter could not understand. At last, there was a pause, and Rider turned to Beehunter and spoke in Cherokee.

"Mose here found this gray horse wandering loose out at his place," he said. "He brought it in for us to deal with."

"That's one of George Panther's horses," said Beehunter.

"You sure of that?"

"Of course."

Rider turned back to the man he called Mose.

"Beehunter knows this horse," he said. "It belongs to George Panther. We'll take it out to him, and I'm sure he'll appreciate its return. Thanks for bringing it in, Mose."

"It wasn't no problem, Rider," said Mose. "I had to come into town anyhow."

Mose climbed back onto his own horse, turned it and rode away. Rider watched him for a moment.

"Beehunter," he said, "I wonder why George's horse was wandering loose, saddled up like that, way over by Mose's place?"

"That's George's best saddle, too," said Beehunter. "He usually puts that one on Lightning."

"Well," Rider said, "there might be something wrong here. I'd better saddle up and get this horse on out there to George."

Behind his desk in his office in Fort Smith, Marshal Crump listened patiently to the tale told by the three deputies he had sent to arrest George Panther. When the tale was done, Crump sat silent for a long moment, fidgeting with a pencil, tapping it on the desk. He was trying to find the right words for his response and the right way to organize his thoughts. At last he looked directly at Harper.

"I don't dispute anything you said, Kit, but it can't go in your damned report," he said. "Not like that." He looked at McGee. "Your report will simply say that you failed to find George Panther at home, and you failed to find any trail indicating which way he might have gone. That's all."

The three deputies, looking dejected, stood up to leave the office.

"If Talmadge Hunt is still out there," Crump said, "tell him I want to see him."

"Yes, sir."

They left, shutting the door behind them, and Crump leaned back in his chair with a heavy sigh. He leaned forward again and opened a desk drawer. He took out a bottle of whiskey and a glass and poured himself a stiff drink. He swallowed it in two gulps and replaced the glass and the bottle in the drawer. Then he took out a cigar and a cutter, nipped the end of the cigar and poked it between his lips. He took out a match, struck it on the edge of the desk top and lit the cigar, puffing out great clouds of blue smoke that soon filled the air in the small office. A moment later there was a knock on the door.

"Come in!" Crump roared.

The door opened, and Talmadge Hunt stepped in. "You want to see me?"

"Come in and sit down, Talmadge," Crump said.

Hunt took hold of a chair and dragged it up close to the desk. Then he sat and took the wide-brimmed hat off his head. Hunt was perhaps thirty years old, tall and lean. He was dressed neatly in dark trousers and a dark vest over a white shirt. A thick black mustache adorned his upper lip, and he spoke in a slow and polite southern drawl.

"Have a cigar?" Crump asked.

"Thank you," said Hunt as Crump passed him a cigar, the cutter and a match. Hunt went through the same ritual as had Crump and returned the cutter. Crump took it and shoved the big ashtray to the middle of the desk where both men could reach it. He thought for a minute, then opened the drawer again, taking out the whiskey bottle and two glasses.

"Whiskey?"

"I don't mind."

"I've got a special assignment for you," Crump said, pouring whiskey into the two glasses. "There's an Indian medicine man over in the Cherokee Nation near Tahlequah who's wanted for murder. His name is George Panther. He killed a white man at his house. Claims the man was trying to steal his horse and took the first shot. He claims self-defense. The problem is, he won't come over here voluntarily to stand trial and prove his claim."

He paused and shoved one glass across the desk. Hunt picked it up and took a sip.

"Glen Jones and Amos Adams arrested him," Crump continued. "He didn't give them any trouble. When they camped that night, they tied him good and tight to a tree. The next morning he was gone. The ropes were there still tied." He took a gulp of whiskey, then continued. "They went back to his house, but it was empty. No sign of him or any of his family. So later, I sent McGee, Billings and Harper after him. They just got back. They found the house empty just like Jones and Adams did, but Harper was full of spook tales. Said an owl attacked him. Swore it was Panther. Oh, yeah. There was no one home in the house, but the corral was full of horses."

"Sounds to me," said Hunt, "like the man's getting warnings of when we're coming, and he just gets out into the woods and hides till the coast is clear. Also sounds like poor ole Harper's been listening to too many ghost stories late at night."

"That's what I think, too," Crump said. "But now, here's what I want you to do. I want you to pick six good men. That'll make seven of you altogether. I want each man to be armed with a revolver and a rifle. Take plenty of ammunition. I want you to out-fit a supply wagon so you can stay just as long as it takes. Take canvas tents, and take a cook. I don't want to see you again or hear from you until you can tell me that George Panther is in jail or dead. Do you understand me?"

"Clear as a bell," Hunt said.

"Do you have any questions?"

"You say I get to pick the men?"

"Take whoever you want."

"I'll follow this Indian medicine man clear to hell if I have to," Hunt said, "but I'll find him and bring him in."

Deep in the woods, Tom Panther stopped running. He needed to rest. It was going to be a long walk on over to Skinny Johnson's house. Damn it, he wished that he could remember what he had done with that damned gray horse. He sat down beneath a large oak tree and leaned back against the trunk. The barrel of the Colt stabbed into his thigh, so he pulled it out and placed it beside him on the ground. He leaned his head back against the tree trunk and closed his eyes. Soon he was asleep, and visions of whiskey, blood, fast horses and naked women swam in his head.

George Panther was sitting beneath his arbor when Go-Ahead Rider came up on his prancing black horse, leading the still-saddled gray. George stood up and squinted. It was his own gray horse wearing his best saddle, the horse upon which Tom had ridden away. He walked forward to meet Rider, a worried look on his face.

"What's wrong, George?" Rider said. "I thought you'd be happy to have your horse back again. He is still yours, isn't he? You didn't sell him or trade him off or anything like that, did you?"

"It's mine, all right," George said. "Tom rode off on that horse. Where'd you get it, Go-Ahead? Has something happened to Tom?"

"Mose Pike found it wandering near his house," Rider said. "He brought it in to Tahlequah to the sheriff's office. I don't know anything about Tom."

"That boy's in some kind of trouble," George said. "I already had a feeling about that."

Andy and Gwed' stepped out the front door of the house just then, curious to see what was going on. "What is it?" Gwed' asked.

"Go-Ahead's brought our horse back," said George. "It's the one Tom was riding."

"Andy," said Gwed', "take the horse to the corral."

Andy moved quickly to do as his mother had told him. Rider handed the reins to Andy, and he headed toward the corral, leading the horse.

"Take that saddle off him," said George. "And give him a good rub. He's been neglected pretty bad."

"I will."

"Step down, Go-Ahead, and have some coffee with us," George said.

Rider swung down out of his saddle. "Thanks," he said. "George, I wouldn't worry too much. Tom likely had a little too much to drink and let the horse wander off. I'll keep an eye out for him."

But even as he tried to console the worried parents, Go-Ahead Rider had a sense that, when the truth was told, there would be much more to the story than that. He'd had a notion for some time that Tom was headed for bad trouble sooner or later.

"I appreciate it," George said, walking toward the house, "but I'm afraid you might be wrong. I got a bad feeling about that boy this time. I think he's in some kind of real trouble. Go-Ahead, if you catch him at something, don't go easy on him. I think that's his whole problem. But it's my fault. I've gone too easy on him all these years."

"It's not your fault, George," said Rider. "You always did the best you could. I know that. Look how Andy turned out. There's not a finer boy around. We do our best, George, but these youngsters are going to go their own way. There's no explaining it."

"I guess you're right," George said, "but it's hard not to feel responsible."

"Things just kind of get set into motion. It's kind of like that prophecy you told me awhile back. Remember? How the whites are going to take over everything. There won't be any Cherokee Nation anymore. But then it's going to come back strong as ever. If you can make a prophecy like that, then whose fault is it when it comes about?"

"You know, Rider, a long time ago, back in the beginning of time, the Creator gave us all of our ways. He gave us all our medicine, too, and it was meant to help the people. It was meant to be used for good. Somewhere along the way, someone who knew the medicine started using it for bad purposes. Whoever it was who did that perverted it. That threw everything out of balance. That's the reason all these bad things are happening all around us. Because someone did that, others started doing it, and there are those out there still today who are doing that. We're suffering because the power is being abused. That's what it's all about."

"I never thought about it like that, George," Rider said.

"Well, that's the way it is. Anyway, that's the way it was told to me, and the reason we're having so much trouble around right now is that a new one has come into the area, and he's a real bad one. It's taking all my time to fight it. Too much of my time."

Chapter 10

George Panther sat beside the river, watching the water flow by, talking to the river, calling it by its traditional Cherokee name of Long Man, asking it for advice and help, watching leaves and twigs float by, staring in near desperation for a sign of some kind to help him in his search for the truth, to locate once and for all the source of all the evil in the neighborhood. He sat patiently for hours, yet no sign came. Nothing manifested itself that would be of any assistance to him in this very serious game, this war of medicine, this battle between good and evil. At last he stood up, his muscles aching from the long stillness, and he turned, disappointed, to walk slowly back home.

The citizens on the main street of Tahlequah stopped and stared as seven men on horseback followed by a wagon driven by a Black man rode into town. Some of the citizens caught glimpses of the badges on the white men's vests as they rode by, and so they knew that the men were deputy United States marshals. They talked in low voices to their neighbors, and in a short time, the word was all over town. These strangers were a posse of deputy

U.S. marshals, and they had brought a supply wagon with them. They must be on some serious mission to have come in so well prepared. They were like a small army. The citizens stood still and watched as the posse rode through town without stopping. They watched as the white lawmen stopped at the edge of the creek just north of town, still well in view, and the wagon turned and rolled along the creek bank while the deputies simply rode their horses across into the field on the other side of the creek.

The wagon driver had apparently gone in search of a good spot to ford the creek with his wagon, for in a few minutes they saw it come back into view on the other side of the creek. The driver pulled it up where the deputies waited. The people on the main street of Tahlequah watched as the men began unloading supplies. Soon they had pitched three large canvas tents. The Black man had built a fire and was preparing a meal. The deputies had unsaddled and picketed their horses.

Then six of the men walked down to the single log footbridge and moved across it single file, walking back into town. The citizens watched as the men separated and walked into stores or stopped to talk to other people standing on the street. Finally, the word had reached all over town that the deputy marshals were there in search of George Panther. They carried a warrant for his arrest for murder, and they meant to get him this time.They had come in force, and they had brought enough supplies with them to stay until the job was done. There would be no rest for George Panther. And there would be no escape.

Of course, the deputies were not getting any help from any of the people they talked to. They received no new information. They already knew where George Panther lived. No one could, or would, tell them anything more than that. They did not get angry, though. They simply moved on to another person with the same questions. They had not really expected any cooperation from the Cherokee citizens of Tahlequah. They were simply going through the motions. They were making their presence and their purpose known. They were showing off their strength and announcing their intentions, making an impression and a statement.

The people began to cluster in small groups and talk in hushed tones about the deputies and what they were up to. The ones who had already been questioned told the others what questions the white men had asked them, and told how they had not given any useful information to them. Those who could speak the Cherokee language used it in conversation. Even so, they still spoke softly. It wasn't long before Sheriff Go-Ahead Rider and his deputy, Beehunter, appeared in the crowd. They moved into one of the small clusters.

"White lawmen are here," said a full-blood, speaking in Cherokee.

Rider nodded. "I see," he said.

"Look up there," the full-blood said. "They made a camp."

"It looks like they mean to stay awhile," Rider said.

"It looks like they're building a town," Beehunter said.

"They've come after George Panther," the other man said.

"Did they say that?"

"Yes. They're asking everyone where they can find him. But no one will tell them."

Rider looked at Beehunter. "I'll be back," he said. He walked across the street, heading directly for the nearest of the deputy marshals. The man looked at him as he approached.

"You the sheriff here?" the deputy marshal said.

"That's right," said Rider. "Who's in charge of your outfit?"

"Talmadge Hunt," the man said. He turned and pointed down the street. "That's him right over there. Tall fellow."

"Thanks," said Rider. He started walking toward Hunt, but as he walked along the street, Cherokee citizens stopped him to tell him what they had heard or to ask him questions. At last he reached Hunt, but Hunt was busy questioning a Cherokee woman. She divulged no information, and Rider wasn't surprised. When he saw a break in the conversation, he spoke to Hunt. "Mr. Hunt?"

Hunt turned to face Rider. "I'm Deputy United States Marshal Talmadge Hunt," he said. "What can I do for you?"

"Likely nothing," Rider said, thinking the man just a little pompous. "I just thought that since you've set up your camp right on the edge of town here that I ought to come over and introduce myself. I'm Go-Ahead Rider, high sheriff of the Cherokee Nation."

"Well," said Hunt, "I guess you've already heard why we're here."

"Oh, yeah," Rider said. "It's no secret. It's all over town."

"We haven't tried to make it a secret," Hunt said. "We're after George Panther, and we mean to get him this time. We want everyone to know."

Rider looked toward the camp at the north end of town. "It sure does look like you mean business," he said. "What are you trying to do down here in town?"

"Just asking questions," said Hunt. "That's all."

"Doing any good?"

"No one will admit to knowing anything," Hunt said, "but that's about what I expected. How about you? You have any information that might help us out?"

Rider shook his head. "I'm like everyone else," he said. "I know where George lives, but then, I reckon you do, too. I sure don't know if you'll find him at home or not, and if he ain't there, I don't know where he might be. You know, you might think you ain't getting any cooperation out of these folks. The truth is likely that they don't know anything more than you and me know about ole George's whereabouts."

"Is that right?" Hunt said. "Well, I think you know a lot more than I do, but I don't think you'll admit it."

Rider shrugged. "Think what you want," he said. "Well, I just thought I ought to come over and introduce myself. I'll let you get on with your business."

He turned and walked away. He crossed the street and found Beehunter waiting there where he had left him.

"They mean to get George this time," he said in Cherokee. "He ought to know about this." Then, as if he were changing the subject, he said, "Beehunter, I think you have a day off coming to you. Why don't you go on and take it now?"

"You're right, Go-Ahead," Beehunter said. "I do have some time coming to me. I think I'll take it now."

Beehunter turned and walked back toward the National Prison while Rider stayed with the group of citizens on the main street, watching the lawmen from Fort Smith.

Tom Panther came out of the woods near the home of the woman he usually bought illegal whiskey from, and he saw a friend of his. It was a young man about his own age called Punch.

Punch saw Tom about the same time. "Hey, Tom," he called out in English. "What are you doing?"

Tom was on his way to the home of Skinny to kill him with the stolen Colt, but, of course, he did not want to say that. "Oh, I'm just messing around," he said. "What about you?"

"I got some whiskey," said Punch. "Let's go to my house and drink it."

Tom thought about his mission of vengeance, and he decided that it could wait. He could find Skinny and kill him anytime. It might even be better to let it wait awhile. Let Skinny stew. Let him wonder about when Tom would be coming after him. Punch had whiskey right now.

"Let's go," he said.

*   *   *

It was about that same time that a man approached Go-Ahead Rider, still standing on the street, still watching the deputy marshals.

"What's going on here?" he asked, speaking English.

"Deputy marshals out of Fort Smith," Rider answered. "Looking for George Panther."

"Hell," the man said, "they ain't going to find him here."

Rider grinned. "You're right about that," he said. "George is pretty safe as long as these guys are all in town."

"Well, that's not what I come to see you about," the man said. "I live over at Dog Town. My neighbor, ole Bood Trainor, he's been killed."

"What happened?"

"Murdered," the man said. "Right in his own home. His wife come home and found him. His head was all bashed in. She's way too upset to come in and report it. That's why I come in after you."

"When did this happen?" Rider asked.

"Don't know. She just come home and found him this morning. She'd been visiting at her mama's house, she and her little girl. It's a terrible thing, Sheriff. Terrible. The little girl's just a year old. Ole Bood had some wild times, I guess. Lots of young men does. But he'd settled down. He was a nice young man. Done some work for me a month or so ago. It's just a terrible thing."

"Yes, it is," Rider said. He thought about what George Panther had told him, about the world being out of balance because of the misuse of medicine. "You have a horse with you?" Rider asked.

"No, sir. Don't own one."

"Walk with me over to the sheriff's barn. We'll saddle one up for you. I want you to ride back out there with me."

"I'll be glad to, Sheriff. And getting to ride back instead of walking is going to be welcome, too. I'm kind of tuckered out from the walk in, and I ain't ashamed to admit it."

Beehunter rode up to George Panther's house, and Gwed', having heard his approach, came out the front door.

"*Siyo*, Beehunter," she said. "Come in and have some coffee."

"*Wado*," said Beehunter. He climbed down from his saddle and walked toward the front door. "Is George at home?"

"He's inside," she said. "Come on in."

Beehunter followed Gwed' into the house. George was seated at the kitchen table. He greeted Beehunter while Gwed' poured three cups of coffee and put them on the table. Beehunter and Gwed' sat down.

"George," Beehunter said, "you have to get ready for big trouble. Seven white lawmen came into Tahlequah today. They brought a wagonload of supplies and tents. They have a Black man with them who is their cook. They made a camp there by Wolf Creek. Just now they're talking to everyone in Tahlequah, asking questions about you. They said they mean to stay as long as it takes this time. They're coming after you."

Gwed' shot a worried look at her husband.

"Thank you, Beehunter," George said. "I'll be ready. Gwed', find Andy. I want all of you, Sally and

Annie too, to go away for a while again. And this time I mean it. Don't come back till I say so."

"Won't you come with us this time?" she asked.

"I can't do that," he said. "My work is right here. I have to get to the bottom of all this evil. That's the only way it will ever end. I want all of you off over there where I don't have to worry about you along with everything else. That way, I'll be able to concentrate better. Please do like I say. It's all for the best."

Rider went into the Trainor house and saw the body. He saw the bloody rolling pin on the floor and the mess that had been left. It was obvious that the killer had been looking for something. After studying the scene thoroughly, he had some of the male neighbors help him lay out Bood's body and cover it. Then he asked about the whereabouts of the young widow. He found her at a neighbor's house, still sobbing. He apologized for bothering her at such a time, but he needed to ask her a few questions that just wouldn't wait.

She explained that she had no idea who might have done such a terrible thing. Bood had been a little wild before they were married, but she couldn't think of a single real enemy he had made. He was a good man. He had been good to her and to their little girl. No, she had not bothered to check around and see if anything was missing from her house. Yes, she did have a place to go. She would take her child and go back to her mother's house. Finally, she reluctantly agreed to accompany Rider back to the house and see if she could tell if anything was missing. It was an ordeal Rider hated to put the woman through, but it had to be done.

After a cursory look around, the woman finally realized that the gun her husband had kept in the top bureau drawer of the bedroom was missing. She also determined that her husband had prepared a meal for two. Then she realized that one of his shirts as well as a pair of trousers were missing. It appeared, Rider thought, that this brutal deed had been done over a suit of clothes and a revolver. Of course, there could be some other reason, but that was all that was apparent. It also seemed that Bood Trainor had been acquainted with his killer. Rider accompanied the tearful young widow back to the neighbor's house and left her there. He started to go back to the Trainor house, but an old woman met him in the yard.

"Rider," she said, speaking Cherokee.

He turned and walked over to her. "Yes?"

"I know who did that," she said.

"Tell me," he said.

"It was that Tom Panther. George Panther's no-good son. I saw him."

"Are you sure it was Tom?"

"I'm sure. I saw him."

"Just exactly what did you see?" Rider asked.

"I was looking out my window over there," she said, pointing. "I saw Tom Panther coming running out the back door."

"The back door of Bood Trainor's house?"

"Yes. That one. And he had a gun. He was running. Then he stopped. He turned around and ran back in. Pretty soon, he came out again, and he had some clothes all bundled up. He ran into the woods there."

"Thank you," Rider said.

He walked up and down the street, visiting with all the neighbors he found at home, and he talked with several who said that they had seen Tom Panther walking toward the Trainor house. Some, who did not know Tom, gave descriptions of a young man they had seen. The descriptions fit. Of course, there was as yet no final and absolute proof of Tom's guilt, but it was beginning to look very bad for him, and Rider remembered the words of George Panther.

I got a bad feeling about that boy this time. I think he's in some kind of real trouble.

Rider walked back to the Trainor house and went around back. The woman from next door had pointed to a spot at the edge of the woods where she said Tom had run. Rider walked in that direction. He found where someone had gone into the woods, all right, and he followed the trail. Rider found the place at the base of a tree where Tom had stopped to rest. The tracks went on from there, but they showed that Tom was walking. They led to a stream, and there beside the stream was a discarded shirt with bloodstains on it, and a pair of discarded trousers. Rider picked them up and continued following the trail, but soon it faded. He started back to Dog Town.

He would have to have a warrant issued for the arrest of Tom Panther, and he would have to begin a search. He would have to send out all his deputies to all of Tom's known haunts. He thought about the irony of the posse of deputy marshals who were searching for George Panther at the same time that he and his own deputies would be searching for Tom. He hoped that some evidence would surface to prove that Tom had not done the deed, but he was doubtful. The way Tom had been going for some time pointed to something like this. It was worse than anything Rider had expected. The killing had been brutal, and apparently calculated, and what made it even worse, it had apparently been done to a host by his own guest.

Go-Ahead Rider did not like the unpleasant task ahead of him. And there was even one more unpleasant aspect of it that he had not yet given full thought to. He was going to have to ride over to George Panther's home and tell George, and that at a time when George had plenty of other worries. Rider thought again about the misuse of medicine. He wondered if George was right about that, and he wondered if there could be any way to put a stop to it.

"Hey, Tom," Punch said. "Where'd you get that gun?"

They were in Punch's home drinking whiskey. It was a two-room log house, dark, cluttered and unkempt. Punch's wife, Dot, was in the house, drinking with them.

"I got it from ole Bood," Tom said. As soon as he said it, he knew that he should not have, but he was already drunk. He shrugged off any regret. "Remember Bood?"

"Yeah, Bood used to drink with us. What happened to ole Bood anyhow? How come he don't drink with us no more?"

"He got married," Tom said. "Settled down. He reformed."

"Hell," said Punch. "I got married, too. See?"

He reached over and slapped the ample buttocks of Dot, who was lying stretched out on her side on the rumpled bed.

"Ow," she said. "Hey, give me some more whiskey."

Tom passed the jug to Dot, and she started to drink from it. Tom reached over and grabbed it away from her.

"Pour some in your glass," he said. "Don't keep the jug."

She picked up her glass and held it out, and Tom slopped some whiskey into the glass, some of it spilling onto Dot and some onto the bed. Then he moved back over and dropped down into the chair he'd been sitting in.

"Hey," said Punch, "how come you got that gun from ole Bood? What you going to do with it?"

"Ah, I got me a plan."

"What is it?"

"I know what I'm going to do. You don't need to know."

"You going to rob someone?"

"Naw. I don't need to rob no one."

"Well what the hell you planning to do? How come ole Bood loaned you his gun anyhow?"

"He didn't," said Tom. "I took it."

"You stole it from Bood?"

"He won't miss it," said Tom. "He's dead."

"Bood's dead?"

"Yeah, and there's soon going to be another dead body."

"Did you kill Bood, Tom?"

"I bashed his brains out."

"God. Who else you going to kill. Not me?"

"Naw. I got no quarrel with you, Punch. Hell, you and me are pals. I'm going to kill that no-good Skinny Johnson."

"Really? How come?"

"A personal matter," Tom said. "Now, you wouldn't go blabbing to no one and spoil things for me, would you?"

"No. Not me, Tom. I won't say nothing to nobody. Killed ole Bood, huh? Damn."

Chapter 11

Beehunter was on his way back to Tahlequah when he met two full-blooded Cherokees on the road, both on horseback. Beehunter knew them both. He greeted them in Cherokee. They returned the greeting, but Beehunter could not help noticing that they seemed a bit sullen. "Is something wrong here?" he asked them.

"Have you been to George Panther's house, Beehunter?"

"Yes. I just came from there."

"Why did you go there?"

Beehunter thought for a long moment before answering the question. He was not used to being quizzed in that way. He could tell that something was up with these two, and he suspected that it had something to do with George Panther.

"Just now," he said, "I'm not working for Rider. I have some time off. I came out here on my own time to see George. I came to tell him about the seven white lawmen in Tahlequah who are planning to come out here after him."

The two looked at each other, just as a third came walking out of the woods. It was not until Beehunter saw the third man, the one on foot carrying a Winchester rifle, that he realized the other two were also armed with rifles. One also had a revolver tucked into the waistband of his trousers. The third man noticed the tension right away. He nodded a greeting to the two facing Beehunter.

"You say there are seven coming?" one of the mounted men asked Beehunter.

"Yes. Seven. But what's going on here?" Beehunter asked.

"Are you with us?" one asked.

"How can I answer your question unless you tell me what's going on?"

Canoe came riding down the road. There were two more with him. They all carried rifles. These three joined the others. Canoe greeted Beehunter.

"Is there some problem here, Deputy?" he asked.

"I don't know," Beehunter said. "I just came from George Panther's house. I went to see George to tell him about the white catchers in town. On my way back I met these men in the road. They won't tell me what's going on, but they want to know if I'm with them."

"We know about the catchers," said Canoe, "and we mean to stop them. We won't let them take George to Fort Smith, and we won't let them kill him. Are you going to try to stop us?"

Beehunter looked at Canoe, and he could see his determination. He looked at each of the other five men. "I wouldn't try to stop you from doing what you think you have to do," he said. "George told me that he'd be ready for the lawmen. Do you not believe he can handle this situation for himself?"

"Usually I wouldn't worry about George," said Canoe, "but lately he's been very busy. It might be that he's working on too many different things. He's working too hard. He's tired. It might be that something or someone could slip up on him."

"That's why I came to warn him," said Beehunter.

"I understand," said Canoe, "but we just don't want to take any chances. George has helped all of us. Some of us would be dead without George. Or our wives or children would be dead."

"Besides," said one of the others angrily, "we have you and Rider. Why should we allow these white catchers to come into our country and take our people? If a Cherokee has done something wrong, we have Cherokee law to take care of it."

"The man George killed was a white man," Beehunter said.

"What does that matter? The man was trying to steal from him, and the man shot at him first. If I went over to Fort Smith and tried to steal from a white man, and the white man shot me, would they let you go over there and arrest the white man? No. They would not. Why should we let them get away with such behavior?"

Beehunter could see that emotions were running high with these men, and no amount of reasoning would make any difference in the way they felt. They were loyal to George Panther and protective of him, but they were also patriotic and were being protective of the rights of the Cherokee Nation against the bullying of the larger and more powerful United States. Beehunter had his job, and he had his own loyalty to Go-Ahead Rider, but he understood these men. He understood their loyalties.

More than that, he agreed with them and so could not argue with them.

"I'm with you," he said. "What are your plans?"

Canoe pointed ahead on the road. "Up there where the road curves," he said, "we'll get on both sides of the road up on the hillside. We'll hide in the trees up there. When the white men come along the road, we'll surprise them. We won't let them get by us and go on to George's house."

"Do you mean to kill them?"

"If they turn back," Canoe said, "then no one will be hurt."

"Where will we leave our horses?"

"Around the bend out of sight from here," Canoe said. "A little ways through the woods up there is the creek. We'll take them in there."

"Is someone going to watch the road so we'll know when the white men are coming?"

"You can do that," Canoe said. He pointed back toward Tahlequah. "There's a high place just down there."

"I know it," Beehunter said. "When I see them coming, I'll ride back and wave my hat. Then I'll put my horse with yours and climb on up to join you."

"I'll be on the right side," Canoe said. "Come up there with me."

"*Howa*," said Beehunter, and he rode toward Tahlequah as the rest rode in the opposite direction. In a short while, he came to the place that Canoe had been talking about. He tied his horse beside the road and began making his way through the thick woods and up the side of a steep hill. He moved with grace and ease, for he was at home in the wooded hills of the Cherokee Nation. Soon, he was on top and could see in both directions for several miles. No one was coming from the direction of Tahlequah. There was no way of knowing how soon the posse of deputies would head for George's house. He would just have to wait and watch.

While he waited, he had time to consider the position he had put himself in. If he were to kill one of the deputy marshals, even shoot at them, or just be in the company of those who did, he would be in violation of the laws of both the United States and the Cherokee Nation. He realized that since the deputy marshals were white men, the white man's law would take precedence over the Cherokee. And he was a deputy sheriff of the Cherokee Nation. He knew that Rider would disapprove of what he was doing. He knew that he would have to tell Rider. He could not violate the law and his own oath by keeping that information from Rider. He knew that he should not be in that place just then, but at the same time, he agreed with Canoe and the other men.

Go-Ahead Rider had a real dilemma, too. He felt bad enough that he was going to have to arrest George Panther's son for murder. He hoped that something would turn up to prove that, in spite of the overwhelming evidence against him, Tom was innocent. But it was not a realistic hope, and he knew that. Arresting Tom Panther promised to be the most distasteful and unpleasant job that had ever faced him as high sheriff of the Cherokee Nation.

But there was even a more pressing dilemma, for Rider had to set in motion the search for Tom, and he felt a need to inform George about what was happening before he did. Yet he could not, for the posse of U.S. deputies was on their way to George's house, and there was no way for Rider to go out there without being seen and questioned by them. More than that, it would be a wasted trip, for if George was hiding from the white men, he would be hidden from Rider as well. The deputy marshals had decided to come to Tahlequah and ride on out to George's house at the worst possible time. Rider was not at all sure what was best for him to do.

George knew that Gwed' and the rest of his family were safe from harm. He knew that they had gone to her sister Polly's house over in the next district, and the white lawmen would have no idea where to look for them. He wasn't worried about his own safety either. He was ready. His barrier wouldn't stop the posse from coming into his house, but his other medicine would prevent them from seeing him. It had worked before, and it would work again. As long as he had ample warning and time to prepare, he could protect himself from those men—or any other, for that matter.

But George was worried sick about Tom. He had no idea where Tom might be, though he did have some idea what Tom might be up to. He would be with his cronies drinking whiskey or trying to figure out how to get some. That much was almost certain. He would be in some kind of trouble or about to get into it. George hoped that Rider had already caught Tom drinking and had thrown him in jail. At least he'd be safe there for a little while. What worried George was that Tom might blunder into the posse coming home to ask for money or something to eat.

His larger and constant concern, of course, remained the same. It was the question he could not answer satisfactorily. Not yet. Was Big Forehead the source of all the trouble in the neighborhood? And if it was Big Forehead, who had paid him to do so much harm? He would not have done it on his own. At least, that did not seem likely. There had to be someone somewhere with a bad grudge against George or against one of the people George helped. And George had to find out who it was, who both of them were, the one who paid, and the one who was making the bad medicine. Only then would he be able to stop it.

In the meantime, all he could do was provide protection to those who came to him for help. When the bad medicine came at them, George's medicine could send it back where it came from. But not knowing its source, he was helpless to stop it. And it would come again. This annoyance with the deputy marshals was something that had been thrown in to weaken him and interfere with the process of looking for the ones who were responsible. It complicated his life and spread him too thin, keeping him too busy to do what had to be done to protect the others and find the source of the evil. But George was determined. He would take care of the white lawmen, and he would find the truth of the larger problem. He would accomplish it all.

Beehunter saw the posse of deputies coming, and he hurried back down to the road. He mounted up and rode fast toward George Panther's house. As he moved below where he knew that Canoe and the others were hiding, he waved his hat back and forth at arm's length. He rode on around the bend and pulled up where he saw the path through the woods that led down to the creek, and he took his horse there and left it with the others. Then he trotted back to the road and climbed the hill where Canoe waited for him.

"Over here," said Canoe.

Beehunter found him quickly and settled down beside him.

"They're coming?" Canoe said.

"Yes," said Beehunter. "It will be awhile yet. You can see a long way from up where I was watching. But they're coming."

"We're ready for them then," Canoe said. "When they get here—right down there—I'll shoot in front of them to make them stop. Then I'll tell them to go back. If they turn around and go back, then all will be well—until the next time they come. But if they keep going toward George's house, or if they shoot at us, then we'll start shooting, and we'll shoot to hit them. I told everyone already, don't try to kill them, but try to hit them. If we hurt some of them, the others will have to take the hurt ones back to town."

"That's a good idea," said Beehunter.

Rider is not going to like this, he thought, but what else could he do? He hoped for the best. Maybe the posse from Fort Smith would turn around and go back when they realized they had ridden into an ambush. Maybe they would not get George Panther and no one would get hurt. That would be best. But if they were determined, then it was almost a sure bet that someone would get killed, and if it was one of the white lawmen, then Beehunter would be a part of it. That would mean that he could no longer work for Rider as a deputy. He didn't like to think about that. He liked Rider, and liked his job. He wished those white men had never come around.

Where did they all come from, and why were there so many of them? He knew that his people had come from back east, from what had become the states of North and South Carolina, Tennessee, Kentucky, Alabama, Virginia, West Virginia and Georgia. He knew that the white people had come from across the ocean and had started taking land away from the Cherokees and other Indian people. He knew about the Trail of Tears, the attempted great removal of all Cherokee People from their ancient homelands. He knew that the Removal Treaty had said that once the people had all been settled out west, they would not be bothered again. And he knew as well that it had all been lies, for the white men were moving in on them again. They were pressing hard on them from the east. There seemed to be no rest for the Cherokees.

Talmadge Hunt had stopped his posse along the side of the road. He had them all dismount and sit on the ground, and he stood before them to give them some last-minute advice and instructions. He felt like the general of an army preparing to go into battle. He liked the feeling of authority and the anticipation of a fight.

"It won't be long now," he said. "It's just a little farther down this road. Now the way I understand it, Panther himself won't give us any problems except that he'll likely be well hidden. The last two times our men have come out here, they haven't found any sign of him. If we don't find him, we'll stick it out. We'll wait.

"Now I talked to the men who came out here last, and they didn't meet any resistance from Panther himself, but someone was hid up on the hillside, and he took a couple of potshots at them. The way it sounded to me was that whoever it was just tried to scare them off, make them turn back, and it sounded like it was just one man with a rifle.

"But we can't count on the same thing happening here today. We have to be ready for anything that might happen. We might just ride on up to the house with no interference, and we might find Panther there and arrest him with no problems. I hope so. We might ride up to the house, and he might shoot at us. Or someone might be lying in ambush for us right now. It might be that same one man, or it might be more. So all I'm saying is be ready for anything.

"If anyone should start shooting at us, don't wait for my orders. Shoot back, and shoot to kill. Up another couple of miles, there's a bend in the road. If they are waiting for us, I expect they'll be laid in on the hillside just this side of that bend. When you see it up ahead, keep your eyes open. Watch the hillsides. If shooting starts, dismount and take to cover on the sides of the roads, but when you leave your horses, take your rifles with you. Without a rifle, you won't be any good at all. Any questions?"

There were none, so Hunt ordered them to mount up, and he led them on down the road. No one said anything. Each man was tense as he watched the wooded hillsides for any sign of danger.

Tom had been drunk for some time, and so were Punch and Dot, but they had been out of whiskey for a while, and they were all beginning to hurt from the lack. Punch had said he was hungry, and Dot had made him get up and fix them some eggs and sausage. Eating kept them busy for a while, but now they were full, and the eggs and sausage were all gone, and they were wanting whiskey again.

"Go get some," Dot said.

"I don't have any money," Punch whined. "I spent all my money on that last jug."

"That's all right," said Tom. "Let's go."

"You have money?" Punch whimpered.

"Come on," Tom said. "We'll get some whiskey."

As he headed for the door, Tom patted the revolver tucked in his waistband. He looked back at Dot and gave her a wink. He went on out the door, and Punch followed him.

"Where's the closest place?" Tom asked.

"That's Jenny Spruell," Punch said. "She's just over the hill that way. Just a couple of miles from here. She always has whiskey. But she wants her money right then."

"Don't worry about it," Tom said.

They walked on for a while without talking.

"I feel sick," said Punch.

"You'll be fine when we get that whiskey," said Tom. He was beginning to feel winded himself from the walk. He had done more walking on this trip than he had done for quite some time. He wished he knew where he had lost his father's horse and saddle. That horse would come in real handy, he thought. They made it to the top of the hill, and looking down, they could see the small cabin. Smoke curled out of the chimney on its far end.

"Is that the place?" Tom asked.

"Yeah," said Punch. "That's Jenny Spruell's house."

They started down the hillside.

"You sure she'll have whiskey?"

"She always has whiskey."

"You better be right," said Tom. "I don't know this woman."

"She's an old white woman," Punch said. "I don't know why she lives here, but she's always got whiskey. Always."

"Okay. Then we'll get some of it."

At the bottom of the hill, Tom stopped to catch his breath. Punch waited with him. In a moment, they resumed their walk. They crossed an open field and walked up to the old woman's door. They stood for a moment and looked at each other. Punch gave a shrug, lifted a fist and banged on the door.

"Who is it?" came a rough voice from inside.

Tom nudged Punch, and Punch called out, "It's me. Punch. You know me."

"I know you," came the croney voice. "What do you want?"

"I want some whiskey, Jenny. Open up."

"You got money?"

Punch hesitated, and Tom gouged him in the ribs.

"Yeah, sure. What do you think?"

The door opened a crack, and watery blue eyes peered out. "Who's that with you? I don't know him."

Tom gave his best smile. "I'm Tom Panther, Miz Spruell," he said. "I'm the one that has the money. Can we come in?"

The old woman hesitated a moment, then opened the door and stepped back. Tom went inside, and Punch followed.

"Let me see your money," she said.

"Let us see the whiskey," said Tom.

"It's right over there," Punch said, pointing to the far side of the room.

Tom squinted in the dimly lit cabin, and he saw jugs piled against the far wall. He smiled. "Go get a couple of them," he said to Punch.

"Don't touch it. Let me see your money first," the old woman demanded.

Tom jerked the revolver out and cocked it all in one motion, swinging the barrel up to point directly at the woman's face. Her rheumy eyes opened wide in fright. Her wrinkled lips parted slightly.

"Go get it," Tom said.

Punch took long strides across the room and started gathering up all the jugs he could handle.

"You're stealing from me," the old crone said.

"What're you going to do?" Tom asked her. "Are you going to tell the law that we come and stole some illegal booze from you?"

Chapter 12

Beehunter held a rifle ready, a shell already cranked into the chamber. He was a little lower on the hillside than any of the others and about in the center of them all. Canoe was just above him and to his right. He could see where some of the others were hidden across the road. He waited with some apprehension for the posse to appear. He had decided that he was going to be in trouble with someone no matter what he did, and these men were protecting George Panther, and so there he was, right in the middle of things. He would worry about what to tell Rider later.

Just then, the deputies came riding around the bend in the road. Beehunter tensed and waited. Canoe was running this show. He would wait for Canoe to make a move. Maybe, he thought, he would even be able to sit through this without firing a shot. He decided that he would try to do just that. A shot rang out from behind him, and even though he had been expecting it, it made him jump. He saw where the bullet kicked up dust in front of the lead rider's horse. The posse all came to a halt. They all looked up at the hillsides.

"Go back!" Canoe shouted.

*   *   *

George Panther was alone in the back room of his house. He was looking into his crystal, but he was not getting any clearer image than he had all the other times he had tried. He could see the figure of a man, but it was still just a shadow, a silhouette. He stared hard, and he talked to the crystal, trying to coax some clear features out of the vague and sinewy image. Suddenly, he heard a rifle shot, and then another. Soon it sounded like a small war down the road near his house. The image in the crystal vanished as George heaved a heavy sigh.

A bullet hit a tree trunk and zinged past Beehunter's head. The deputy marshals had all dismounted and had taken cover along the sides of the road. They were firing rapidly up into the hillsides. The Cherokees were firing back. Down below, a deputy called out. He had been hit. Behind him, Beehunter heard a Cherokee yelp from taking a bullet. He spotted a deputy creeping along the left side of the road, and he took careful aim and fired. Even from that distance, he could see the blood spurt when his bullet tore into the man's right calf. He had hit the man exactly where he intended. He had forgotten his earlier resolve to hold his fire. The heat of battle had taken over and drawn him in. Beehunter looked for another target.

Talmadge Hunt searched the hillsides for something to shoot at. He thought he detected a movement in the thick brush, and he fired. Another shot rang out from the hillside, and just behind him, a man cried out in pain.

"Damn," Hunt said. He turned to the only man he could see clearly and who was near enough to hear him. "See if you can find out how many are hit," he said. The deputy turned and ran back in a crouch. Hunt searched for another target and finding none, wasted a shot out of frustration.

In another moment, the other deputy came up beside him. "We've got four hit, Talmadge," he said.

"Shit," said Hunt. "How bad are they?"

"None of them's too bad," said the other, "if we could get the bleeding stopped and get them bandaged up."

"Damn it!" Hunt said. He blew out an exasperated sigh. "Can you get to your horse?"

"Yeah. I think so."

"Well, get on him and get back to town. Bring the wagon out here. We'll have to load up the wounded and take them in to the doc."

The deputy was on his way. Hunt was frustrated and angry. Crouched in high weeds, he considered his situation. He knew he had made a big mistake. He had fallen into the same ambush as the previous deputies who had tried to arrest George Panther. It was obvious now that Panther had a good many supporters. Hunt figured that he would never get to Panther along this road. He had thought that with enough men and supplies, he would fare much better than the others, but here he was pinned down with four wounded men. A shot rang out and another man yelled out in pain. Five wounded men.

"Hey, back there," he called out. "Someone get to bandaging the wounded. Tear up your shirts if you have to. Just try to stop the bleeding."

He did not want to go down in Marshal Crump's

book as another failure. He must not. He made up his mind that he would not ride back to Fort Smith to report this fiasco. He would go back to Tahlequah to his camp and get the wounded men to a doctor, then rethink his whole approach to the problem. He might send word back to Crump that he needed some men to replace the wounded, maybe even boost his numbers some. It couldn't hurt. A bullet spanged into the ground near him, and he huddled up more tightly.

Goddamn that George Panther, he thought. Goddamn that Indian. He was determined not to let Panther ruin his career. He had a good record as a deputy marshal, and he had his mind on bigger and better things. Maybe an appointment as a U.S. marshal. He had no intention to remain a hireling all his career. But he had to keep his record clean. George Panther was trying to besmirch it in a big way.

A big brown owl stood in the yard just outside George Panther's house. It puffed out its feathers and spread wide its wings. It gave a slight squat, then sprang off with its legs as its big wings began to flap. The bird took to the air. It flew higher and higher, sailing toward the scene of the big fight. Shots were no longer being fired as rapidly as they had been earlier, but they still sounded now and then. The owl flew in a wide circle, looking down on the scene below, taking it all in. Then it began to glide toward a specifically selected spot. It came down in the woods on the hillside, silently, just behind where Canoe and the others were hidden. It landed lightly on the steeply slanted ground and cocked its big shaggy head to one side.

* * *

There had to be another approach to the Panther house, Hunt was thinking. If he could get himself and his men out of this current mess, he would try to find out what that other approach might be. He would try to get his men up close to the house the next time, maybe sneak up from behind it—get them close to the house without anyone even knowing that they were approaching. He would surround the house, then catch George Panther before Panther or any of his loyal friends knew anything was up. That was the way to do it. But he had to find that other approach to the house. He heard the wagon on the road behind him, and he got to his feet, keeping low in a crouch, and hurried back to meet it. His planning would have to wait. He had five wounded men to get into the wagon and back to Tahlequah for medical attention.

"Beehunter," said Canoe.

"What is it?"

"What does it look like down there to you? Do you think they're leaving?"

"I don't know," Beehunter said. "I think their wagon came. I think they're loading up the wounded to take them back to town. I don't know if they'll all leave or not."

Just then Canoe felt a presence beside him, and he jumped with fright. He turned his head to see George Panther standing there.

"George," he said. "How did you get up here?"

"I told you not to do this," George said harshly. "I told you to stay out of it, and now you've gone and got these other men involved. I want you to get all these men out of here, and I want you to keep your-self and them out of this fight from now on. Do you hear me?"

"George, we were just—"

"I know what you were doing. I don't want you to do it. That's all. You've already gotten some people hurt. You could get someone killed. Now get everyone out of here."

"I don't know if I can get them out right now," Canoe said. "I can't get word to those across the road. If we start to move, the lawmen will see us."

"Canoe," said Beehunter, "I think the posse down there is leaving."

"Okay," George said to Canoe. "You heard that. Now's your chance. Get everyone out of here."

The shooting had stopped. The wounded deputy marshals were all loaded into the wagon, and the wagon started rolling back toward Tahlequah. Hunt and the other able-bodied men continued watching the hillsides until the wagon was well down the road. Then they mounted their horses and followed. A part of Hunt wanted to continue the pursuit of George Panther, but his wiser part told him that there would be another time. Enough was enough.

Canoe and his followers, including Beehunter, made their way down the hillside. George stayed where he had been, watching them go. A little ways down the hill, Canoe looked back over his shoulder. "Are you coming, George?"

"You just keep going," George said. He waited. He had his own way back, and no one else needed to see what it was.

Canoe kept moving, Beehunter close behind him. After a little while, Canoe glanced back at Beehunter. "George is really mad at me just now," he said.

Beehunter thought that maybe George was as mad at Canoe as Rider would be at him when Rider found out about all this.

Sheriff Go-Ahead Rider saw the deputies' wagon leave the camp site in a hurry, and he guessed what was going on. They would be returning soon with wounded. He wondered how many, and whether or not any Cherokees had gotten hurt. He figured that George Panther was safe enough, but he wondered what Beehunter might be up to. He hoped that Beehunter had not gotten himself caught in the middle of the fight. It was then that he noticed a man in black walking toward him. He thought for a moment before he remembered where it was he had seen the man before. It had been at the last big race. Rider had been curious about the man then and had asked one or two people about him, but no one seemed to know him or anything about him.

"Sheriff Rider?" the man said, extending his hand.

Rider took the hand. He did not like the feel of it. It was cold, clammy. "That's right," he said.

"I'm called Big Forehead," the man said, speaking in Cherokee. But there was something about his Cherokee speech. It was correct, and it was understandable, but it did not sound local. Nor did it sound like North Carolina Cherokee. Rider had talked with Cherokees from North Carolina. They talked differently from the people in the Cherokee

Nation out west, but this Big Forehead did not sound the way they did, either.

"What can I do for you?" Rider asked.

Big Forehead shrugged. "I'm new here," he said. "I just wanted to introduce myself."

"Where did you come from?" Rider asked.

"Up north. Those white lawmen over there—I heard they were after a man named George Panther."

"That's what they said."

"Is that the man with the big white horse? The horse that won the race?"

"That's George," Rider said.

"They said that he's wanted for the killing of a white man," said Big Forehead.

"So I heard."

"You don't know?"

"When it's federal business," Rider said, "it's not my business. I stay out of it. Are you Cherokee?"

Big Forehead smiled. "I'm a Real Person," he said. He touched the brim of his hat, gave a nod, turned and started walking away.

A Real Person, Rider thought. Of course, Cherokees used to identify themselves that way. Big Forehead might be speaking formally and a bit old-fashioned by referring to himself as a Real Person. Or he might have used the term in the contemporary sense to mean only that he is an Indian. It had been a sneaky answer, Rider decided, one calculated to obscure. Rider did not like the man, but he wanted to know more about him.

George Panther returned to his house quickly. When Canoe and the others arrived unexpectedly,

he was sitting beneath the arbor. He could see that
several of the men had been shot. He would have
some work to do. He had already given Canoe a
talking to, so he decided to say nothing more about
it. He would do the doctoring and let the rest go. As
the men came toward the arbor, they looked at the
ground. George could tell Canoe had told them all
what George had said. They had the look of children who had just been scolded. George had to fight
to keep from smiling.

Rider was sitting behind the desk in his office
when Beehunter came in. He looked up, but he did
not say anything.

"The wagon just brought the wounded white
men in," Beehunter said.

"How many were hurt? Do you know?"

"Five, I think."

"Five out of seven," Rider said. "I'd say they lost
the day. Any hurt badly?"

"Not too bad. The men who were fighting them
only shot to wound so they would have to quit the
fight and bring the hurt ones back to the doctor."

"That's an old trick," Rider said, "but it's still a
good one."

"Yes," said Beehunter. "It is. Go-Ahead?"

"What is it?"

"I was there. I shot at them, too."

"You shot at the white lawmen?" Rider pressed.

"Yes. I had been to see George. I was coming
back, and Canoe and some others met me in the
road. They asked me where I had been and where I
was going. They said, 'Are you with us'?"

"And you said—"

"I said yes. The white lawmen were coming to get George, and these men were there to protect George. I didn't know what else to do. What should I have done?"

Rider sat for a moment in silence.

"If I had been there instead of you," he said, "I might have done the same thing. I don't know. I know that it must have been a difficult decision to make. These are not easy times we're living in."

George Panther's prophecy came back into Rider's mind, as well as the reason for all this trouble, all these bad times.

"Do you want me to give back my badge?" Beehunter asked. "Will you put me in jail?"

"I didn't see you do anything wrong, Beehunter," Rider said, "and no one has come in to file any complaints against you. Why should I take your badge? I'd be shorthanded without you, and the council might not give me the money to hire a replacement."

"But I—"

"You've had a long day, Beehunter. Why don't you go on home?"

"*Howa*," Beehunter said. He turned to leave the office.

"Beehunter," said Rider.

Beehunter stopped and turned around. "Yes?"

"Did you actually hit anyone out there—when you were shooting?"

Beehunter smiled. "There was a lot of shooting," he said. "Five white men got shot. Maybe three Cherokees. It was loud, and people were running all around. Who can tell?"

After Beehunter had left, Rider went to the sheriff's barn and saddled his big black horse. If the posse had just returned, it would be a good time to ride out and see George. He would ride around the long way out of town, though, because he did not want the federal lawmen to see him riding toward George's house. If they did see him, they would be suspicious. They might even follow him. At the very least, they would question him about it later, and he did not want to have to fool with them.

Big Forehead walked casually over to the wagon where the deputies were helping their wounded companions out of the wagon and into the doctor's office. He saw the tall lawman standing to one side, and something told him that was the man in charge. He strolled over to meet him. "Are you the one in charge of this posse?" he asked in English.

"Yes," said Talmadge Hunt. "I am."

Big Forehead extended his right hand. "I'm called Big Forehead."

"Talmadge Hunt."

"You've been after George Panther," Big Forehead said. "People have been talking about it in town."

"And as you can see," said Hunt, "I ran into some trouble."

"Yes, I see. You know, they tell me this George Panther is a powerful medicine man."

"Yeah. They told me that, too. Do you know him?"

"I've met him."

"He has a mess of friends," said Hunt. "Are you one of them?"

Big Forehead shrugged and smiled. "I hardly

know the man," he said. "I bet against his horse, and I lost a lot of money."

Hunt looked up and down the street. There was no one close enough to overhear them. He decided to make his try. This was the most promising prospect yet. "Do you know where Panther lives?" he asked.

"I know."

"Do you know," said Hunt, lowering his voice, "a way to get there without going on the main road? Maybe a way to come up behind the house?"

"Oh, you mean you want to go back out there, and you don't want anyone to give him a warning that you're on the way, and you don't want anyone to see you coming. Is that right?"

"You've got the right idea," Hunt said. "Can you help me?"

"I think I know just the path you want to take," Big Forehead said. "Can we go somewhere and sit down with pencil and paper? I can draw you a beautiful map."

When Rider arrived at George Panther's house, George had just finished patching up the last of the wounded Canoe had brought to him. Rider stayed in his saddle until Canoe and the others all left. He watched them go, and he could see their guilty looks.

George looked up toward Rider. "Come on down, Go-Ahead," he said. "Let's have some coffee."

Rider dismounted and followed George into the house. George poured them coffee, and they sat at the table.

"Thank you," Rider said. "Where's the rest of your family?"

"I sent them to a place where they'll be safe from all this."

"I see."

"Do you come about those men who just left?" George asked. "You know, they were just protecting me. I told them I was okay. I told them not to do it, but they did it anyway. They didn't kill anyone, did they?"

"They didn't kill anyone, but the deputy marshals will want to arrest them anyway—if they ever find out who was involved. I don't know who was involved. I didn't recognize any of those that just left here."

George smiled. He knew that Rider knew who the men were, probably even knew that Beehunter had been among them.

"Anyway," Rider continued, "that's not the reason I came out here. I just had to wait until that bunch was out of the way. George, I have bad news."

"It's Tom then," George said.

"Yes. A man named Bood Trainor was murdered in Dog Town. The killer took some clothes and a gun. Some of the neighbors told me that it was Tom who did it. There's no proof yet, but there are those witnesses. I'll have to try to find him and arrest him. He'll be charged with murder."

George drew in a deep breath and tilted his head back, looking up at the ceiling. "I knew he was in bad trouble, Go-Ahead. I even told you that, didn't I?"

"Yes. You did."

"I won't interfere," George said, "and I won't hold it against you."

"I know that, George," Rider said.

"He's done a murder?"

"It sure looks that way, George. I'm sorry."

"That's a hanging offense."

"Yes. It is."

"Go-Ahead, I must ask you a favor."

"What is it?" said Rider.

"If it's you that catches up with Tom," George said, "and I hope it is, just remember this one thing: I don't want to see him hang. You know what I mean, Go-Ahead? I don't want my boy to hang."

Sheriff Go-Ahead Rider knew exactly what George Panther had meant. Riding slowly back toward Tahlequah, he thought about the tremendous impact of George's words. It had been tough enough to have to go to George's house and tell him about his son Tom. But this was more—much more. George Panther had just given Rider a most terrible burden, something that could change the course of Rider's entire life. And George was a friend. He was also Rider's elder, and he was a highly respected medicine man. Rider could not see how he could refuse George Panther's request.

But what if Tom did not resist arrest? What if Rider did turn out to be the one who found Tom, and then Tom just quietly submitted? Would Rider be able to shoot him to death in cold blood? That was exactly the thing that George Panther had asked him to do. He had asked Rider to murder his son. Yet Rider was sworn to uphold the law. He could not refuse George, but neither did he know if he would be able to do as George had asked, if and when the time should come.

Rider tried to sort out in his mind the conflicts that seemed to be raging all around. Representing the law of the Cherokee Nation, he was looking for Tom Panther. The deputy marshals, representing the law of the United States, were trying to apprehend George Panther. There was apparently a bad Indian doctor causing havoc all around, with whom George was engaged in a medicine war. Beehunter had just dealt with his own conflict—to fight against the U.S. lawmen on behalf of George or not. Rider now had a terrible conflict to deal with. And then there was Tom and his personal devils, whatever they might be. And looming in the background over it all was the United States government insinuating itself ever deeper into the affairs of the Cherokee Nation and the Cherokee People. Rider thought that one more conflict added to all this just might finish them all.

Chapter 13

Canoe was asleep in his house when something started scratching at his door. The scraping sounds grew louder and louder, and at last the noise brought Canoe awake. He lay still for a moment listening, his eyes opened wide. The scratching soon stopped. Canoe lay still listening to his own heartbeat, hearing his own heavy breath. A moment later, he heard the scraping again, but this time it was just outside his window, only a few feet away from his bed, separated from him only by the thickness of the wall. Then a peculiar odor came to his nostrils. It came right through the wall. It was a bad smell, yet sickly sweet. He could not identify it. It filled the room, and Canoe felt as if it might make him gag. Summoning all his courage, Canoe got up quickly and found his rifle. He cranked a shell into its chamber. Then he found his pipe and the tobacco George Panther had prepared for him. He filled and lit the pipe, sat down in a chair with the rifle across his knees and smoked, puffing almost furiously.

With the first light of day, Canoe headed for George Panther's house. He had not slept again, not since he had first heard the scratching. He had spent the night smoking and listening to the dreadful noises of the evil thing that seemed close enough to him to touch. He carried his rifle with him as he walked, but he knew that it would really do no good against whatever was tormenting him. When he finally reached George's house, he found George outside.

George saw him coming, saw the rifle and frowned.

"I'm not going out to the road," Canoe said. "I just brought this along because something is after me. I guess it won't do any good, but it made me feel better to carry it. It was right at my house, first at my door and then at my window. It was trying to get in all night long."

He told George more about the scratching and the strange smell and how he had not slept for the rest of the night. George listened, then had Canoe wait for him while he went inside the house. He looked into the crystal again, but he saw only the same hazy form. He knew that the same man was responsible for all this trouble, but he could not pin him down. The shadow would never seem to come clear. He finally put the crystal away and selected some herbs from several different pots around the room. Soon he was back outside near the arbor with Canoe, boiling the herbs in a pot of water.

"This what I'm fixing for you," he told Canoe. "Take it home and sprinkle it all through your house, and then go outside and sprinkle it all around your house, and then I want you to drink some of it. It will make you vomit and throw out all that bad air you breathed into your lungs. And keep smoking that tobacco I fixed for you. Do you still have plenty?"

"Yes. I have enough."

"Good. Keep using it. This will protect you. It won't stop it—I can't till I know just who it is doing it. But it will protect you and your wife and daughter."

George watched Canoe leave, thinking about all of the evil and mischief that was bothering so many of his friends and neighbors and was doing its best to prevent him from helping them. I've got to find this man, or woman, whatever it is, and stop it, he told himself. I have to stop it soon. All of these problems were connected. Canoe's troubles. George's trouble with the lawmen from Fort Smith. Tom's problems. Even Charlie Horse. All of it. It was coming from the same source. George could sense it. He just could not get close enough to that source to do anything.

Canoe met with the other Cherokee defenders of George Panther, those who had not been hurt during the fight, at his house. Everyone had coffee and bread, and they sat around outside in chairs, on benches and on tree stumps. They were all carrying their guns, revolvers, rifles and whatever other weapons they owned.

"I think we should keep watching the road," Canoe said. "Next time, when those lawmen come, maybe we won't fight them, because George said not to. Maybe we'll just go tell him they're coming. Or maybe we can put some problems in their way. We can cut down a tree or something to block their path and slow them down. I don't know, but I think

we should keep watching. George said he can protect himself, but we can't take a chance on anything
happening to him. What do you say?"

"I don't know," one man said.

"Listen," said Canoe. "Last night I was sleeping,
and a thing started scratching at my door. Then it
scratched at my window. It woke me up and frightened me. It made a stink that filled my house and almost made me sick to breathe. I hurried to George
this morning, and he made me some medicine.
What would I do without George? What would any
of us do?"

"I say we keep watching," said one of the men,
and the rest murmured agreement and nodded
their heads.

Beehunter knew that something was bothering
Go-Ahead Rider. Rider seemed distracted, and dis-
tant. Beehunter could not remember seeing Rider
like that before. At first Beehunter was afraid that
maybe Rider was mad at him for his having taken
part in the fight with the white lawmen, but after a
little time he could tell that it was something else.
When the sheriff was alone, he went into the office
and sat down facing Rider across the desk. Rider
looked up.

"What is it?" Rider said in Cherokee. "Do you
want to talk with me about something?"

"I want to know what it is that's bothering you,
Go-Ahead," Beehunter said.

"Why do you say that?"

"I'm your friend. I've known you for a long time.
I can tell. What is it?"

Rider thought for a moment. Then he decided

that he would tell Beehunter what George Panther had asked of him. He needed to tell someone. "Beehunter," he said, "you know I went to tell George about Tom. I had to tell him that we're going to arrest Tom for murder."

"Yes," Beehunter said. "I know."

"When I told him, he said he wanted to ask me one favor. He said to me, 'I don't want my boy to hang.' I couldn't refuse him, Beehunter, but I don't know what I'll do when the time comes. If Tom's resisting arrest, shooting at me, that's one thing, but if he's just standing there, it would be murder."

Beehunter thought it through. He took in the deep significance of what Rider had just told him. He considered the source of the request, and he considered not only Rider's position in the Cherokee Nation, but his personal importance to the people.

"It will all work out," Beehunter said, and he hoped that it would, because he knew that he would not leave that burden on Rider. Beehunter made up his mind right then to go out looking for Tom Panther. He would find Tom and kill him. That way, Rider would not have to make that awful decision. And Rider's position as high sheriff would not be endangered. "Don't worry, Go-Ahead," he said. "It will work out."

Talmadge Hunt gathered his able-bodied men around him in their camp across the creek from Tahlequah. He had a plan, and it was time to let them in on it. They had just finished their noon meal, and they were all drinking coffee.

"Listen to me, boys," Hunt said. He did not feel quite so pompous as he had the time before. "I've got some more men coming over here from Fort Smith. Our supplies are still holding out just fine. We'll hang around till the new men get here, and then we're going out again. But it's not going to happen like it did before.

"There's another way over to Panther's house. I just found out about it. When we get ready, we'll go around the long way. If those Indians who ambushed us are waiting there again, they won't see us come in. We'll get ourselves right up close to the house through the woods. We'll be right on top of him before he knows we're even on the way. We'll surround the house, and we'll give him one chance to surrender. If he refuses, we'll blast him out of there. We've got enough ammunition to do it, too."

"What about any wounded we might have?" a deputy asked.

"We'll take the wagon with us," Hunt said. "It won't be right up there by the house with us, but it'll be in reach. There'll be enough of us to handle it. If someone gets hit, someone else'll take him back to the wagon. I mean to stay out there at Panther's house till we get him this time."

"Well, we're all ready to go," said a deputy. "Long as we get some help, like you said."

"Say, Talmadge," said another. "I got an idea."

"What is it, Mike?"

"If we have enough men, what if someone was to go in the same way we did before? That way, if there's anyone waiting there, like there was that other time, they'll start shooting. Then for sure, everyone's attention will be out on that road. The rest of us could move on in from the new way you're talking about. If anyone's around the house at all, all their attention'll be out there on the road where the shooting's going on."

"Yeah," said Hunt. "That's a good idea. Then even if there's not any ambush this time, we'll still be coming at him from both sides."

"Yeah."

"Good. We'll do it that way, Mike. Everyone understand that?"

"How soon will them other men be here, Talmadge?"

"Give them four more days," he said. "I expect they'll be here by then. In the meantime, we'll just rest ourselves up here. Check all our weapons out. We'll be ready to go whenever the others show up."

Marshal Crump looked up from his paperwork as Deputy Fields stepped into his office. "Come on in, Fields," he said. "I'll get right to the point. You've heard about that damn George Panther?"

"Yes, sir."

"I just got word from Talmadge Hunt that Panther's managed to outwit them again. Actually, this time, they never even got to his house. A bunch of Cherokees caught them in an ambush before they could reach it. Wounded five men. Talmadge has sent me word that he needs some replacements. I already told him that I don't want to see him back here till he's got Panther in custody—or dead."

"Yes, sir."

Crump picked up a sheet of paper from his desktop and handed it to Fields, who took it and looked it over. It was a list of names.

"I want you to gather up those men," Crump

said. "Take them with you to Tahlequah and find
Talmadge. Join up with him and get that damn
Indian. Listen to me, Fields. When you see Talmadge,
you tell him what I'm telling you: George Panther is
making us look like a bunch of incompetent fools.
The judge is not happy. I'm not happy. I want this
case wrapped up, and I want it wrapped up fast. I
don't care what you have to do. Do you understand
me? Just get it done. That's all."

Tom Panther tipped back the jug and drained it
of whiskey. He tossed it aside and reached out a
hand. "Hey, Punch," he said. "Pass me that other
jug."

"That was all," said Punch. "That was the last
one. You just finished it all off."

"Bullshit," said Tom. "There's one more."

"No. We drank it all."

"You'll just have to go get some more," said Dot,
"or else dry up and blow away."

Tom tried to sit up, but he fell back again. "Shit,"
he said.

"What're you going to do?" Punch asked. "You
going to dry up?"

"You go get us some more," Tom said. "I can't get
up."

"I don't have no money," said Punch.

"We didn't have no money when we got that last
batch," said Tom. He picked up the revolver from
beside him on the bed and held it out toward
Punch. Punch's eyes opened wide.

"I can't do that," he said.

"Why not?"

"I never pointed a gun at no one in my whole life."

"Go on, Punch," said Dot. "Take it."

"I can't do it, Tom," Punch whined.

"You don't have to do nothing," said Tom. "Just go in her house and get some whiskey and let her see the gun. She won't do nothing. What can she do? She ain't going to pull a gun on you, and she can't tell the law. It's against the law for her to sell the stuff. Hell, it's against the law for her to have it in her house."

"Go on now, Punch," Dot said.

Punch took the gun. He stood still holding it in both hands and staring at it.

"Go on," urged Tom. "Go on or I'll take it back and use it on you."

Dot laughed, and Punch turned and walked out of the house.

"He's afraid," Dot said. "He's not much of a man. I don't know why I ever married him. I must have been drunk or something."

"He'll get the whiskey," said Tom. "He wants some more almost as bad as I do. He'll come back after a while with some more whiskey. Hey. Come here."

Dot turned her head to look at Tom lying there on her bed. She knew what he wanted. She smiled a half-grin, as if to say, I know what's on your mind. I know men.

"Come on," he said. "Ole Punch will be gone for a while. He won't ever know. What's the harm?"

Dot walked over to the side of the bed and looked down at Tom. Tom reached out and took her by an arm, pulling her down roughly on top of him.

He tangled his fingers in her hair and pulled her face to his, mashing her lips with his. She pulled away from him.

"Wait a minute," she said, and she started to remove her clothing. Tom watched her with greedy eyes, and he rubbed himself between the legs. Once naked, Dot sat on the edge of the bed and began unfastening Tom's trousers. Soon she had him stripped, and she crawled back on top of him.

Go-Ahead Rider was not just Beehunter's employer. He was the best friend that Beehunter had ever had, and Beehunter wasn't going to let anything bad happen to Rider if he could help it. Any time Rider had told Beehunter to do something, Beehunter had done it without question. Many times when Beehunter had known that Rider needed or even just wanted something to be taken care of, even if Rider had not told Beehunter to do it, Beehunter had done it.

Now he knew that Rider had been given not only a very difficult task by George Panther, but also a task that could cost Rider his position as high sheriff, maybe even his self-respect. If Rider was not very careful, it could even get him charged with murder, and then, if convicted, hanged. Beehunter could not let that happen. He was riding the countryside around Tahlequah in search of Tom Panther. Beehunter meant to kill Tom before Rider was faced with that terrible choice. Beehunter would try to get away with it, but if he failed to cover his tracks well enough, then so be it. He would be the one to hang, not Rider.

Beehunter had no idea where Tom might be hiding. He did not expect him to be at home, so he did not ride to George Panther's house. He would not likely be seen anywhere around Dog Town so soon after he had murdered Bood Trainor. But there were other places to look. Beehunter knew some of the people with whom Tom hung out and got into trouble. He would check them out, looking for Tom. He also knew where to find some of the whiskey sellers, and he knew most of the drinkers. He could try to make them tell him where other whiskey sellers were located.

He rode to the home of a young man he had only just let out of jail for drunkenness, a man named Billy Flores. Beehunter thought that Billy was part Cherokee and part Mexican. He found Billy at home with his mother, still looking pretty rugged from the wild time he'd had followed by a few days in jail.

"What do you want with Billy?" the mother asked in Cherokee.

"I just want to ask him some questions."

"Are you going to put him in jail again?"

"No. I only want to talk to him. That's all."

"He can't speak Cherokee," the mother said.

"I know," said Beehunter. "Will you stay and interpret for us?"

Reluctantly, she agreed, and she called Billy out. He sat down, glaring at Beehunter, his arms crossed over his chest.

"He just wants to ask you some questions," the mother said in English. "He don't want to put you back in jail. Talk to him. Tell him what he wants to know, and maybe he'll go away."

"What's he want to know?"

She turned to Beehunter. "What do you want to ask?"

"Tell him I'm looking for Tom Panther," Beehunter said, "and ask him when he saw Tom last."

The mother asked.

"I ain't seen Tom for a week or so," Billy said.

The mother put Billy's words into Cherokee for Beehunter.

"I know he's not at his father's home," Beehunter said. "He's not over at Dog Town. Who else does he run with? Where might he be?"

After the mother interpreted, Billy said, "I don't know who he'd be running with. He's made just about everyone mad at him. When he gets drunk, he's mean. Nobody I know wants to hang out with him anymore."

Beehunter left the Flores' home with no more information than he had when he had arrived. He knew that this was going to be a tough job. He would just have to find someone else. If none of Tom's former running mates knew anything, or would admit to knowing anything, the next thing was to check all the illegal booze dealers he knew about or could find out about. If Tom was out running wild, he would certainly have been in to see one of them. The problem was that none of the drinkers and none of the dealers would want to talk to Beehunter about where whiskey could be obtained. No one would talk to a lawman about whiskey.

Of course, Beehunter still knew who some of them were. He had put them in jail more than once, and they always went right back to doing what they had done before. They did not seem to know of any other way to make a living. Well, he knew of a couple more of Tom's old running mates to check with first. If that led nowhere, he would start on the list of whiskey dealers. He had to find Tom Panther.

Go-Ahead Rider was getting awfully tired of having the Fort Smith deputies hanging around Tahlequah. Rider was usually a pretty patient and tolerant man, but just their presence was annoying. He understood why Canoe and the others were doing what they were doing. He knew why Beehunter had joined with them that one time. He wished they would just go away. He could not say that he wished they would get their job done and leave, because their job was to get George Panther. Rider just wanted them to leave.

But he knew they would not. In fact, he wondered if they were just another step in the awful process outlined in the prophecy George had told him. He wondered if from now on, he would see more and more white people flocking into the Cherokee Nation. He knew the talk about white people lurking around in Kansas just north of the Cherokee Nation, saying that the Cherokee land ought to be taken over by the U.S. government and turned over to white people. He figured it was just a matter of time. He was afraid that he was already witnessing the truth of the terrible prophecy, and he did not like it one bit.

When Punch returned with the whiskey, Tom and Dot were dressed again. They gave no indication that they had been doing anything other than waiting around for him to return with something to drink. Tom made out he was asleep and Punch woke him up coming in the house. He rolled over and gave Punch a bleary-eyed look.

"You have any trouble?" he asked.

Punch grinned. "No trouble," he said. "No trouble at all. But that old woman told me not to come back anymore. She said if I was to come back, or if you come back, she's going to have a man there waiting for us, and he's going to kill us. That's what she said. He's going to kill us. When I left with all this whiskey, she said, 'Maybe he'll come and kill you anyway for what you already stole from me.' I took another jug for that and laughed at her. It was fun."

"Well, maybe we'll just go back over there and kill him . . . and her too," said Tom.

Punch put down the jugs of whiskey he had stolen from the unfortunate woman and pulled out the gun. He waved it around in the air. "You get a lot more respect when you have one of these things," he said. "I should have got me one a long time ago."

Dot looked at Tom. "Oh, look what you done, Tom," she said. "Look what you made Punch into."

Tom laughed.

"He's a gunfighter and a badman," he said. "Maybe he'll be a famous bank robber."

Punch turned this way and that, pointing the revolver. "Bang," he said. "Bang. Bang. Maybe I *will* rob me a bank. Maybe I'll kill me somebody, too. Bang. A lawman. Bang. Bang."

"Hey, that's enough of that," said Tom. "Put it down before you kill me or your wife. Or your own damn self. Have a drink of whiskey with me before I decide to get up and kick your ass."

Punch whirled and leveled the revolver at Tom. "Bang," he said. He stepped over to the table and put the gun down. "Let's have a drink."

Chapter 14

Canoe sat watching the road to George Panther's house and looked around quickly when he heard someone walking toward him. He relaxed when he saw that it was one of his fellow guards. The man walked over and squatted down.

"No one's come down that road now for a long time," the man said.

"That's good," said Canoe.

"Yes, but Sam just left."

"Where did he go?"

"He said the white catchers have given up. He said he had other things to do, and he didn't believe that they were coming back again anyway. So he left."

"What about the others?" Canoe asked.

The man gave a shrug. "Mostly, they think like Sam. They're all talking about going home. They think it's all over with."

"And you?"

"I don't know, Canoe. Maybe they're right. And besides, we know that George doesn't want us to be doing this. George said he can take care of himself. I believe him. Look how he takes care of all of us."

"That's why I think we should take care of him

now," Canoe said. "George has always been ready to help us when we needed anything. Now it's our turn to help him."

"But not if he doesn't need our help. Not if he doesn't want it."

"He's just trying to look out for us," said Canoe, "as always. Maybe we rely on him too much. Maybe we should do something for ourselves now and then. Something for George. We can't expect George to do everything, can we?"

"We ran those men off one time," the other man said, "and George got mad at us. I think we should do what he told us to do and just go home. The others are going home. So am I. I think you should go home, too."

"Listen," Canoe said, "those white catchers have not given up. They never give up. They'll be coming back with more men than before."

"I don't know," the other said. "I don't like to argue with those men over there."

Canoe sat on the hillside alone. He watched the road below. No one came riding along. He was sulking. The men he had thought were his friends had all deserted him. He knew as well as they that George had told them to stay out of this business. But he also knew that George was only trying to protect them by fighting his own fight. Why couldn't the others see that they needed to help George? This was not a medicine fight. This was a fight with guns. This was a war with the white men. George needed all the help he could get. George was fighting too many fights all at the same time. And the deputies would come back, just as he had said. They would add to their strength, and they would come back, full of anger and determination. Well, let them desert him, he concluded. He would stay. He would never desert George. As far as Canoe was concerned, George Panther was the most important man in the whole Cherokee Nation, and for Canoe, the Cherokee Nation was the world. Canoe would die for George Panther if he had to. He would certainly kill for him.

The new deputies from Fort Smith had ridden by rail as far as they could go. From there they picked up horses and started on the last leg of their trip to Tahlequah. Along the way, they stopped for a rest beside the road, and Fields stood up in front of them.

"Men," he said, "I want to tell you a few things before we get on over there to Tahlequah with Talmadge. I think all of you know ole Talmadge. He's a good man. We all like him. But he's been having more than his share of trouble with this Panther case. It seems simple enough. Just go out to a man's house and arrest him. That's all. Only thing is, the man never seems to be home. The Indians say that he is home, but only we can't see him on account of he's invisible. He's some kind of big medicine man."

A chuckle went through the group of deputies.

"Anyhow, I don't believe that no more than you do, because for one thing, the last time old Talmadge went out there with his posse, a bunch of Indians ambushed them and shot the posse up. Talmadge had five men injured. If that there George Panther is invisible, then how come he has a mess of armed Indians ambush the posse? It don't make sense.

"Well, the thing is, we got to go on and act like Talmadge is still in charge of this operation, but if things gets bogged down again, I just might have to take it over. I want you to know that and be ready for it if it should come to that. But if it don't come to that, don't let on. Just go on and do whatever it is ole Talmadge tells us to do.

"But what I got from Marshal Crump was some special instructions, and they was very clear. Marshal Crump wants us to get that George Panther in the worst way. He told me to do whatever it takes. Whatever it takes. That's just how he said it. He don't care how we do it, long as we get the bastard. If ole Talmadge has that same idea by now, then we'll be all right with him. If not, well, like I said, we just might have to take matters into our own hands."

Jenny Spruell peeked out her window when she heard the wagon wheels squeaking outside, and she recognized the white man from Arkansas, the man from whom she bought her wares. He would have a wagonload for her. She opened the door and stepped out. "Hello, Hiram," she said.

Hiram Knott grinned wide and wiped sweat off his brow with a shirtsleeve. "Howdy, Jenny," he said. "How's business?"

"Business been good," she said, "but I got robbed. Twice."

"You got robbed? Who done it?"

"Two no good young men," she said. "One's that Punch Doak. He just lives over that hill yonder. I don't know the other one. Never seen him before. He said his name, but I don't recollect it. They come in here to buy whiskey, they said. When I asked them for their money, the stranger, he pulled a gun. They took the whiskey. The boy with the gun, he said, 'Who you going to tell?' That's what he said to me. 'Who you going to tell?' Later, Punch Doak come back. He was by hisself this time, but he had the gun. He stole some more whiskey."

"We can't have that, Jenny," said Knott. He climbed down off his wagon seat. "Let me get this stuff unloaded for you, and then we'll talk some more about those two boys. We'll see if we can't figure out what to do about it. We can't have that sort of thing going on at all. That's awful bad for business—and for our reputations."

"I want some eggs, Dot," said Tom Panther. "Can you fry me up some?"

"I ain't got no eggs," said Dot.

"Hey, Punch," said Tom. "Go out and get us some eggs."

"I ain't got no money, Tom."

"You didn't have no money when you went and got that whiskey either, did you? Does that give you any ideas?"

Punch sat up, a smile on his face. He picked up the gun and held it lovingly. "Yeah," he said. "It does. Bang. I'll be back. I'll get some eggs."

He hurried out of the house and headed through the woods. He was thinking about a neighbor whose house was not far if he cut through the woods. It would be a few miles more taking the road. The neighbor had chickens. He should have eggs. Punch figured that he'd sneak in and steal the eggs, and if the neighbor happened to catch him, well, he'd have the gun. But the closer he got to the neighbor's place, the wilder his ideas became. The man also had some good saddle horses. It would be a lot more fun as well as more practical to go out robbing and stealing and shooting on horseback. Tom Panther had introduced him to the business of stealing with a gun, and he liked it. It sure as hell beat working. With a couple of good horses under them, Punch and Tom could terrorize the whole countryside. Hell, they could ride over into Arkansas and up into Kansas and rob banks all over the place.

He came out of the woods and was looking down into a green valley onto a prosperous farm. There was a house and a barn and two fine-looking horses in the corral. There were cleared fields. Punch pulled the gun out of his britches and checked it over. It was fully loaded. He spun the cylinder. He cocked it, then eased the hammer back down. The gun was ready, and so was he. He started walking boldly down to the farm.

When Punch got close to the barn, he met an unexpected surprise. The farmer stepped out of the barn right there in front of him.

"Hello, Punch," the man said.

"Oh, hi, Mr. Morton."

"What can I do for you?"

"I, uh . . . You got any eggs?"

"Sure have. You want a dozen or two dozen?"

"Give me a dozen," said Punch. "No. Make it two dozen. I got company at my house."

While Morton went to gather the eggs, Punch

walked slowly toward the corral, looking greedily at the two horses there. They sure did look fine. Saddle them up, he thought, and he and Tom could ride out anywhere. They could head out of the neighborhood to someplace where they wouldn't even be recognized, and they could rob some store along the way. They could get another gun and more ammunition and some money. Lots of money. They could rob a bank. They could rob a train. That would be some kind of thing, to rob a train. If they only had those horses.

"Anything else for you, Punch?"

Morton's voice startled him. He turned around. "Yeah," he said. "Saddle up them two horses there."

"What?"

"Saddle the horses. I want them."

"They're not for sale, Punch, and even if they were, I doubt that you could afford them. Here. Take your eggs and run along."

Punch jerked the revolver out of his waistband and pointed it at Morton, cocking it. "I want you to saddle them horses."

"Punch, you're making a big mistake. Put that gun way. Here. Take your eggs. I won't even charge you for them. Just take your eggs and go on your way."

"Mr. Morton," said Punch, "you better put them eggs down and fetch out the saddles and get them horses ready for me. If you don't get to it, I'll kill you. I really will. I'll shoot you dead."

Morton went into the corral. The saddles and the rest of the gear were thrown over the top rail of the fence. Morton took his time and seemingly did the job right. Punch watched as Morton put on the blankets, then the saddles, then cinched them up. He watched Morton fit the bridles. All done, Morton turned to face Punch.

"I wish I could talk you out of this," he said. "You know, the law will be after you. You could hang for this."

"They'll have to find me to hang me," Punch said, "and I ain't easy to find when I don't want to be found." He took up the basket of eggs and went into the corral. He looked from one horse to the other, selected one and tried to mount up. He put a foot into a stirrup, took hold of the saddle horn with the same hand that was holding the revolver, then started to swing on up into the saddle. But the saddle swung down under the horse's belly instead, dumping Punch hard onto his back. Eggs spilled all around. Punch yowled. The horse stamped and nickered. Morton came running at Punch fast, trying to take advantage of his upset situation. Punch panicked and swung the revolver around and fired. Morton stopped, a stunned look on his face. His hands went up to a fresh, bloody hole in his chest. He looked at Punch unbelieving. Then he fell forward dead.

Punch stood up and looked at Morton's body. "Son of a bitch," he said.

He looked around and saw that a few eggs were unbroken. He picked them up and put them back into the basket. Then he walked over to the second horse and gave a tug on the saddle. It too rolled under the horse.

"The dirty bastard," he said. "He didn't tighten the cinches. He done that on purpose. Son of a bitch."

Punch decided that it was more work to straighten up the saddles and get them back where they were supposed to be than it would have been to saddle them properly in the first place, but he finally got the job done. The horses were ready to go. He wanted more eggs, though. He went to find them, and he filled the basket. Then he left it beside a post by the corral and walked over to the house. He opened the front door and stepped inside the living room.

Mrs. Morton was crouched behind a chair, trembling. "Don't hurt me, Punch," she said.

"You know me," he said. He raised the revolver and shot her in the head. Then he started rummaging through the house. He found another revolver and some boxes of bullets. He found a rifle and a shotgun. He found clothes: shirts and trousers that might fit him and Tom Panther and some dresses that Dot might be able to wear. He found a few dollars and some coins he put into his pocket. Finally, he pulled a quilt off the bed and used it to wrap all his ill-gotten gains into a bundle. Throwing the bundle over his shoulder, he walked back to the corral. When Punch rode out of the farm, he was riding one fine horse and leading another. The second horse carried the bundle of stolen goods in its saddle.

The shortcut through the woods would have been difficult to negotiate on horseback, so on his return trip, Punch kept to the road. It was farther, but at least he was riding along happily, feeling exhilarated from his spree. The killings hadn't been bad. He had actually kind of enjoyed them. He wondered what Tom would think—and Dot. They wouldn't make so much fun of him now. He rounded a curve in the road and found a wagon blocking his path. A man sat on the wagon seat. Punch stopped. He put his hand on the butt of his revolver.

"You're blocking the road, mister," he said.

"Would you be Punch Doak?" the man said.

Punch was startled. He felt as though he'd been ambushed and caught. "Who wants to know?" he said.

"My name ain't important to you," the man said, "but my business might be. You see, I sell whiskey. I'm what you might call a wholesaler. You know what that means?"

"Uh, no."

"Well, you see, a wholesaler don't sell to folks like you. A wholesaler sells to a person that's called a retailer, and the retailer is the one you go to to buy your stuff. You understand?"

"I guess so," Punch said. He was looking sideways at this strange man, wondering what the hell he was up to.

"One of the retailers I sell to is a woman named Jenny Spruell. Do you know Miss Spruell? A fine lady."

"No," Punch said.

"I think you're lying to me now, Punch. How come you think I know who you are?"

"How would I know that?"

"Well, I know who you are because Jenny told me who you are, and she also told me what you done, you and your friend. Now, Punch, we can't have that. We can't let you get away with that. How are me and poor ole Miz Spruell supposed to make a living with you and your friend doing us like that?

If she can't make a living, then she won't have no money to buy more whiskey whenever I come around. Then we all lose, Punch. She loses, 'cause you stole from her. I lose, 'cause she's got no money to buy more whiskey from me. You lose, on account of you can't find no more whiskey to buy—or steal. You following that line of reasoning, Punch?"

"You get out of my way and leave me alone," Punch said.

Just then Punch realized that he was looking down the barrel of a big revolver. He didn't know where it had come from. He didn't know if the man had just pulled it so fast that he hadn't seen it, or if the man had been holding it all along and he had just failed to see it. Punch's hand gripped the handle of his own revolver and pulled it out an inch.

"I wouldn't do that, Punch," the man warned. He fired a shot that whizzed by Punch's right ear, and Punch flinched and squeezed his eyes tight shut. "What do you think we had ought to do about our problem?" the man said. "You have any ideas for me?"

Punch made no response. The man fired again. This time the bullet sang past Punch's left ear. Punch flinched again. "Don't," he said. "Don't shoot."

"Oh," the man said. "So you ain't lost your tongue. See, I could kill you right here and now real easy. I could kill you as an example to anyone else who might take it in his head to do what you done. But my whiskey is still gone, and I haven't been paid for it. Now, I'll ask you again, do you have any notion whatever how we could resolve our little problem?"

"I have an idea," said Punch.

"Well, I'm anxious to hear your idea."

"You don't have to kill me and Tom for what we done, mister," Punch said, his voice trembling. "I . . . I didn't know he was going to do it. I was just with him. That's all. It's his gun."

"That was the first time. The second time you done it all on your own."

"Well, yeah, but it was Tom's idea. And Tom's gun."

"Tom who?"

"Tom Panther."

"Where is Tom Panther?"

"He's over at my house. With my wife."

"That must be cozy for them," the man said.

"What?"

"Never mind. Go on then with your idea. You said that I don't have to kill you and Tom."

"No. You don't. We can pay you for what we took. That way, you don't have to kill us. And you get your money."

"You have some money?"

"I got some," said Punch. He started digging into his pocket and came out with the money he had just stolen from the Morton place. He held it out toward the wholesaler.

"Get down and come over here," the man said.

Punch dismounted and walked over to the wagon. The man held out his left palm, and Punch dropped the money into it. The man looked it over quickly.

"Is that all you got?"

"Ever' penny."

"It ain't enough, Punch," the man said.

"I can get the rest," Punch said. "Give me a little while. I can get it."

"I've got to head back to Arkansas," the man said. "Just how much time you think you need?"

"Tomorrow," said Punch. He slapped his own forehead. "No. Next day. Yeah. It'll take me two whole days. I'll get it. Me and Tom. We can get it. Just like I got that there. We can—"

"Hold it," the man said. "I don't need to know what you're fixing to do. I don't want to know. It ain't none of my business. All I want to know is that you're fixing to bring us the full amount of what you owe, and you'll be bringing it over to Miz Spruell's house day after tomorrow. Have I got that all right?"

"Yes. Yes, sir. Day after tomorrow. I promise you."

"If I don't see you then," the man said, "I know where your house is at, Punch. I'll come calling. You be at Jenny Spruell's house day after tomorrow with all the money. I'm counting on you now."

Chapter 15

The shabby raven circled a small shack in a valley below. Now and then a small feather fell from one of its wings or from its tail. A thin wisp of smoke rose up from the chimney on one end of the shack. The wretched-looking bird flew in a lower and tighter circle. Closer, it soared right through the wisp of smoke and sniffed at it. It wheeled again, so low that it was circling the shack and looking in its windows as it flew by. It spotted an open window and flew over to rest on the window ledge. On the rumpled bed inside the shack, a naked man lay on top of a naked woman. The eavesdropping raven watched them with evil red eyes. It listened to their heavy breathing and watched their labored movements.

Tom Panther moaned out loud and lay still for a moment. Then he rolled over onto his back to stretch out beside Dot. Both of their naked bodies were covered with sweat, and the bedclothes beneath them were wet and sticky.

"Is that all?" Dot said.

"All what?" said Tom.

"Is that as long as you can go?"

"Ka! Ka!"

Tom and Dot both turned their heads toward the window from which the noise had come. The raven was gone. Instead, a naked man was perched there, and he was leering through red eyes at Dot on the bed in her nakedness. She let out a small cry and jerked damp sheets up over her body. Tom laughed.

"It's all right," he said. "I know him."

"What are you laughing at?" Big Forehead said.

"I ain't never seen you like that before," Tom said.

"I've been traveling," said Big Forehead.

"Yeah," said Tom, "and I guess I know how you been traveling."

"I think you left the lady unsatisfied," Big Forehead said, changing the subject.

"Well, come on over and help yourself," Tom said. "See if you can satisfy her if you're so worried about her. Her husband can't do it, and I guess I can't either. I don't know what it would take to satisfy this one, what you just called a lady."

"Shut up, Tom," said Dot.

Big Forehead put his bare feet down onto the floor and walked the few feet over to the bed. Dot pulled the sticky sheet up under her chin and stared up at him with fear in her eyes. But mingled with the fear was an inexplicable fascination. Big Forehead grinned. His red eyes stared directly into hers, and they did not blink. His long, raven black hair hung loose over his shoulders. He reached down and took hold of the sheet and jerked it off with a flourish, flinging it across the room. Dot did not scream. She did not move. As Big Forehead put a knee on the bed, she slowly spread her legs.

Tom got up from the bed seemingly disinterested. He walked over to the table and picked up a whiskey jug. He poured himself a drink, ignoring the moans and groans and the creaking of the bed behind him. He emptied the glass and poured himself another. He chuckled, for a thought had just popped into his head. He wondered what poor ole Punch would think if he were to come into the shack at just that moment to find his wife with two naked men, one of them on top and at work on her.

But Punch was not yet near his home. He had been given a terrible fright by the whiskey peddler from Arkansas who had not told him his name. He had to come up with some more money and fast. The man meant to kill him if he failed. When he had almost stopped shaking from fear, he started riding toward his house. He meant to tell Tom Panther what had happened and then talk Tom into going with him to rob a store or a bank. No, a store would be better this first time. The store couldn't be too far away, though. They would have to get back in time to pay the man. He sure did not want the man coming to his house.

Then he wondered what Tom would actually say when he heard what all had happened. Punch wouldn't be able to tell just part of the story. He would have to tell it all, if he told any, and he wondered if he should tell Tom about old Morton and hsi wife. He wondered if he should tell Tom that he had allowed this white man from Arkansas to get the drop on him and scare him the way he had done. Tom would probably call him a coward and say that he should have killed the man. He might call him a fool. Tom and Dot had sent Punch out to get some eggs. That was all. And he had run into all kinds of trouble, and he had not handled it so good. Of course, he did have the eggs. He handled that part of it all right.

But the more he thought about it, the more he felt that he should solve the money problem before going back to the house and telling Tom what had happened. There was a country store not too far away. When he had first considered robbing stores, this one had not been in his plans. It was too close to his home, and the man who ran the store would know him. Of course, Morton and his wife had known him, too. He decided to head for the store. There would be plenty of money there. Old man Cash always did a brisk business. Old man Cash. Punch thought that the man was well named.

Having made up his mind, he was anxious to get into the store and throw down on old Cash. It would be a whole lot better, he thought, to go back to his house with plenty of money. Maybe he would even go back to Jenny Spruell's house and pay the mean old man from Arkansas the money he owed him, and then go home and not bother telling Tom and Dot anything at all about what he had done other than get the eggs. Yes, he thought, that was the best way. That was what he would do.

Go-Ahead Rider walked through the front door of the Cherokee National Capitol. He moved to the stairway and went up to the second floor to the office of the principal chief. He started to knock, but the chief looked up from behind his desk through the open door.

"Come in, Go-Ahead," he said.

"You wanted to see me, Chief?"

"Yes. Take a chair. Thanks for coming over so quickly. I've got a letter here I want to read to you. It's from Judge Parker over in Fort Smith."

"Okay," said Rider.

The Chief picked up the letter and started to read, skipping the greeting.

As you are certainly aware, I have issued a warrant for the arrest of one of your citizens by the name of George Panther, for the murder of a white man, and not an Indian. By this writing, my deputies have made several attempts at serving the warrant, so far, all unsuccessful. On their last attempt they were fired upon by several parties thus far unknown, but an investigation will be made into that matter as well.

I am writing this to you to inform you that my deputies have made me aware of a disturbing lack of cooperation from your high sheriff, not to mention from average citizens. I find that news very vexing. I would think that any law enforcement officer worthy of the name and the badge and the oath he has sworn would be more than willing to cooperate with other law enforcement agencies in the apprehension of a wanted murderer, and I am requesting with this letter that you look into the matter at your earliest convenience. I am doing everything in my power to make the Indian Territory, including your Cherokee Nation, a decent and safe place for law-abiding citizens and good Christians to raise their families. I would hope that you would want the same thing and would therefore give me every possible cooperation in my sincere attempt to bring civilization to your homeland. Yours sincerely.

The Chief put the letter down on his desk and looked up at Rider.

"Well," Rider said, "he's not lying. About me not cooperating with his deputies, that is."

"Is there anything more you want to say?"

"No, sir. I reckon not."

Actually, there was much that Rider would have liked to say. He would have liked to say the things to Judge Parker, though, and not to his chief. He would have liked to go into Parker's office and tell him just what he thought about his deputies wandering freely through the Cherokee Nation and arresting Cherokee citizens. He would like to tell the judge to get those deputies out and keep them out. And he would like to tell him a thing or two about his notions of civilization.

"I've written a response," the chief said. He took up another sheet of paper from the desktop and began to read again.

As you are well aware, your country has chosen to exercise its own powers of jurisdiction within the boundaries of our country any time a white person is involved in a case. That is an imbalance of justice, but it is one which we are not powerful enough to oppose openly. That does not mean we welcome it.

And while we are powerless to prevent you from exercising such jurisdiction, you, on the other hand, are powerless to insist that the law officers of the Cherokee Nation assist you in your infringement on our sovereign powers. High Sheriff Go-Ahead Rider is a man in whom I have total and complete confidence. I stand firmly behind him in his actions—or in-actions.

The chief put the letter down and leaned back in his chair, looking at Rider.

"Thank you for that, Chief," Rider said.

"I meant every word," said the chief. "I wish I could have stated my feelings more strongly, but I think I had better let it go at that."

"I think you got the idea across all right," said Rider.

"If I could have my way, the United States would get clear of our borders and stay out. It's the great-est bully in the history of the world. Sometimes, Rider, I long for the old days, the days of Dragging Canoe and our great war chiefs. Sometimes I wish I'd been born a hundred years ago so that I could fight the sons of bitches."

"If that was possible, sir," Rider said, "I'd be right there alongside of you."

The chief sighed. "We were born at the wrong time, Rider. We were born at the wrong time."

Rider thought about the prophecy again. The wrong time indeed.

Walking back to his office, Rider thought about the chief's words, and the prophecy he had heard

from George Panther. He sighed. He guessed that
he and the chief were caught in the middle. They
were living in the time of decline. They were witnessing the first part of the prophecy, the part that
said the white people would take over the Cherokee
Nation. And they would be long dead before the
second part came about, the part where the
Cherokees would come back strong.

But then someone had to hold things together
until the rest of the prophecy would be fulfilled.
Thinking about it in that way, maybe that was the
most important time of all, the time of holding it all
together. And he was glad that George had told him
about the prophecy. He decided that if he had to
watch his government crumble, it would be a little
easier to take, knowing that it would come back
again one day as strong as ever. And he was glad to
think that he would play his part. He would do the
best he could.

Beehunter rode into a small community a few
miles east of Tahlequah. He knew most of the people there, and as he rode by, most of them greeted
him in Cherokee. He rode slowly, waiting for someone who might be of help to him in his search for
Tom Panther. He was almost all the way through
the hamlet when he saw Esau Sanders. He knew
Esau to be a good man, but one with a weakness.
Now and then Esau just had to have a drink of
whiskey. And when he had that drink, he had to
keep going. On those occasions, more often than
not, Esau wound up spending some time in jail.
Beehunter called out to Esau as he dismounted,
and, leading his horse, walked over to shake hands.

"Beehunter," said Sanders, speaking Cherokee, "how are you? I haven't seen you since the last time you put me in jail."

"I'm good," Beehunter said. "How are you doing?"

"Doing well. I haven't been drinking since that time. What are you doing over here?"

"I'm looking for someone, Esau. Maybe you can help me."

"I will if I can."

"You know Tom Panther, don't you?"

"Yes. George's son. I know him. Is that who you're looking for?"

"Yes. Most of his old friends say they don't go around with him anymore. They don't know where he is."

"He's not staying with George?"

"Not lately."

Esau scratched his head and wrinkled his brow. "Well, I don't know, Beehunter," he said. "From what I hear, Tom really has run off all his old friends. He's pretty bad when he's drunk, and he's been drinking more and more lately. He used to be all right, even fun. But he's worse lately. He gets mean, from what I hear. Have you seen Bood Trainor?"

"Bood's dead," said Beehunter.

"Oh. How?"

"He was killed. It looks like Tom did it. That's why I'm looking for him."

"Oh, that's too bad. Well, let's see. I know that Tom used to run with a young man called Punch. Punch something or other. Let's see. Doak, I think. Punch Doak."

"Where might I find Punch Doak?"

"That's not easy," said Esau. "Punch is one of those who moves around, you know. The last I heard, he was going up north somewhere. I don't know where, but what he'll do is look for a house that's already built but nobody lives there anymore, and he'll just move in. He doesn't like to work, that Punch."

"Somewhere up north?"

"Yeah. Up north. Punch and his wife. He's got a wife named Dot. I don't know who her parents are. Don't know what her name was before she married Punch."

"Esau, who's selling whiskey around these days?"

"Ah, I don't know, Beehunter."

"I'm not out to arrest anyone for selling whiskey," Beehunter said. "I'm looking for Tom Panther and now for Punch Doak. Do you think that they'd be anywhere too far away from a good supply of whiskey?"

"Oh. Well, if I was looking for whiskey up this way"—he paused and pointed north—"I'd probably go to Jenny Spruell's house. She's pretty well known up that way. She's an old white woman. She always has whiskey. Anyway, that's what they say. I don't know. I'm not looking for whiskey now."

"Can you tell me how to find her, Esau?"

Big Forehead sat up on the bed and smiled. Dot was lying beside him. Over at the table, Tom Panther was drinking whiskey.

"I came here looking for you, Tom," Big Forehead said.

"How come?"

"Because of that medicine I set into motion for you."

"What about it?"

"It's strong."

"So? I asked you to make it strong."

"It's out of control, Tom. Your father could be killed."

Tom turned up his glass and drained it of whiskey. Then he poured it full again. "Do you think I care about that?" he said. "He's got no respect for me. I ask him for something and he don't want to give it to me. What kind of a way is that for a father to act? I'm his son. If I want to ride his horse, he ought to let me take it. If I need some money, he ought to give it to me. Don't you think so? What do I care what happens to him? He don't care about me. He only thinks about Andy—my good brother, the smart one. He goes to school. My father wonders how come I'm so worthless and Andy is so good and so smart. Let the medicine kill the old man. I don't care."

"I just wanted to talk to you because when you first came to see me, you didn't say that you wanted him killed. I started doing things to him because he cost me some money at the horse race, and then when you came and said what you said, I decided to go after him, even though no one had paid me anything to do it. I started doing things to him and to those around him, but he fought back. He fought back too hard. I had to use stronger and stronger medicine, and now it's out of control. I couldn't hold it back if I wanted to. And I don't want to, but I wanted to tell you about it."

"That's all right," said Tom. "I don't give a shit.

Hey, how did you find me all the way up here anyhow?"

Big Forehead grinned wide. "You can't hide from me, Tom," he said.

"Hell. I wasn't trying to hide from you. I just wondered how you come to find me. That's all."

"Pour me a glass of whiskey, Tom."

Tom got up and found another glass. He poured it full and carried it over to Big Forehead, who drank it down in great gulps.

Punch Doak rode up to the country store. Two horses were tied to the rail out front. He did not like the look of that—it meant customers, witnesses. He held back and waited. Finally, a man came out of the store, mounted one of the horses and rode away. Punch waited impatiently for the last one to come out. He had never been much good at patience. Finally he saw the man come out the door and linger there on the porch. Old man Cash followed, and they stood talking. Punch thought it rude of the old man to take up more of Cash's time like that when his business was done and there was someone else waiting to be taken care of. Finally, the man got on his horse and left.

Punch nudged his horse forward. He tied both horses to the rail, felt the handle of the revolver and pulled his jacket around him tightly to cover the weapon. He looked around. No one was coming. Cash should be alone in the store. Punch walked up on the porch, stood for a moment gathering his courage, opened the door and stepped inside.

"Hello, Punch," Cash said. "Haven't seen you around for a while."

"I ain't been around," Punch said, " 'cause I ain't got no money." He pulled out the revolver and cocked it. The barrel pointed at Cash's chest. "That's how come I'm here. Give me all your money."

"Punch?"

"Come on. Give it to me. Hurry up or I'll shoot."

With trembling hands, the old man reached under the counter and brought out his cash box. He placed it on the counter and opened it. Punch stepped over to take a look. It was full of money, more than Punch had ever seen at any one time in his entire life. Keeping the revolver aimed at Cash, he reached into the box with his left hand and began taking out handfuls of money and stuffing them into his jacket pocket.

"Punch," the old man said, "take it all, but don't shoot me. Money's not worth dying for. Hell, I can always make more. Just go ahead and take it all. I won't say anything to anyone."

Punch was picking with his fingers to get every last coin. Finished at last, he looked into the eyes of his victim.

"Thank you, Mister Cash," he said, and he pulled the trigger.

Talmadge Hunt was sitting with Deputy Fields by a campfire just outside of Tahlequah. He wiped a spot of ground clear and picked up a stick. He drew a square and then some lines.

"Now, Fields," he said, "this is how the road runs out to ole Panther's house. This right here is where we got hit the last time we went out. Here's my plan for this time. I want you and a few of the boys to go on ahead and ride that same road. When you come

to this curve right here—you can't miss it—go slow
and keep a sharp eye. If they're up there where they
was before, they'll shoot at you. Be careful, but keep
them busy. And here's why.

"I found me another way to the house, and it's
around here." Hunt pointed to some new lines he
had drawn on the ground. "While them ambushers
are busy with you and your boys, I'll take the rest in
this way. We'll come through the woods on foot for
the last leg of it, and we'll get in around the back of
the house. If Panther's at home, we'll get him. And
what's more, we'll be on both sides of them ambushers, and we'll get them, too. How's that sound
to you?"

"It's a good plan, Talmadge," Fields said. "When
do we go?"

"First thing in the morning, if you and the new
men are rested up enough for it."

"We'll be ready, Talmadge," Fields said. "Hell,
the boys are all raring to go."

George tried his crystal once again, and again he
saw the shadowy figure, but this time there was
something else, something he had not seen before.
He could not make it out either, not exactly. But he
could tell now that the reason the sinister figure was
obscure was because there was something in front
of it, something between George and the figure he
wanted to see. Whatever was standing between him
and the shadowy figure was something George did
not want to see or know about. Despite that feeling,
he tried to peer into the crystal even harder. For
even though he would not like it when he saw it, he

knew that he would have to see it in order to accomplish his goal.

At the shabby cabin where Big Forehead was staying, the scraggly raven flew down from the sky. Its flight pattern was crooked and wobbly, and when it came in close and aimed for the open window, it flew into the side of the house instead and fell to the ground. Two feathers fell out of its tail. It stood up and shook its head and remaining feathers.

"Ka," it croaked.

It hopped up to the windowsill, staggering slightly. It stood there on unsteady, skinny legs, and belched.

"Ka. Ka."

Chapter 16

Punch came out of the store, his left jacket pocket stuffed with money and his revolver still clutched in his right hand. As he ran down the steps of the porch, four men on horseback suddenly appeared from around the side of the building.

"Hey, boy," one of them called. "What was that shot we heard?"

Panicked, Punch flung a shot at the man. The unarmed riders all turned their mounts and hurried back around the building. Punch climbed into the saddle and started riding hard away from the scene, leading the extra horse. He heard one of the men behind him yell out, "Check inside!" Punch rode as hard as he could, kicking the horse underneath him, lashing at it viciously. Looking back over his shoulder, he saw two of the men go into the store. Shit, he thought, there are guns in that damn store. He hurried on. A part of him wanted to turn loose of the reins to the extra horse, but all of the things he had taken from the Morton place were tied onto that horse. Tom's eggs were also on that horse. He clutched the reins tight.

Punch was aware that he was riding in the opposite direction from his own house, but he was afraid to turn around. Why the hell had he fled in that direction? he asked himself. The four men were back there, between him and where he wanted to go. He would just have to outrun them, get away and hide until he had lost them, and then make his sneaking way back home. He looked back again and did not see anyone coming after him. He felt a sense of relief for a moment. Then he realized that when they found the body in the store, they would likely get guns and ride after him. He lashed harder at his horse. Then suddenly the horse stumbled, flinging a surprised and frightened Punch high into the air and off to the side of the road. He landed hard on his back.

The breath was knocked completely out of him, and he could not move. He sucked hard for air. At last, able to breathe once again, he sat up just in time to see both horses running away, taking all the clothes and all the guns and all the eggs along with them. He stood up and yelled at the horses as if they would listen, understand and obey.

"Hey!" he called out. "Come back here! You horses. Come back!"

Of course, they did not. He considered for a moment running after them, but he knew that he would never be able to catch them.

"Son of a bitch," he swore. But it made no difference. It was too late. The horses were long gone and so were all of the things he had stolen from the Morton house, including Tom's damned eggs. The Mortons had been killed for nothing, nothing except the thrill of it. At least he still had money in his pocket from Cash's store. He stuck his hand in his pocket to feel it. That was reassuring. He looked back down the road the way he had come. He still saw no one coming. He started to walk the way he had been going, after the horses, but that suddenly felt foolish. That was not the direction he wanted to go, and if the men rode after him, they would find him fairly quickly. If he turned around and walked back the other way, he would meet them somewhere down the road. He stood there for a moment in a quandary, then walked into the woods.

He knew that the four men on horseback would be after him, knowing that he had killed old Cash and robbed him. They would almost certainly have picked up some guns and ammunition from the store. Maybe they did not yet know that he was unhorsed, afoot in the woods, an area that he was unfamiliar with. Maybe the sons of bitches would miss him entirely as they raced down the road after him. He chuckled at the thought.

He had not gotten far into the woods and away from the road when he heard the sound of approaching horses running fast. His heart began to pound. He turned around and ran back to the edge of the woods, squatted down in some bushes behind the trunk of a large tree and watched as they came pounding by. Sure enough, it was the four men from the store. It would not be long before they came upon the two horses he had lost. Then they would double back. They would know that he was on foot somewhere along the way. He turned and ran farther into the woods.

Outside of Tahlequah, the federal posse split up, Fields and his bunch staying on the main road according to Hunt's plan. Hunt and the rest turned off on a side road. Fields rode at the head of the secondary group. He realized that Hunt had planned this operation so that he would be the one to get all the credit for its success. He would be the one to move in on the house while Fields and his bunch kept the unknown waylayers busy on the road. But that was all right, he told himself. After all, Hunt had been at it longer. It had been his operation in the first place, and his plan. Fields had told himself that he would give Hunt this one last chance. Anyhow, who could tell what might still happen?

Maybe there wouldn't even be an ambush. Maybe Fields and his men would move in on the front of the house and catch Panther themselves. Or maybe, as had happened before, they would all arrive at the house with no opposition and find it abandoned. He would just wait and see what would happen. His musings stopped when he saw the sharp curve in the road ahead. He held up a hand to halt the posse.

"That's the place right up there, boys," he said. "According to Talmadge, if they try to stop us, it'll be just around that curve. Be ready for anything. Keep your eyes on the hillsides up ahead, and if anyone starts shooting, dismount and take cover quick. And fire back. Shoot to kill."

George knew they were coming. He wasn't ready for them. He was weak from searching the crystal and from having had little sleep for several days. He wasn't at all sure he had the strength to be able to avoid them this time using his usual methods. He would have to resort to ordinary flight this time. He walked to the corral and put a saddle on Lightning,

then mounted up and rode out. The road on which
the posse would be coming went right on by his
house and continued north. He rode north with no
particular destination in mind.

It bothered George a little, having to run away
like a common fugitive, but this time he had to do it.
It was all the fault of that one he could not identify,
the dark figure with the red eyes. He wondered if
that one was watching him flee on horseback with a
sense of smug satisfaction. Well, he thought, the
posse would not just hang around his house forever.
When they discovered that he was not at home
again, they would leave. Then George would go
back to his house and get back to his work. He was
tired, but he would not let this happen again. He
could not afford to let it happen.

Canoe sat on the side of the hill, hidden from the
view from the road below by the lush, green foliage.
Two other Cherokee men were with him. He was
glad that he had been able to talk them into coming
back around, after the others had all left him. He
was proud that he was not the only one left who recognized the importance of this work. He was especially glad of that when he saw the posse appear
from around the curve in the road below.

"Go back!" he shouted suddenly. Of course, he
did not expect them to heed his warning. They
never did. It was simply a polite thing to do, to
warn them before starting to shoot at them. This
time, though, the posse did not turn back, nor did it
continue on. It did not even wait for the warning
shot. Instead, all the men dismounted quickly and,
taking their rifles with them, ran for cover. It was as

if they had planned it. It looked like a rehearsed military action. Canoe fired quickly, but his shot went wild. The other two men beside Canoe started shooting then, and a moment later, shots were returned from the sides of the road.

For the first time since he had started this business, Canoe felt fear. The men down there impressed him as efficient and determined. For the first time, he felt as if those men down there meant to kill him, and that they just might be able to do it. And because of all that, he felt anger. He wanted to kill them as well. He began looking carefully for his targets. He wanted his shots to count.

Punch Doak ran through the strange woods for as long as he could. He fell down a couple of times, looking back over his shoulder, and while he ran, his skin was scratched and his clothes were pulled and torn by the thickness of the undergrowth. At last, he could stand it no longer and stopped. He stood for a moment, weaving and panting, trying to catch his breath, and then he staggered a few steps more and dropped down heavily at the base of a large oak tree. He leaned back against the trunk of the tree and soon he was sound asleep, his dreams full of wild adventures of riding and shooting and robbing banks. He also dreamed of eggs—eggs in a basket, eggs rolling on the ground, eggs broken, eggs frying in bacon grease in a hot iron skillet.

Fields crouched low beside the road. Now and then he sent a shot at the hillside in the vicinity of where the ambushers seemed to be. If he could only see a target, he would be happy to shoot at it, but not being able to locate one, he wasn't really too concerned. It seemed that Talmadge Hunt's plan was working. They were having a shoot-out on the road just as Talmadge had planned. Anyone in the house ahead or near it would hear the shots, and his attention would be drawn to the fight. Hunt and the others would be able to sneak right up at the back of the house. They were probably working their way through the woods at that very moment. He fired another shot at the hillside.

He guessed it would be all right if Hunt's plan worked out this time and Hunt wound up getting all the credit for the capture of George Panther. No matter how it turned out, Fields knew that he would look good in the marshal's eyes, for even if Talmadge Hunt should get the official credit, Crump would know that Talmadge had failed until Fields had come to his aid. That would be good enough for Fields. A bullet suddenly zinged off a rock near where Fields crouched. He stopped his musing, squinted at the hillside ahead and fired a rifle shot, hoping that it would find a target.

"Where's that no-good worthless husband of yours at anyhow?" Tom asked. "He went out to get us some eggs hours ago."

Dot shrugged. "No telling," she said. "You said it."

"Said what?"

"No-good and worthless. That's just what he is."

"Hell," Tom said, "I want them eggs. He should oughta been back a long time ago."

"Oh, I know where to get some eggs," she said. She started to put her clothes on.

"Where you going?"

"To get some eggs. That's what you want, ain't it? It won't take long."

Tom grabbed up his trousers and started to pull them on.

"What're you doing?" she said.

"Hell," he said. "I'm going with you. I don't want you to run out on me, too."

"I'm just going for eggs. That's all."

"Yeah. That's what Punch said."

"Suit yourself."

"I mean to."

Both dressed, pulling on their rumpled clothes rather hastily, and left the house together. Dot led the way. She led Tom along a path through the woods to a clearing on the other side. There a small log cabin stood alone, a thread of smoke rising lazily from its stone chimney. Chickens gawked around the yard on all sides of the house, pecking and cackling. Dot gave Tom a look and a sign to keep quiet. She crept along the edge of the woods to a tiny shed that just peeked out from the trees and brush. Looking toward the log cabin to make sure she was not being watched, she ducked inside the shed. Tom waited outside, lurking in the shadows. He heard loud clucking sounds from the shed. He looked back and forth quickly from the shed to the cabin. A moment later, Dot reappeared, a half dozen or so eggs cupped in her hands. Tom pulled off his shirt and spread it on the ground, and Dot placed the eggs on the shirt.

"Get some more," Tom said. "Hell, I'll eat all these at one time."

She ducked into the shed again and came out

with two handfuls of eggs, which she put with the others. She gathered the shirt into a bundle, picked it up and led the way back to the path through the woods.

Talmadge Hunt heard the shots from the road, and he knew that Fields and the others had been ambushed just as he had been during his last attempt at arresting George Panther. He felt a sudden thrill. His plan was working. He and his bunch would be able to make it to the back of the house without being detected. They would surprise Panther for sure. This time, he felt certain he would be successful. He dismounted. The horse would be no use where he was going.

"Follow me, boys," he said, and he cut quickly into the woods just at the place Big Forehead had described to him. It was a narrow path, in danger of being reclaimed by the thick growth on both sides. Hunt and the others had to protect their faces with their arms as they rushed along the trace. He moved as fast as he could, and he was beginning to get winded, for the trail was longer than he had imagined from the description he had been given. He trotted the length of it, for fear the fight would be resolved before he and his men were in place. He did not want that to happen. He had to be there for the finish.

He could still hear shots when he finally came out of the woods and found himself looking at George Panther's house from a new angle. His heart pounded. Here he would either make or break his reputation. He made signs to the men behind him to begin working their way through the woods into a wide semicircle, and begin surrounding the house. He was afraid that the rustling of the undergrowth as the men moved clumsily through the thicket would be heard in the house, but there was nothing he could do about that. Nothing but hope for the best. At last, all was still again, all except the noises of the various forest creatures. Everything was in place.

He heard another rifle bark out, and then three more rapid shots. The deputies on the road still had the full attention of George Panther's protectors, and that was good. Hunt stepped out into the open and waved an arm. The long line of deputies came out into the open, and began to close in on the house. The house was completely surrounded. There was no way anyone inside could escape.

"George Panther!" Hunt cried out.

There was no answer, so he called out again. He still received no answer.

"Anyone in there," he yelled, "come out with your hands up! Now! Come out or we start shooting!"

No one answered.

"All right, boys," Hunt called out, "start blasting."

Everyone fired at once and the noise was deafening. There seemed to be no break between gun shots, no silence in between. It was like one long continuous barrage. The air filled with the acrid smell of burnt gunpowder. Splinters and chunks of wood flew from the walls of the house where the bullets struck. Shutters on the windows broke apart, and the front door was soon pockmarked and bullet-riddled. Two deputies were slightly wounded in their own crossfire.

Canoe thought that someone had started a war behind him when he heard the shooting. It caught him completely by surprise, not only because of its whereabouts but also because of the loudness. He wondered for a moment if it might be a troop of U.S. cavalry back there.

"Hey," he said to the other two. "That's at George's house. Let's get out of here."

He started moving as fast as he could, uphill and through the woods, as his two companions followed him, trying to keep up as best they could. A few shots rang out from the deputies down along the road, but soon they stopped.

"They're fighting up at the house," shouted Fields. "Get to your horses."

The deputies all caught up their mounts and swung up into their saddles. Fields led the way at a fast gallop. Rounding the curve, they came onto the final straightaway, and then they could see what was happening. Hunt and his men had the house entirely surrounded, and they were firing into the house as fast as they could.

Fields reined in, and so did his followers. "Damn," he said. "If there was anything alive in there, it's dead now."

There was no sense in moving in to help. He could tell that it was all over. In another minute, he heard Hunt call out a ceasefire. He had to call out more than once. Finally, the shooting stopped. The foul smell of burnt gunpowder wafted through the eerie silence. From somewhere, a bluejay scolded. A slight breeze rustled the leaves in the trees.

"We got two men hit, Talmadge," someone called out.

"Tend to them," Hunt said.

Fields and the rest watched as Talmadge Hunt stepped boldly out of line to approach the front door. They watched as Hunt reached for the door and gave it a shove. The door did not open—it simply fell onto the floor in the house. They watched, holding their breath as Hunt stepped inside. The wait seemed interminable. What was he doing in there? Suddenly, they all heard him shout from inside the house.

"Goddamn it!"

A moment later, Talmadge Hunt came stamping back out in view. "There's no one in there!" he shouted. "No one."

Fields rode in close. He stayed in his saddle.

"Then who the hell shot me?" asked one of the two wounded deputies.

"Hell, boys," said Fields, "you shot each other."

Up on a nearby ridge, Canoe and the other two men had been watching. They too heard Hunt's shouts of frustration with a great sense of relief. They looked at one another in stunned silence. Then Canoe grinned. "He's not even there," he said.

"They did all that shooting at an empty house," said one of the other two.

"Yes," said the other one. "They even shot each other."

All three men laughed.

"Let's go home," Canoe said.

* * *

"Come on," said Hunt. "Give me a hand."

"What're you doing?" asked a deputy.

"Gather up all the dry shit you can find. Grass, twigs, anything." As he talked, he began gathering himself, and he shoved the pile he had scooped up against the wall of the house. "Put it right there. Come on. Load it up there."

Several of the deputies joined in the effort.

"That's enough," said Hunt finally, reaching into a shirt pocket. He brought out a match, then squatted by the dry kindling. He struck the match and held it to the pile. In a moment a small flame broke out. Hunt watched it for a moment. Then it went out. "Damn it," he muttered. He pulled out a second match and tried again. Again he produced a small flame. This time he stood up and stepped back to watch it grow. Flames soon rose and began to lick at the dry logs on the side of the house.

"He's never here anyhow," Hunt said. "The son of a bitch. He shouldn't even miss the goddamn place. But if he does ever come back to it, he won't find nothing but a pile of ashes. If I can't get him, he'll damn sure know I was here."

Then Hunt shivered as he felt a cold chill run through his body as the ground was covered almost at once in shadow. He looked up to see fast-moving, black clouds blocking out the blue sky. The breeze became a howling wind that made the treetops bend and wave. There was a flash of lightning, and then rain fell, and the flames were doused. Hunt looked up, allowing the large drops to pelt his face. They fell harder and faster, and he ducked his head and pulled his coat collar tight around his neck. It would be a good long run through the woods in the rain back to the place where they had left the horses. He made a quick decision.

"Come on," he said. "Let's get inside."

George Panther's house was soon packed with the large posse. When all the men had crowded in, there was nothing left to sit on but the floor. Coming in out of the sudden driving rain, the men took off their hats and slapped them against their legs to knock the water off. They pulled out bandanas to wipe at their faces. As they cursed and stamped around, some poked into cupboards or into tins and jars they found around the room. Some found food that they quickly ate. They rummaged around in shelves and in drawers, throwing things around and on the floor.

Fields made his way through the crowd to stand beside Hunt. "Talmadge," he said. "I'm sorry."

"Yeah. Me, too."

"I got to tell you something."

"Okay," said Hunt disgustedly. "What is it?"

"When Crump called me in to the office to give me this assignment, to send me out here to join up with you, he said we got to get this George Panther. He said he don't care what we do, or how we do it, but he said we got to get it done."

"Yeah?"

"Talmadge, your way ain't working. We got to get tough."

"What do you mean? Tough how?"

"Just coming out here time after time like this and hoping to catch the man at home ain't going to get

it done," Fields said. "Someone out there somewhere knows where the hell he's at."

"We've questioned people. No one will admit to
knowing anything."

"There's ways of making them talk," said Fields.
"Like I said, we got to get tough to get this job
done."

Dot was frying eggs, and Tom was lying on the
wretched-looking bed, drinking whiskey.

"Hurry up, will you?" he said.

"Eggs only cook so fast," she said. "They'll be
ready in a minute."

"I'm hungry," Tom said. "And I been hungry for
eggs for a long time now."

"They're almost ready."

"Where's that damn shitty husband of yours anyhow?"

Dot shrugged and scooped eggs out of the skillet
onto a plate. She turned and tossed the plate onto
the already cluttered table. As she was getting a
fork, Tom stepped to the table. He sat down as Dot
threw the dirty fork down beside the plate. Tom
picked it up and began eating ravenously.

"I don't know where that no-good bastard is at,"
Dot said. "You know, he left here with your gun,
and I think he was meaning to rob somebody. Likely
he tried it and got hisself killed. He don't know
nothing about robbing no one, and he don't know
nothing about using a gun neither."

"If he went and got hisself killed," said Tom, his
mouth full, "then he don't know nothing at all no
more." He took another drink of whiskey and went
back to eating the eggs.

"Tom?"

"What?"

"Who was that man?"

"What man?"

"You know what man I'm talking about. That man that come naked through the window there. That man that . . . you know."

"How come you want to know?" Tom asked. "You like him? You want him to come back and do it again?"

Dot sat still. She didn't answer.

"I might get him to come back if that's what you want."

"Who is he?"

"He's nobody," Tom said. "I mean, he's just some guy I met. That's all. Shut up about him."

"He said something about using strong medicine against your papa."

"That's none of your business. Shut up and cook some more eggs."

As Dot moved to do as Tom demanded, Tom poured himself another glass of whiskey.

"There was something strange about that man, Tom. Something real strange. He scared me. Is he a conjuring man?"

"You didn't look to me like you was scared of him," Tom said. "You looked more like you was having a fine old time."

"Yeah?" she said. "Well, what about you? Did you like watching it?"

"I didn't watch," he said. "I don't give a shit about that."

"I never seen a man quite like him before," said Dot. "Never."

Out in a strange patch of woods, Punch Doak woke up sitting beneath a tree. It took him a moment to remember where he was and why he was there. It took another moment to orient himself, and then he started walking in the direction he thought would take him home. Now the story he would have to tell was even more embarrassing than before, for now he had no horse. He had no eggs. He had no other choice anymore but to go home and tell Tom and Dot about all he had done, about all he had been through. And he would have to tell them about the Arkansas whiskey peddler who wanted his money. But Punch was tired and hungry, and he wanted a drink of whiskey.

If he could get home, he would rest and he would eat, and then he would tell the tale to Tom and Dot, and together they would figure out how to deal with the whiskey peddler and what to do next. For the time being, he would try to push it all out of his mind and concentrate on getting himself home.

Chapter 17

When the unexpected driving rain as unexpectedly stopped, Hunt and Fields and the other deputies abandoned the home of George Panther, leaving it a mess. Hunt and his bunch took the path in the woods through which they had come. It was wet and muddy. They sloshed their way through to where their horses waited at the other end. Fields and those with him caught up their own horses outside the house, then mounted up and rode off toward Tahlequah on the main road. They had traveled only a few miles when Fields noticed that the ground was dry. Seemingly it had rained only on George Panther's house, or at least, in a small radius around the house. He pushed the thought from his mind. Such things happened sometimes. Then he saw a road shooting off to his right. He stopped and studied it for a moment. He was not yet ready to write this day's venture off as a total failure. He remembered the charge of Marshal Crump and his own resolve to take things over if Hunt's methods proved ineffective.

"Let's check this out, boys," he said, turning his horse onto the side road. "It's got to lead somewhere. Might be some friendly folks living down there."

The small posse followed Fields through the woods to the end of the lane, where a lonely one-room cabin stood. A thin trail of smoke was pluming from its chimney. A red hound slept in the sun beside the house. Guinea hens strutted about the yard, clucking and cackling. Fields dismounted right by the front door.

"Looks like someone's at home all right," he said.

"If I had me a dog like that one there that didn't bark when strangers come riding up," said a deputy close behind Fields, "I'd shoot the lazy son of a bitch."

Not bothering to knock or even call out, Fields opened the door and stepped inside. A Cherokee man who looked to be in his early sixties and a woman a little younger, probably in her fifties, stood up from their chairs.

"Howdy, folks," said Fields. "Just looking for a little information. That's all."

"What do you want here?" the man questioned. "Who are you?"

"We're deputy United States marshals," said Fields. "We're looking for George Panther. You know him?"

"We know George," the man said.

"Well, he ain't at home. Where can we find him?"

"We don't know."

Fields looked at the woman. "What about you?"

"She don't know," the man said.

"Can't she talk for herself?"

"She don't know English."

"Well, you tell her what I asked, and see what she has to say."

The man spoke to the woman in Cherokee, and as she responded, Fields walked over to the table in the middle of the room. There was a coffeepot on the table and some cups, a coal oil lamp in the center. Fields took hold of the edge of the tabletop. He stood looking at the woman, waiting to hear her response. When she had finished talking, the man looked uneasily back toward Fields.

"She said she don't know neither," the Cherokee man said. "Like I told you. We don't know."

Suddenly, Fields flipped the table over with an angry and violent motion of his arm, spilling the coffee, spilling coal oil, and scattering the lamp, the pot and cups over the floor.

"Hey," the Cherokee man cried, and the woman yelled out something in Cherokee. "What you do that for? We don't know what you want to know. You don't have a right to do that. Leave us alone. Get out of our house."

Fields stepped over to the man and slapped him hard across the face. "I think you do know," he said. "I think you're a lying son of a bitch. I think all you damned Indians know all about each other. I think you're protecting George Panther. You're protecting a wanted criminal. A fugitive. Goddamn it, Panther's wanted for the murder of a white man, and I mean to find him. Now you tell me what I want to know."

"I know where he lives," the man said, "but you said you been there and he ain't home. If he ain't home, I don't know where he's at. He could be anywhere. We don't know. Leave us alone."

Fields slapped him again.

"I don't know nothing."

The woman said something in Cherokee in a desperate voice.

"Maybe you don't mind getting slapped around a bit," Fields said to the man, "but let's see how you like this."

He stepped over to the woman and looked into her face with an ugly leer. She covered her face with both hands.

"Don't you touch her," the man said.

Fields grabbed a wrist and pulled one hand away from the woman's face. With his other hand he slapped her hard three times. She shrieked and started to cry.

"Stop it!" the man cried, rushing to the woman's rescue. "Stop. I tell you, we don't know where George is at."

Fields shoved the man away so hard that the man fell to the floor. He stood for a moment looking down at him, then he heaved a sigh.

"We don't know," the man murmured, and he too began crying along with his wife.

Fields turned and walked out the door.

"They don't know nothing," he said to the other deputies as he mounted his horse. "Let's get out of here."

Fields started to ride, then paused. Looking at the man who had made the comment earlier about the lazy hound, he said, "Shoot the damn dog."

Bobby Stump was a big full-blooded Cherokee. At least he always referred to himself as a full-blood, as did most of the people who knew him, although some whispered that his grandfather on his mother's side had been a mean Dutchman. No one said it when Bobby was around, though. Such a thing might easily have caused a fight, and not many wanted to get themselves into a tussle with Bobby. He had been known to thump quite a few heads. Bobby Stump did not like white people. In fact, he had little use for Cherokee people of mixed-blood. He always referred to them as either half-breeds or whites, never as Cherokees. Bobby had a bad temper and a surly disposition, too, and be-cause of that, he did not have very many friends, full-blood, mixed-blood or otherwise.

Bobby knew George Panther, and had even gone to George a few times for help. George had always helped him, as he helped anyone who came to him with problems or ailments, except for the times when Bobby had asked George to do some mean-ness to someone he had it in for. George had refused him on those occasions, because George would refuse anyone such a request. George did not make bad medicine. Because George had refused him on those occasions, Bobby did not really like George. If the truth were told, Bobby was probably more than just a little bit jealous of George. Still, if Bobby needed help, he would go to George.

But something special had come up, a special op-portunity, and Bobby meant to take full advantage of it. Bobby, like everyone else, had heard that the deputies from Fort Smith were looking for George Panther for the killing of a white man. He had not concerned himself too much with that, although it did annoy him on principle that white lawmen could come into his Cherokee Nation and arrest

Cherokees. He kind of liked the fact that George had killed a white man, but he had not said anything to anyone. He was really jealous of that act. He had also heard that Canoe and some others had been shooting at the deputies to drive them away from George's house. At first, he thought it was stupid, for they might easily get themselves shot that way, and if George was as powerful as everyone said, he could take care of himself. But this latest news was something else again.

Bobby had just found out that the deputies were going into the homes of innocent Cherokees, sometimes old people, and harassing them, asking them where to find George Panther, and when the people did not know the answer or refused to tell, the deputies beat them. This angered Bobby. But in spite of the possible danger, it gave him a reason to do something he really wanted to do deep down in his heart and soul. Bobby wanted to kill a white man. So Bobby sought out Canoe.

"Did you hear about those lawmen?" he asked.

"I know they're looking for George," Canoe said.

"And I know you been shooting at them and driving them off," said Bobby. "Everyone knows that. That's not what I'm talking about."

"What is it then?"

"They been breaking into people's homes and beating them up," said Bobby.

"I hadn't heard that," Canoe said.

"They break in and surprise people, scare them. Then they say where's George, and the people say they don't know, and then the deputies beat on them to try to make them tell."

"That's not right," Canoe said.

"Well, they're doing it. They're going all around. I'm going to find them and kill me one or two of them," Bobby said. "I've never killed me a white man yet. This is a good reason to do it. Are you going with me? You and the others?"

"If they're doing what you said, then we have to stop them," Canoe said. "Yes. We'll go with you. I'll get some men together right away."

Talmadge Hunt had not found out what Fields and the others were doing until they had all arrived back in Tahlequah. After leaving the home of George Panther, Hunt and his men had made their way back to the main road, but they had not met up with Fields and his band. Figuring that Fields was ahead of them on their way back, they rode on. They reached the camp on the creek ahead of Fields. So when Fields and the others came on in later, Hunt found out what had been going on.

"Damn," said Hunt. "You been harassing innocent people? You ain't supposed to do that."

"Marshal Crump said to get the job done no matter what we have to do or how we have to do it. Remember? I told you that. Now, your way ain't worked so far. We can't find the son of a bitch at home. These bastards know where to find him, but they ain't telling. That means they're guilty of aiding and abetting. Now, are you with me or what?"

Hunt scratched his head. Reluctantly, he said, "I guess when you put it like that . . . hell, I don't know what else to do."

"Let's go then," said Fields. "We'll hit every house in the damn country if we have to, but we'll find him."

So Fields had taken over the operation. It was obvious. No one said anything about it, but when the reunited posse moved on down the road, Fields was in the lead. Hunt let it happen. He did not like Fields's methods, but he knew that he was in a tight spot. He knew that the marshal and the judge were both losing patience with this manhunt, and he had a feeling that he had better get the job done or he might soon be looking for other work. So he decided that he would have to go along with Fields. And letting Fields take over the posse eased his own conscience a bit. It took the decision, and therefore the responsibility, out of his hands. He was only a follower. Damn it, but he knew he wanted this job over and done with.

Canoe, Bobby Stump and two others found some horses. They rode out armed with Winchester rifles and revolvers. They had heard about where the posse had been operating, and they headed in that direction. They meant to find them and put a stop to their depredations. They had ridden well into the evening by the time they spotted the lawmen. Most of them were sitting on their horses just outside a small house. Three of the horses were riderless. That meant that three of the men were inside the house, tormenting the occupants. Stump leveled his rifle.

"Wait," said Canoe. "If we shoot at them now, they might hurt the people in the house."

"They already hurt them," said Bobby. "They're hurting them right now."

"They might kill them," Canoe said. "Wait till they come out. Let them ride back out this way.

We'll hide along the side of the road and shoot them
as they go by."

Bobby lowered his rifle, a serious pout on his
face. He knew that he could have picked one of
them off real easy. He was itching to kill a white
man, especially a white lawman. Canoe and the
other two men dismounted, so Bobby did, too. They
led their horses into the thickness of the under-
brush.

"Take them in deeper," Canoe said.

When they had the horses hidden far enough in
the woods, they made their way back closer to the
roadside. They readied their weapons and waited.
They could see the house and the posse from their
vantage point, for the road was straight from there
to the house, and it moved uphill from the house to
their position. They watched as three men came out
of the house and mounted up. The posse turned
their horses and started riding in their direction.
Then an old man come staggering out the front door
of the house, wiping at his face and looking at the
backs of the riders. Bobby chambered a shell in his
rifle, waiting anxiously for a good shot.

"Let them get past us," Canoe said. "That way
they won't be able to go back to the house for
cover."

The riders came closer. Bobby's finger was itching on the trigger. They came right up to where
Bobby and Canoe and the others waited. They rode
past so close that Bobby thought he could have spit
on them. He could smell them. The noise of the
horses' hooves and the creaking of saddle leather
was loud in his ears. They rode on by, and Bobby
stepped quickly out into the road, lifted his rifle to

his shoulder, gobbled like a turkey, and fired. One of the riders to the rear of the group jerked and fell back. Just then the other three Cherokees began firing from their hiding places, and three more deputies dropped from their saddles.

The white men started yelling and dismounting and running for cover. Talmadge Hunt turned in his saddle and jerked out his revolver. His horse was dancing around in the middle of the road in all the excitement, but Hunt managed somehow to get a bead on his target, even while fighting to control his horse. He fired.

Bobby Stump felt the bullet go into his paunch. He looked down at the small hole and saw the blood begin to run out on his belly. He looked up just as Hunt fired again, and the second slug tore into his chest. He raised his rifle and fired again, and he saw blood fly from the white man's shoulder. Bobby turned and staggered into the woods.

Hunt dismounted and ran into the cover at the side of the road. The rest of the posse, except for those who had fallen at the first shots fired from behind them, had already ducked into the thickness.

"You hurt bad?" Fields asked.

"Bad enough," said Hunt. "I'll live, though, unless I bleed to death here in the woods."

"You peppered that one ole boy real good," Fields said.

"I hit him a couple of times, but he's thickset. Hell, he might not even have felt them."

"Here. Let me see if I can't get that shoulder wrapped up, maybe stop the bleeding."

Several of the other deputies fired shots in the general direction of where they believed the attackers were hidden, and shots were returned, but no one on either side could actually see whom they were shooting at. In a little while, the shooting slowed. Finally, things were quiet.

"We got to get you into town to a doc," Fields said to Hunt. "All I done was just a crude patching job. I can't do no more."

"If we step out into the road again," Hunt said, "we'll be perfect targets."

"The horses moved ahead some when the shooting started," Fields said. "Maybe we can work our way up to them through the woods here, then ride out fast."

"It's worth a try," Hunt agreed. "Let's pass the word."

Soon the deputies were moving slowly through the tangled brush away from their attackers. Fields decided to take up the rear so that if the attackers should start shooting again, he would be ready to fire back, giving the other men some cover.

"What's going on up there?" one of the Cherokees asked.

"I think we got them running," Canoe said. "Bobby shot that one in the shoulder. I bet they're going to leave and try to get him to a doctor."

"What'll we do then?" the man asked.

"I don't want to shoot anymore," said Canoe. "Not if they're leaving. We already killed four. That's enough"

The deputies moved out into the road to catch and mount their horses, and Fields stepped into the middle of the road behind them. He faced back toward the attackers, holding his revolver ready. He looked this way and that, but saw no one. No one took a shot at him. He glanced quickly over his shoulder and saw that the other men were all mounted and ready to go. He turned and ran for his own horse, calling out to the posse. "Get going."

The posse started riding, except for one man who sat in his saddle, holding the reins of Fields's horse. When Fields reached the horse and vaulted into the saddle, the man handed him the reins, and both riders kicked their horses in the sides and hurried after the others. They abandoned the bodies of their fallen comrades as well as the four loose horses.

Canoe stepped out into the road and watched the posse flee. He felt good. They had done their job. They had driven them away. The two other Cherokee men stepped out to stand beside him.

"We chased them off," said one.

"We'll have to keep watching," Canoe said. "They'll come back."

"Let's get our horses," said the third man. "I want to ride down to that house and see if the people there are all right."

They turned to walk into the woods, and Canoe hesitated. "Wait a minute," he said. "Where's Bobby?"

"He was right over there," said one.

The three men moved back into the thicket.

"Bobby?" Canoe called. There was no answer. "Bobby, where are you?"

"Here he is," said one of the other men. Canoe walked toward his voice. He saw the man standing there looking down. He made his way to the man's side, and saw Bobby Stump sitting with his back against a tree trunk, his chin on his chest, his eyes closed, his chest and belly covered with blood. Bobby Stump was dead.

The people in the house were bruised and a little bloody, but they would be all right. Though Canoe was glad they had killed a few of the deputy marshals, he was also worried. He knew that the more they killed, the more would come back. He worried that the United States might even send in the Army, and then the Cherokee Nation would be at war with them. He decided that if it came to that, he would go in and confess rather than let other people suffer for what he had done, but he would not do that until he knew that George Panther was safe.

He was pleased at the success of his mission. He was happy that the posse was gone, if only for a little while. But he was not elated, for there was something else that dampened his spirits. One of the Cherokees had been killed this time. Bobby Stump's body was still back there in the woods.

Chapter 18

George Panther sat with his wife, Gwed', and her sister, Polly, in the sister's home some miles away from his own house. Andy was there, too, as were Big Joe, Polly's husband, Sally and Annie. They had just finished the evening meal and were sitting around the table drinking coffee.

"George," said Gwed', "will we ever get to go back home and stay?"

"I don't know how soon," George said. "What I'm guessing has happened is that those lawmen went to the house again and then when they didn't find me at home, they headed back to Tahlequah again just like before. Unless Canoe didn't listen to me any better than he did last time, they had another shooting fight. Anyhow, in the morning, I'll take Andy and we'll go over to the house and see what we can find out. I'll send Andy on back here to let you know what's going on."

"No," she said. "I'm going home with you."

"I don't want you in the middle of all this trouble."

"George, just being your wife is being in the middle of trouble. I knew that when I married you. I'm not going to hide from your trouble now. Your trouble is my trouble. I'm going home with you in the morning. I mean it, George."

George looked over at his sister-in-law with a frustrated expression. "Polly, talk to her, will you?" he asked.

"I think she's right, George," Sally said. "If my Joe was in trouble, I'd stay right by him."

"I feel the same way," Andy said. "We're all in this together."

"It's time for you to go back to school, Andy," his mother said.

"Not when there's trouble at home," he said.

"Your mother's right, boy," said George. "Right now, the safest place for you is at school. Those lawmen would never think to look for any of my family there." Then he glanced over at Joe.

Joe shrugged his wide shoulders. "When these women make up our minds for us," he said, "we might as well not waste our breath arguing."

George looked at his sister, who had not said a word during all this discussion. "Well, Sally, what do you think?"

"I think my house is not finished," she said, "and if we don't all go home, it will never get finished."

"I want to be at home with you, Uncle," Annie said. "Besides, everything will be all right. You'll see."

George suddenly had a strange feeling about this little girl, his sister's daughter. He looked at her intently for an instant. She was a beautiful child, but there was something more about her. Something that was difficult to explain. He believed what she had just told him. He believed that there was deep wisdom in her pretty little head.

*   *   *

Canoe and the other two men left the home of the
people who had been attacked by Deputy Fields
and the others. They had comforted the man and his
wife, daubed at their wounds and made sure that
they were all right. Then they had made their ex-
cuses and taken their leave. Just before leaving,
Canoe, having noticed that the couple had a wagon
and team, asked if he could borrow it. He would
have to do something with Bobby Stump's body. He
couldn't just leave Bobby sitting there like that.
Then there were the bodies of the deputies. He wasn't
worried about them. Let the white lawmen deal
with their own. He and the others went back to the
place where Bobby's corpse waited.

"Let's get him in the wagon," Canoe said.

It took them all to load Bobby's body. He had
been a heavy man, and he was even heavier in
death. The job done, they all leaned on the wagon
and wiped their brows.

"Where will we take him?" one asked.

"Well," said Canoe, "we have to take him to his
people."

"Who are they?"

"His parents are dead," said the third man. "His
wife left him. They had no children."

"What about brothers or sisters?" Canoe asked.

"He had a brother, but he left a few years ago. I
think maybe he went out to California."

"Well, we have to do something with him," said
Canoe. "I guess we'll have to take care of it ourselves. Maybe I'll ask George—"

He stopped in mid-sentence. He suddenly had
what he thought to be a brilliant idea. Something

that would solve this whole problem. Perhaps they should take care of the bodies of the deputies after all. He quickly sketched out his idea to his two companions. They all smiled broadly at the plan, and they all agreed that it was inspired.

"But will they believe you?" one asked.

Canoe gave a shrug. "I don't know," he said. "All I can do is try it and find out."

"I think it will work," said the other. "Let's do it."

They loaded the bodies of the four deputies into the wagon along with that of Bobby Stump, and then they set about rounding up the fallen deputies' horses.

Hunt and Fields sat across a small campfire from each other. Hunt had been to see the doctor in Tahlequah and had his wound tended to properly. The rest of the deputies lounged around. Some had already gone to sleep. It was a dark night, and some lights could be seen in windows in Tahlequah down below.

"I think we better send you on back to Fort Smith, Talmadge," Fields said.

"What for?" Hunt asked.

"You're hurt."

"Hell," said Hunt, "I'll be all right. What are you planning to do from here?"

"The same thing we been doing," said Fields. "We keep banging on enough doors and enough heads, someone's going to talk. We'll get Panther sooner or later that way."

"I just wish there was some other way."

"We can't just keep going out there to his house hoping that he'll be waiting for us at home," said

Fields. "He won't ever be there. He keeps getting word from someone."

"Yeah," said Hunt, and he let out a long breath. "You're probably right. Well, I think I'll hit the hay."

"Think about what I said."

"What's that?"

"About going on back to Fort Smith. Hell, you done your part today, and you've been hurt. There wouldn't be no disgrace in it."

"I'd sure like to see this thing through," Hunt said. "I'll see how this shoulder's feeling in the morning."

"All right," said Fields. "We'll talk about it again in the morning. Get a good night's sleep, pard."

Canoe had driven through part of the night, and he rolled up in the borrowed wagon right into the camp of the deputy marshals just north of Tahlequah. Four horses were tied onto the back of the wagon. It was early morning, and the deputies' campfire had gone out sometime during the night. The ashes were still smoldering though, and the smell of burning wood was in the crisp morning air. No one was up, but when the wagon rattled into the camp, a couple of men stirred. Talmadge Hunt sat up and winced at the pain that shot through his shoulder. Maybe he should go back to Fort Smith after all, he thought. Fields sat up and looked over at the wagon that had just been driven into his camp, noting the Indian man driving.

"You want us?" he asked, squinting through still sleepy eyes at the wagon driver.

"Are you the deputy marshals?" Canoe asked.

"That's right," Fields said. He swung his legs out

from under the blanket and reached for his boots. He had not taken off his trousers the night before. He pulled his boots on and stood up. Then he hitched the braces up over his shoulders, looking at Canoe and the wagon. He thought that he recognized the four horses tied onto the back.

"Talmadge," he said, "tell Cookie to get the coffee going, will you?" He strolled over to the wagon. As soon as he got close to it, he could see the bodies in the back.

"I found these in the road," Canoe said. "I thought I should bring them in here to you."

Fields stared for a moment at the bodies. Four of them were the deputies that they had left abandoned in the road. The four horses tied to the wagon were indeed the horses those dead men had been riding. The fifth body in the wagon was an Indian. Fields knew that Hunt had hit one of their attackers at least once. Maybe twice.

"Who's that one?" he asked.

"That there?" asked Canoe, playing dumb and pointing at the body of Bobby Stump.

"Yeah," said Fields, "that one there. Hell, I know the others."

Talmadge Hunt approached and looked at the corpses in the wagon, recognizing the man he had shot.

"I didn't know if I'd killed him or not," he said. "He was a tough one."

"So who the hell is he?" asked Fields.

"Why, that's George Panther," said Canoe. "I thought you knew him. Everyone knows you been chasing him all this time. Didn't you ever see him yet?"

*   *   *

The word was quickly all over Tahlequah. Go-Ahead Rider was sent for, and before he was halfway to the camp, he knew why he had been summoned. They were saying that the body of George Panther had just been brought in. As Rider walked across the creek by the footbridge, Fields came to meet him. He wanted to question the sheriff before he'd had a chance to view the body.

"Rider," said Fields, "you know George Panther?"

"Yeah, I know him."

"What's he look like?"

"He's a big man," Rider said. "What can I tell you more than that? He's a full-blood Cherokee. One description would likely fit us all as far as you're concerned."

"You're real funny, Sheriff," Fields said. "I want you to take a look at a body over there in that wagon."

Rider walked to the wagon, followed by Fields. He was dreading what he might see. It was hard to believe that anyone could get the best of George Panther, but then, the U.S. Court at Fort Smith had thrown everything they had at him. And there was talk that George had been fighting something else, someone much more sinister and more powerful. Rider guessed that no one was unbeatable. He stepped up close to the wagon. He looked at the bodies, and, with a tremendous sense of relief, he recognized that of Bobby Stump. He had put Bobby in jail a few times. A serious look came over his face, and he took his hat off.

"That's George, all right," he said. He looked up

t Canoe, who was still sitting on the wagon seat.
'Where'd you find him, Canoe?"

"Just up the road from old Terrapin's house, Go-
Ahead. These deputies were there, too. These dead
ones. I thought I'd better bring all the bodies in here
o this deputy marshals' camp."

"You did exactly the right thing, Canoe," Rider
said. He turned back to Deputy Fields. "Well," he
said, "you men did your job, all right. I guess the
case is closed, and you all can go on back home."

"Not quite," Fields said. "There's the little matter
of the men who ambushed the posses and wounded
some men and killed these three here."

"How many would you say there were?" Rider
asked.

"That's hard to say."

"Did you ever get a look at them?"

"No. Not really. Just this one here."

"I'd say that this one here—George Panther—
was the only one who was shooting at you. He's the
only one you ever saw, ain't he? Ole George was
real good with a Winchester. He could almost make
you think there was an army after you. Any time
you went to his house, he wasn't there, was he?
Hell, boys, he was out there on that hillside with his
rifle."

"I never seen anyone that good," said Fields.
"Just one man."

"I don't know," said Hunt. "It could've been just
him."

Fields couldn't get over the feeling that something was being pulled on him. Exasperated, he
turned away from Rider and Hunt. But then he

turned back again. "Who was it that arrested Panther that first time?" he asked.

"It was Glen Jones, I think," Hunt said. "Yeah. Amos was with him."

"I say we take this body back to Fort Smith and get an identification from Glen and Amos."

"Weather like this," Rider said, "that would be an awful mistake."

"I think he's right," said Hunt.

"You got two of us right here that identified him for you," said Rider. "You need some more, I can round them up for you in just a few minutes. Most everyone around knew ole George. Besides, Hunt here shot him. You were after George, and this here is the only man you ever seen taking shots at you."

"Rider," said Canoe, "these four dead ones were breaking in people's houses and beating them up. They asked them to say where George was at, and when they didn't know, these four beat on them. What can we do about that?"

"There ain't much we can do, Canoe," Rider said. "They're already dead. Ole George killed them, I guess. There's nothing more to complain about, unless there was more than just these four breaking into homes."

Rider looked at Fields.

"Hell," said Fields, "I guess this case is closed. Let's pack it up and head on home." He looked over at Hunt. "You come out of this just fine," he said. "Crump sent you to get George Panther, and you got him."

Big Forehead picked up a pot off his table and flung it hard into the wall across the room, smashng it to bits. He screamed in rage as he stood up, knocking over the chair he had been sitting in, and with both hands, he overturned his table. He kicked at it then turned and picked up the chair, and taking it by the back rest, smashed it again and again against the overturned table until he had broken it to bits. Then he roared around the small room, knocking everything off the shelves, shouting and screaming as he went. Finally, he stopped. He stood still, gasping for breath. His eyes were blazing red with fury.

When George, Gwed', Andy, Sally and Annie came up to their house, they could see immediately that something bad had happened there. George got down from the wagon bench and went up to the house first and looked more closely. He went inside. A moment later, he stepped back out. He looked at his wife and son.

"They shot the place up pretty bad," he said. "I guess they were hoping that I was inside. Then it looks to me like they stayed in there for a while— probably to get out of the rain."

He walked around on the outside. Stopping at the spot where Hunt had tried to set fire to the house, he studied it for a moment. "They tried to burn it down, too," he said. "It rained them out. The medicine's still strong. When they tried to burn the house, the rain came, and they went inside."

"I better get busy cleaning this place up," Gwed' said. She walked toward the house determinedly. She stopped at the door and looked in. "They sure made a mess of things."

"I'll help you," said Andy.

"Me, too," said Sally. "There's a lot to be done."

"I can help, too," Annie said. "We'll fix it all up nice again. It'll be better than ever. You'll see."

They were still cleaning and straightening up in the middle of the afternoon when Canoe came riding into the yard. George saw his big smile and walked over to meet him. "What's got you smiling so wide?" he asked.

"I need you to wash me off, George," Canoe said. "I been handling dead bodies."

"Well, come on over here to my arbor," said George.

Gwed' came out of the house, a curious look on her face. "Tsiyu, *Siyo*," she said.

George told her what Canoe had told him. "Will you mix up the medicine?" he asked her. She went right to work on it. Soon the pot of water was boiling on the small fire just outside the arbor. Gwed' put certain plants into the water.

"So tell me what's been going on," George said to Canoe. "You haven't been fighting with those white lawmen again, have you? You know what I told you about that."

Canoe smiled even wider. "We killed four of them," he said. "That's why I had to come here."

"Canoe, you know what I told you. Now it's not only you, but you're getting other people in trouble doing those things. I—"

"George," said Canoe. "It's all over."

"What?"

"It's all over. They won't be coming back. They won't bother you anymore."

"You'd better explain what you mean," said

George. "If you just killed four deputy marshals, they'll be coming back. You can be sure of that."

"Get Andy out here with us," Canoe said. "You and your sister and niece. You all need to hear this."

Gwed' called the rest of the family out, and while they waited for the medicine to steep long enough, Canoe told his tale.

"I tried to do the way you said, George, but Bobby Stump came by to see me. He said those men were breaking into people's homes, sometimes old people, and they were beating on them, slapping them around, trying to make the people tell them where they could find you."

"I didn't know about that," said George. He looked at his wife and son with a long, sad face. "I'd better go turn myself in. I can't have them doing our people like that. Not because of me. I'm the one they want."

"Wait a minute," Canoe said. "I told you, it's over. Bobby came to see me and told me about all that, and he said we should go stop those men. He said he wanted to kill a white man anyway. So we went looking for them, and we found them, and Bobby killed one or two. Maybe three. I don't know. Four of them got killed, but everyone was shooting. Even me."

"Canoe," George said.

"Wait. Please. Bobby stepped right out in the road in full view, and he was shooting lawmen in their backs, but one lawman turned around and shot back, and he shot Bobby two or three times. Bobby fired some more, then walked into the woods. He sat down there and died. The lawmen all ran away back to Tahlequah.

"So I thought about how I could fix all this trouble. I borrowed a wagon and loaded up all the bodies and drove to Tahlequah to the lawmen's camp. I said I found the bodies in the road and thought I should bring them in. They knew the dead lawmen, of course, but they asked me about the other one, about Bobby. Who is that one? they asked me. George Panther, I said."

George, Gwed', Andy, Sally and Annie stared wide-eyed and unbelieving at Canoe.

"Yes," he said. "That's what I told them. Then Go-Ahead came over, and he looked at the bodies, and he said, yes, that's George Panther. Your case is closed and you can go home now. And you know what, George? The deputies all agreed. The case is really closed. So you're dead. To the white men, you're dead. They won't be back here again. It's over. Only thing is, you might have to get you a new name, I guess."

"See, Uncle," said Annie, "I told you it would be all right."

Beehunter rode to the top of a rise and looked down on the house that should be of the woman Jenny Spruell, if Esau Sanders's directions had been good. Smoke was rising from the chimney, and a wagon and team were parked at the side of the house. Clearly, someone was home, and from the looks of it, she might have a visitor. Beehunter had not worried about it before, but looking down on the house, he wondered if anyone there would be able to speak or understand Cherokee. He himself knew no English. He decided there was nothing for it but to go ahead.

As Beehunter drew close to the house, the door opened and a sweaty white man stepped out. He spoke to Beehunter, but Beehunter did not understand him. Beehunter showed his badge. The man said something else.

"Jenny Spruell," Beehunter said.

If this man knew what Jenny Spruell's business was, or if he was a customer or an associate of hers, Beehunter realized, the badge would have put him on guard. But it was too late. The man had seen the badge.

"Jenny Spruell," repeated Beehunter.

Just then an old woman poked her head out the door and looked at him. She then looked at the white man and said something to him. The old woman must be Jenny Spruell, Beehunter thought.

"Tom Panther," he said.

She squinted at him.

"Punch," he said. "Punch Doak."

Beehunter could tell from the look on her face that she had recognized that name. He said it again. "Punch Doak."

And he made some motions with his hands to indicate that he was looking for Punch Doak. Jenny Spruell looked at the white man. She appeared to be feeling relief. She pointed at the next hill behind her house and made a motion as if going over a hill.

"Punch Doak," she said, and she made the motions again.

Beehunter looked at the hill. He looked back at Jenny Spruell, and he touched the brim of his wide black hat. "*Wado,*" he said, and turned his horse and started riding toward the hill.

At last, he seemed to be on the right trail. If the

old woman had understood him and had told him the truth, Punch Doak's house was just over there. And if Tom Panther was really with Punch, then Tom was just over there, too. Beehunter meant to ride over to Doak's house and kill Tom. He knew that he might be setting himself up for a murder charge, and that he could hang for what he was planning to do. But he also knew that he could not let that sure fate befall Go-Ahead Rider.

Chapter 19

Punch Doak was tired. It had been a long walk since he had lost those horses. He was limping, as blisters had formed on his feet. He wasn't thinking about all the trouble he could be in for the recent evil deeds he had done. He was thinking about his home and his wife. He didn't want people chasing him anymore. He didn't like hiding in strange woods. It did not enter his whiskey-enfeebled mind that the law might come looking for him at his home, and that he should probably run away to some far-off place and start over, someplace where no one could find him, where no one knew him, where he might be safe.

Punch had never been one to think ahead much, but he could remember things. He did remember Tom Panther, and he wondered if Tom would still be there at his house. He remembered that Tom had wanted eggs. Those damned eggs had caused all this trouble, and now they were lost. He wondered if there was any whiskey left back at his house. Then he recalled the money in his pocket, and he checked it again. It was still there, so even though he had lost the eggs and even if there was no more whiskey, he could give the money to Dot, and she could go get some eggs and some whiskey. It had been a long walk, but he was almost there. His house was just over the next hill.

He was feeling better having remembered the money in his pocket, but then he remembered the white man who had stopped him on the road and threatened his life. The white man was over at Jenny Spruell's house. Punch did not want to see the white man again. He thought hard. He had promised to bring some money to pay for the whiskey he and Tom had stolen. He tried to remember why the white man cared about Jenny's whiskey, but he only remembered the gun and the threat. Maybe he would give the money to Dot and tell her to go to Jenny's house and pay the man off and then buy some more whiskey. While she was out, she could get some eggs, too. There was enough money for all of that, he was pretty sure.

Tom Panther finished another glass of whiskey. There was still a little left in the last jug, but he knew that he would have to find a way of getting some more very soon. It was getting late in the evening, and he thought that he had drunk enough for that day. He might finish the jug in a little while. Either way, morning would be time enough to worry about getting some more. He wondered where the hell that little shit Punch was anyhow. Punch had taken his revolver, and should have been back with eggs and whiskey and money. But Punch was not back, and Tom thought that he should continue to take full advantage of the situation as he looked over at Dot. He thought that Punch was sure stupid to leave her there with him like that. This was just what Punch deserved. Tom got up and reeled for a moment. Then he walked over to the bed and began pulling off his clothes, all the time looking at Dot with a drunken leer. She looked back at him and smirked. She pulled off her dress and crawled into bed. A moment later Tom was on top of her.

Just then the door was flung open and Punch Doak stepped in, ragged, dirty and weary. "I lost the eggs," he said, "but I got—"

He stopped. His wife and his friend were naked right there in front of his eyes in his own house. Naked in bed. His eyes grew wide in disbelief and astonishment. He felt an outraged sense of betrayal. Tom was supposed to be a friend. He was a guest in his house. They had gotten drunk together.

Tom rolled off Dot and turned to sit on the edge of the bed. He smiled and reached out his right arm in an explanatory gesture. "Hey, Punch," he said, "it ain't—"

Punch jerked the revolver from his waistband, leveled and cocked it, pointing it straight at Tom's bare chest.

"Punch, don't—"

"You double-crosser," shouted Punch. "You dirty bastard. I trusted you."

Punch pulled the trigger, and the blast and acrid smoke filled the small room. Dot gave a shriek. Tom looked down at the fresh hole in his bare chest, at the dark blood seeping out of his body and running down his belly, into his pubic hairs and pooling there on the sweat-stained sheet between his legs. He looked up at Punch. His mouth opened. "Punch, why—"

Punch fired again, and Tom gave a jerk as the ball

tore into him not an inch from where the other had struck. Then Tom slumped forward, his head falling between his knees. Slowly the weight of his head and shoulders dragged him forward off the bed. He landed with a dull thud on the floor and lay there still in an obscene wad.

"Punch, you're crazy!" Dot screamed. "You killed him. Why? You killed him, you stupid bastard."

"I ought to kill you, too, for what you done," he said. "With my friend." He rushed across the room to the bed and grabbed a handful of sheet, lifting it up to his face. "Right there. On my own bed. God. I can smell it. I really ought to kill you."

"Well, go on then!" she shouted back at him. "Go on and shoot me if you got the guts."

"Well, I had the guts to shoot Tom, didn't I?"

"Go on then," she said. "It ain't hardly worth it living on with you anyhow. Go on. Shoot me."

Punch lowered the revolver and turned to run out of the room. He was confused. He felt lost and betrayed. He did not know what to do or where to go. But no sooner had he run out the front door than he saw a rider approaching. He looked up, wondering who it might be.

The rider came closer, and Punch recognized the deputy sheriff from Tahlequah. He had spent a few nights in the jail there before. He thought about turning around and running back into the house. He thought about running around the house and trying to make it to the woods, but he was tired, tired and confused. None of the things he could think about doing made any sense, so instead, he raised the revolver and fired a shot at the deputy sheriff. The shot was wide.

"Punch! *Hlesdi!*" Beehunter shouted.

Punch fired again and missed wide again. Calmly, Beehunter removed the rifle from the boot on the side of his horse. He cranked a shell into the chamber, raised the rifle to his shoulder, took aim and fired. Punch jerked as the heavy lead smashed into his chest. Then he slumped forward and did not move again. Beehunter rode on over to the body and dismounted. He nudged Punch with the toe of his boot. Punch was dead.

Beehunter looked at the house. Tom had already killed once, and he might be inside, so Beehunter was cautious. The situation was puzzling. The front door was standing open, so he walked over to it slowly, watching the doorway carefully and staying to one side. A yard away, he stopped and waited.

"Anyone home in there?" he called out in Cherokee.

There was no answer. He stepped inside quickly, rifle ready. He saw a naked woman sitting on a bed, seemingly unconcerned, and the body of a naked man on the floor beside the bed. Almost immediately, he figured out what must have just happened. He spoke to the woman in Cherokee, but she did not answer. Perhaps she did not understand. He walked over to the naked body and rolled it over. It was Tom Panther. Go-Ahead's big dilemma was solved, and Beehunter had not had to perform the unpleasant deed for him. He thought about George Panther, and he knew that George and Gwed' would be sad. Andy too. But he also knew that they would receive the news with a certain sense of relief.

He looked around the room and saw the dress

that had been dropped to the floor. Walking over to it, he picked it up and tossed it to the woman. He looked the other way while she pulled it on. He took hold of a quilt that had been shoved to the foot of the bed, and he dragged it off to throw over the body of Tom Panther. Then he motioned for the woman to go with him. Quietly, she stood up and followed obediently as he left the house.

Back in Tahlequah the next day, in the office of the National Prison, Beehunter told the whole story to Rider. He told about meeting Jenny Spruell and the white man, and how Jenny had pointed the way to Punch Doak's house. He told about being fired upon without warning by a frantic Punch Doak. He told Rider what he had found inside the house, and why he thought that Punch Doak had killed Tom Panther. Then he told Rider how he had looked around the neighborhood until he found someone who could understand Cherokee. With the help of that interpreter, he had borrowed a wagon and team to load the bodies and bring them back to Tahlequah, keeping the woman with him the whole time. He did not know if there was anything that the woman could or should be charged with, but he figured that at least she would be wanted in Tahlequah as a witness to the killing of Tom Panther. When Beehunter had finished with his story, Rider assured him that he had done the proper thing.

That same afternoon, news of the other killings up north began coming in to Rider at his office. He took down all the information that was given to him. Even though the facts seemed to be clear enough—that the murders had all been committed by either Tom Panther or Punch Doak—there would have to be a hearing and an official determination for the record, even though both men were now dead. Rider questioned Dot, and she told him what had happened, just as Beehunter had surmised. He gave Dot a note to take to the hotel with instructions to stay in town until after the hearing. The sheriff's office would pay the hotel bill and pay for her meals. She was not charged with any crime.

The following morning, Rider and Beehunter left Tahlequah. One purpose was to return the borrowed wagon and team, and to reimburse the owner for their use. Beehunter drove the team, and Rider sat beside him on the bench. Two saddled riding horses were tied on behind. Their other purpose was to visit the scenes of the murders and interview any witnesses. It was necessary for the investigation, even though the whole case seemed clear cut.

And although he had not yet mentioned it to Beehunter, Rider had a third purpose. Jenny Spruell and her illicit wares had caused way too much mischief in the Cherokee Nation. He meant to bring her in. He was not at all sure whether or not Spruell was a citizen of the Cherokee Nation, but if it turned out that she was not, he would hold her for the deputy marshals from Fort Smith. He meant to shut down her operation one way or another, once and for all.

There was yet another thing that had to be done, and Rider and Beehunter had talked about it and decided that they could take care of it along the way. It was not something that could wait for their return. George Panther's house was not much out of the way, so they drove there first.

George, Gwed', Andy, Sally and little Annie had pretty much cleaned up and repaired their home by the time the two Cherokee lawmen arrived, although there was still some evidence of the shooting that the posse had done. Andy had gone back to school in Tahlequah. When the wagon rolled up in front of his house, George came out to see who was coming and to greet his visitors. Annie was right beside him.

"Go-Ahead, Beehunter," George said, "welcome. Come inside and have some coffee with us. Gwed' and Sally will be glad to see you, too."

"Thank you, George," Rider said. "We're always glad to see you and your family, but we're on business. We can't stay long."

"George," said Rider, once inside, "Gwed', I have some bad news for you." He glanced at Sally and Annie who were also sitting at the table, and added, "For all of you."

"It's about Tom, isn't it?" George asked.

"He's dead," said Rider.

There was silence for a moment. A single tear ran down Gwed's cheek. She brushed it away with the back of her hand.

"How did it happen, Go-Ahead?" George asked.

Rider looked at Beehunter. "I wasn't there," he said. "I'll let Beehunter tell you."

"He was staying with that Punch Doak and his wife in a house north of here," Beehunter said. "They had been drinking whiskey. They got it from that old white woman up there. Punch shot Tom and killed him. I came along just then. I heard the shot, and I killed Punch after he fired at me."

George knew that there must be more to the story. There had to be a reason for Punch to have killed Tom. There were probably a good many more sordid details to the whole affair, but the two lawmen, George's two friends, had chosen to spare them all that. It was enough. He, too, would let it go. Tom had murdered a man, and Tom had to die. George had asked Rider to see that Tom did not hang, and now, although Rider had not done it himself, Tom had been spared that hanging. He was grateful. George and Gwed' thanked Rider and Beehunter. They finished their coffee, and the two lawmen went outside to climb back onto the wagon seat. George followed them outside.

"You've been around too much killing," he said to them. "Too many bodies. I'm putting up a new sweat lodge. I have to have a funeral first, and I want you to come to that. But we'll do the sweat after that. I'll let you know when. We'll have a sweat and big meal. Plan to spend the day."

"We'll be there, George," Rider said. "Thank you."

When the two lawmen were out of sight, George went back into the house. He stepped over to Gwed' and put his arms around her. While she sobbed, they held each other tight.

"Well, Jenny," said Hiram Knott, "I've wasted about as much time here as I can afford. That boy should have been back here two days ago. He would have come back by now if he'd really meant to. I guess I went too easy on him. I'm just too soft-hearted. Now I'm going to have to go out there and find him and teach him a real lesson."

"Just kill him," Jenny said, "the little son of a bitch."

"I may just do that."

Knott walked to the door and opened it. He went outside and started toward his team. He meant to hitch them to his wagon and drive off toward Punch Doak's house. But he saw two riders coming, so he stopped and waited. As they drew near, he recognized the one Indian who had come by Jenny's place a few days ago, the one who could not speak any English. He recognized both of these men as lawmen, but he was not worried. He was a white man from Arkansas, and these Cherokee lawmen could not touch him. He stood waiting for them, a smirk on his face.

As they pulled up their mounts, Beehunter said to Rider in Cherokee, "That's the white man who was here before. I think he's the one who brings her the whiskey she sells."

"Howdy, gents," Knott said. "Anything I can do for you?"

"Is this Jenny Spruell's house?" Rider asked.

"It is."

"Who are you?" asked Rider.

"Hiram Knott's the name. Out of Arkansas. And who might you be?"

"Go-Ahead Rider, high sheriff of the Cherokee Nation. This is my deputy, Beehunter."

"Yeah," said Knott. "We've met before."

"Mr. Knott," said Rider, "what are you doing

here at the home of Jenny Spruell in the Cherokee Nation? Do you have business here?"

"Business? Why no. I'm just visiting. Jenny's an old friend of the family, so to speak. I was just getting ready to hitch my team and head for home when you came riding up."

"Mr. Knott, I believe that you came here to do business with Jenny Spruell."

"Now, what kind of business could I possibly have with an old woman out here like this?"

"Jenny Spruell is a known whiskey peddler," said Rider. "I believe you to be her supplier."

"That's nonsense. Why, I'm a clothing salesman over in Van Buren."

"I don't care what you do in Van Buren," Rider said. "All I care about is what you're up to here in the Cherokee Nation."

"Well, what difference does it make?" Knott said, a smug look on his face. "Even if you did find out that I was engaged in some illegal activity—which I am by no means admitting to you—but even if you should find out such a thing, there's nothing you could do about it, is there? I'm a white man."

"I can take you in and throw you in my jail," said Rider. "I could hold you there for the deputy marshals from Fort Smith. I understand the judge over there takes a very dim view of whiskey peddling in Indian Territory."

The smug look fled Hiram Knott's face. He began to fidget. "Well, you can't prove anything on me," he said. "I mean to hitch up and get out of here, and you can't stop me."

He turned his back on Rider and Beehunter as if to walk on over to his wagon, but instead, he pulled the revolver out from under his coat. Cocking it, he whirled and fired at Rider. Rider saw it coming just in time, and he leaned far to his right, nearly falling out of the saddle. Beehunter pulled out his own revolver. He cocked, aimed and fired quickly. His bullet smashed into Hiram Knott's forehead. His head bounced on his shoulders for a moment. Then his body collapsed.

Jenny Spruell appeared in her doorway. Horrified, she looked down at Knott, then up at Rider and Beehunter. "You killed him," she said. "What did you kill him for?"

"He fired first, ma'am," Rider said. "We didn't want to kill him. We wanted to turn him over to U.S. law. He forced it."

"What am I going to do now?" she said, "What'll I do now?"

"For now, ma'am," Rider said, "I'm afraid you'll have to come along with us to Tahlequah."

"How's a poor old woman to make a living?" she said. "Oh, Lord, Lord, what'll I do now?"

Chapter 20

They buried Tom Panther not far from George's house in a clearing in the woods, near the graves of George's parents and grandparents in the Panther family cemetery. Conducted in the old ways, the ceremony was solemn, and was attended by a large number of people from all around. Canoe was there, as were Rider, Beehunter, Hard-luck Henry, the young Creek couple, Tom Grimes and even Skinny Johnson. There was much weeping and much talk of Tom's finer points, even though people had to reach back a few years in their memories to come up with those.

The funeral done, George and Gwed', with assistance from Andy, who had come back from school for the ceremony, performed the washing off of all those present. That done, the women laid out the food, and everyone ate. Late in the evening, most of the people began heading for their homes. Now George could not practice his medicine for a specified period of time. He had things to do and people to take care of, and he still had the evil one to worry about, but that would all have to wait until the time was right again. He hoped that the medicine he had made for his home was strong enough to last. When the period was over, he would have the sweat lodge. All the bad things that had piled up on people would be removed. Everything would be renewed.

Big Forehead knew what had been happening with George Panther. He knew about Tom, and he knew about the funeral. He knew that George could not work now, not for a while, so he redoubled his efforts. In several ways, George had defeated him all along the way. But this was a vulnerable time for George, and Big Forehead meant to take full advantage for his own evil ends. He tried everything he knew, but he managed only to increase his own frustrations. George was not working. Yet Big Forehead still could not break through his barrier. And soon, the time of George Panther's inactivity came to an end.

The people began gathering at George Panther's house early in the day, his friends and their families, all people he had helped, most of them more than once at any time they had problems of any kind, ailments, injuries or just worries in their lives. They all brought food with them on this day. Some of it was already prepared, some not. They brought venison, hog meat, beef, crawdads, fish, squirrels and rabbits. They brought wild onions, mushrooms, greens, corn, potatoes and other wild vegetables as well as garden produce. Canoe was there, of course, as were Go-Ahead Rider, Beehunter, Charlie Horse, Adam Diwali, Tom Grimes and the young Creek couple. They sat and visited with one another, drinking coffee. The women helped Gwed' begin preparing the big meal. Children ran around the house and out into the woods. But George was not around.

He was out behind the house, a good distance away in a small clearing under the trees just a little way into the woods. Andy, home again from school, was there with him at the new sweat lodge George had just built. A large dome made of a framework of boughs, it was covered with U.S. Army issue white canvas. Two old buffalo hides were thrown over that, but they were not large enough to cover all of the canvas. The dome was large enough so that George could stand up straight if he stood right in the very center. Inside the lodge, tree stumps, stools and one bench were lined up around the circular canvas wall. A pit had been dug in the very center of the dirt floor. George and Andy were outside at another and larger pit. In this larger pit were rocks ranging in size from the size of a fist to that of a man's head. A fire had been built by laying logs over the rocks.

Andy was tending the fire. "I think the rocks are hot enough."

"Bring on the first bunch then, Andy," said George.

Andy walked back along the narrow path through the woods to the house and gathered up Canoe, Rider, Beehunter, Adam Diwali and two other men. They followed him back out to the sweat lodge, where they began pulling off their shirts, boots, trousers, hats and other items of clothing. George had already gone into the lodge. Andy took a pitchfork and dug into the fire. He came up with four rocks. Walking over to the lodge where the flap covering the door was already opened, he ducked inside and placed the rocks in the pit. He went back out and left the pitchfork near the fire.

"All right," said George. "Bring them in."

Canoe went in first, ducking low to get through the door. Once inside, he turned right, then walked around the circle to his left, going almost all the way around to the door again before he sat down. He sat down, leaving room for one person to sit between himself and the door. He was followed by the others. The last one to go in was Andy, who moved to his left and sat by the door in the spot reserved for him by Canoe, and closed the flap.

George took up a hollowed-out gourd and scooped out a dipper full of liquid from a bucket at his feet, pouring it over the hot rocks. It hissed and popped, and hot steam rose from the rocks and filled the lodge. The heat was intense and immediate. It burned the flesh. The men inside the lodge could not see one another through the thickness of the steam. George dipped and poured four more times.

Sweat ran freely from the naked bodies of the men inside the lodge. At last, George dipped from the bucket, took a mouthful of the medicine in there and passed the gourd to his right. He swished the medicine around in his mouth, then spat it out on the ground between his two bare feet. The next man in line did the same. The gourd went all the way around, and when it came back to George, he dipped it yet again.

"You can take a drink this time," he said.

He took the first drink and passed the gourd along. Each man had a drink by the time the gourd came back to George. George sat still and quiet for another moment. "All right, Andy," he then said. Andy opened the flap and went outside. The rest followed. In sharp contrast to the intense heat in the lodge, the air outside felt cold.

"How do you feel?" George asked.

"I feel boiled," said Rider. "But it's good."

"That was a good one," said Canoe. "I feel fresh and clean."

"Everything that's been on you has been cleaned out," George said. "There's just one more thing to do. Andy, bring the bucket."

Andy brought out the bucket and placed it beside George. George gestured to Canoe to step up to him. Canoe held his hands out in front of himself, cupping his palms, and George poured the liquid into Canoe's palms. Canoe ducked his head forward, brought his hands up and washed the liquid through his hair and over his head. George poured the medicine onto Canoe's right arm, and with his left hand, Canoe washed his right arm with a downward motion. Then George poured the medicine onto Canoe's left arm. Then his right leg and his left leg. Canoe pulled on his trousers and boots, took up his shirt and headed for the house. The next man stepped up to stand beside George for the same administrations.

When George had finished with the washing, Andy went back to the house and brought another group of men to go through the same ritual, the sweating and the washing. When they were done, he brought another group, and then another, until all the men had gone through the ceremony. When the men were all done, Gwed' took in some of the women. Andy carried the rocks for her, too. It was early evening before they were done.

The sun was low in the western sky, already hiding behind a dark curtain of trees. A slight breeze rustled the leaves overhead and cooled the evening air. The women began serving the food, and the hungry men all sat down to eat. When the men were done, the children would be fed, and finally the women would eat. The mood was festive, for it had been a good day.

When the long day was done at last, a few of the people went home, but many of them who lived too far away stayed overnight. They slept outside on the ground, in wagon beds, or inside the house on the floor. George sat alone under his arbor for a while relaxing. He felt good. Everyone had told him that things were better in their lives. Those who had been ailing were well. Those who had been experiencing bad fortune were prospering. It had been a long and hard fight, but George was winning it. That much was clear. Then he saw a flash in the sky. A purple light shot up from the ground, rose high, then arched right at him. Some distance away from his house, still high in the sky, it burst, as if it had shattered itself against something solid and impenetrable. It was followed by another flash, and another. Soon the purple lights were bursting in the sky all around George Panther's home like fireworks.

"He knows he's lost," George said to himself, "but he's fighting back now with everything he's got."

The next day when all of the people had gone

home, and Andy had left to go back to school in Tahlequah, George hitched the team to his wagon. He said good-by to Gwed' and drove to the home of Hard-luck Henry. He was not too surprised to find Henry with several large bundles of tobacco ready to go. George helped Henry load the tobacco into the wagon, then the two of them climbed aboard, and George turned the wagon around. He drove into Tahlequah, and stopped the wagon on the main street of town, right in front of the store owned and operated by Tom Grimes, the white man who was part Cherokee who had come to him for help. He got down out of the wagon and went inside the store. Grimes was behind the counter taking someone's money. When he had finished with his customer, he looked up and saw George. He smiled.

"How's your business going, Mr. Grimes?" George asked.

Grimes came hurrying out from behind the counter to meet George and shake his hand. "Business is great, thanks to you," he said. "I'm doing just fine. I'd say I'm prospering. So, how are you today?"

"Oh, I'm just fine," George said.

"Well, is there anything I can help you with? Just ask, and if it's in my power, it's yours."

"I would like for you to step outside with me for just a minute, if you don't mind."

"Not at all," said Grimes. He followed George out to the wagon where George introduced him to Henry. Then Grimes's gaze went to the load in the wagon bed. His eyes lit up. He picked up a twist of tobacco and felt it, sniffing at it. "This is quality goods," he said.

"You think maybe you can do some business with Henry?" George asked.

"I know I can," Grimes said. "I'll do right by him, too. You can trust me on that. Come on, Henry. Let's you and me get this stuff into the store."

"I'll give you a hand," said George.

He looked over at Henry, and Henry smiled a broad, happy smile.

Big Forehead knew that he was fighting a losing battle, yet he had not totally given up. Giving up was not in his nature, nor was losing. He had to try again. To admit defeat was to die. He needed to get out and investigate, to see first-hand what was going on. This had all started out as such a simple thing. He had been annoyed at George Panther because of his white horse, and then after the race was over, he had met George's son Tom quite by accident. He had made the remarkable discovery that the son resented the father almost to the point of hatred.

Slowly, Big Forehead had let out the information that he dabbled in bad medicine, and Tom had almost begged him to use some of it to, as he put it, teach his father a lesson. To make his medicine not work. To make bad things happen. Tom had told him the names of the people who went to George for help. He had told him where the people lived, and had given him all the information Big Forehead asked for. And then Big Forehead had gone to work. It had been a simple enough task. But he had not counted on the power of George Panther.

He just could not get through to George. At first, he was hurting some of George's people and causing George some real personal problems, too. But now, George's people were all well and prospering. And the white lawmen had even stopped looking for George, believing him dead. Even George's troublemaking son Tom was dead. George was winning, but Big Forehead could not allow that to happen, not that easily. He would make a last powerful effort. He would give it everything he had. He would risk his very life, for if he failed at this task, life would not be worth living.

He would figure out just exactly what needed to be done, how and when and where. He was standing inside his small house, looking out the open window, and his clothes lay in a rumpled heap on the floor. He cackled, then hopped on his skinny legs right up to the window ledge.

"Ka, ka," he croaked.

A feather fell out of his rumpled left wing and landed on the ledge.

"Ka, ka."

He looked up into the sky with red eyes. He spread his wings, gave a hop and flapped his wings, rising higher and higher into the sky.

"Ka, Ka."

He loved to fly. He felt free and powerful, and could look down on all the world. He could void himself on people's heads, or fly down close to them and frighten them. He could perch on their windowsills and make them nervous. He could watch men with their wives at night through their windows while they made love. He loved to fly, but this was not a pleasure flight. This was serious business. This flight was for a specific purpose: to spy and see what he could find out about this fight with George Panther.

George Panther was at home, alone in the back room of his house, lying on his stomach in his bed, holding his crystal in both hands and staring into it intently. He had talked to it. He had sung a song to it seven times. And now he was seeing the silhouette inside the crystal again, the same dark and dim image as before. Silent and sinister, it undulated there before his eyes, taunting him.

"Who are you?" he commanded. "Show yourself."

The image almost faded, but George stared unblinking. He concentrated all his will, all his energy. He tried to make daggers of his eyes. "Who are you?" he said firmly. "Let me see you clearly just one time."

The image cleared a bit, and still George did not blink. "Show yourself," he said.

The crystal suddenly filled with a black cloud. Furious, George closed a fist around it and shook it. "Show yourself!" he shouted.

He opened his fist and looked. The image in the crystal was clearer, and suddenly the figure in the crystal turned sharply and at once to face George, looking him straight in the eyes. As it did, the crystal cleared completely and in another instant, George found himself looking directly into the evil red eyes of Big Forehead.

The nasty black bird soared high. It was riding on an updraft, not flapping its wings, just gliding. It would have been enjoying the flight were its mind not so intent on its mission of hatred and revenge. It was headed for the home of George Panther, anxious to see what it could see, anxious to find out if it could fly through the invisible barrier that George had set up around his home. Anxious, above all, to discover a way to finish this fight in his own favor. He saw the house far below, and he headed down. He spiralled lower, and he had to flap his wings again to control the direction of his flight. He would be there soon.

But something was wrong. He felt heavy. He tried to flap his wings, and he found that he was only waving his arms. His feathers were gone. He was plucked bare, no longer a bird. He was only a naked old man, alone and high up in the sky. He looked down through his still red eyes at the winding dirt road beneath him. He saw the trees and the houses getting larger, the road growing wider, much too fast. Big Forehead's head was swimming. He was falling, plummeting through the air. He flailed his arms wildly and desperately. He rolled helplessly over and over. Nothing he could do would slow his travel. He felt himself hurtling downward faster and faster, picking up momentum, gaining speed. It would be over in an instant. He opened his mouth wide with a hideous scream, a shrill shriek that did not stop until his bare body smashed and splattered onto the hard-packed earth of the well-traveled road below.

"Uncle George," said Annie, "look what I found for you."

She ran into the arbor where George was sitting

and smoking a cigarette. He leaned forward in his chair. "What do you have there?" he said.

She held out her hand and opened it up to reveal five four-leaf clovers.

"For me?" George said.

She nodded her head.

"I found them for you," she said. "They're for good luck."

George held out his own hand, palm up, and Annie dumped the little treasure into his big palm. George looked at them carefully and counted them.

"You got five of them," he said. "That's real good. How did you do that? Lots of people look for these and can't even find one."

"Oh, it's real easy," said Annie. "They just stand up and wave at me."

"Well, baby," George said, "you got five, and that's real good, but, you know, seven is the real special number. You think you can find two more to make it seven?"

Annie turned away from George. She put her hands on her hips and turned her face to the right. Slowly she moved her head to the left, searching the ground. Suddenly, she ran out into the yard, and squatted down for a moment. Her back was to George, so he couldn't see what she was doing. She got up, looked again, ran a few steps, squatted, then turned and ran back to George.

"Here," she said.

He held out his hand, and she dropped two more four-leaf clovers into his palm.

"Now there are seven," she said.

George gave her a hug, congratulating her again and thanking her. She said she had to go inside and help her Aunt Gwed', and turned and ran inside the house. George stared after her. He looked at the tiny plants in the palm of his hand, and he thought about Annie for another long moment.

She's the one, he said to himself with sudden revelation. I've been slow to see it. She's the one I've been looking for and waiting for. She was revealed to me, put right here in front of my eyes, and I was so busy with everything else, I didn't see. I see it now, though. I see it clear. It wasn't a boy at all, but a girl. My sister's girl, Annie. Little Annie. I'll have to talk to Gwed' and Sally right away. Annie's the one who will take over from me when my time comes. I'll have to start teaching her real soon now. Annie is the one.

Afterword

The prophecy of George Panther is well on its way to being fulfilled. In a few short years following the events of this story, the Curtis Act was passed by the United States Congress calling for the allotment of Cherokee lands in severalty to individual Cherokees. In order to accomplish this purpose, it called for the creation of a "final Cherokee roll," and when that roll was completed in 1914, the Congress "closed the Cherokee roll." Legally speaking, there were to be no more Cherokees. Tribal laws and courts were abolished. The National Council was stripped of all its powers except the power to adjourn.

The property of the Cherokee Nation was taken over by the U.S. government and distributed to individuals or to the newly created state and county governments. The Cherokee Female Seminary became a state normal school. The Cherokee Nation's public school system became a state school system. The old capitol building at Tahlequah became the Cherokee County Court House, and the National Prison became the Cherokee County Jail. The newspaper was sold and taken to Muskogee. It is still in operation today as the *Muskogee Phoenix*.

But the Cherokee Nation, as a legally recognized

government, was not totally demolished. It was put into a state of near-dormancy, for the business of land transfers was much more complex and time-consuming than Congress had foreseen. Because of the importance of property law in the U.S. legal system, someone had to be in place to sign the legal documents involved in the transfer of property.

The Curtis Act had taken elections away from the Cherokee people and given to the president of the United States the right to appoint a chief of the Cherokee Nation. For all practical purposes, the government of the Cherokee Nation was in a coma. And the result of all this on Cherokee people was devastating. According to the U.S. census, by 1970, only 63 years later—just one lifetime—the average adult Cherokee had only five years of school. Most Cherokee people were living in poverty. Many people had lost their allotments. The first part of the prophecy had come about.

But in the 1970s the national mood regarding Native Peoples everywhere had changed. The American Indian Movement (AIM) was in the news, bringing attention to issues of concern to Indian People. This change in attitude came to the Cherokee Nation in the form of returned elections in 1971. For the first time since before statehood, the Cherokee Nation had an elected principal chief.

In the nearly thirty years since that election, the Cherokee nation has grown tremendously, operating millions of dollars worth of federal service programs. Once again it is operating under a constitutional government with executive, legislative and judicial branches. Elections for principal chief, deputy chief and fifteen Council positions are held every four years. The Cherokee court system is fully operational, as is a Cherokee Nation Marshals Service.

The second part of George Panther's prophecy has not yet been fulfilled, but great strides have been taken in that direction. The present principal chief, Chad Smith, has been quoted as saying, "One hundred years from now, we want to be where we were one hundred years ago." When that day comes, the circle will be complete. The prophecy will have come true.